ACQUAINTED WITH THE NIGHT

Lesli Richardson

http://www.LesliRichardson.com

Acquainted With the Night
Copyright © 2020 by Lesli Richardson

ACKNOWLEDGEMENTS

All poetry quoted in this book is by Robert Frost, various copyright dates.

The Road Not Taken (1916)
Bond and Free (1916)
To Earthward (1923)
Bereft (1928)
Acquainted With the Night (1928)

Note: This book was originally published in 2010 under my Tymber Dalton pen name. It has been revised and expanded for release under my Lesli Richardson pen name.

DEDICATION

For Tessa, Holly, Harley, Valentine, Bubbles, Scudder,
Apache, Gidget, BW, Callie, Bogey, Pickles—and all the others
I hope are waiting on me.

CHAPTER ONE

I never asked to be here. Like most other healthy Terran males between the ages of eighteen and still able to walk on their own two feet, I was drafted by the military to fight in their stupid, senseless war.

I wasn't a warrior.

I wasn't a fighter.

It wasn't my war.

Some fucking bureaucrat in some fucking shithole office somewhere decided we needed to teach the Algonquans a lesson for daring to send their ships to explore a sector of the galaxy we'd only thought about getting around to looking at one day.

Yes, that's right, it was a pissing contest. Mostly because the Terran government no doubt thought the Algonquans would be an easy race to roll over and intimidate, based on their peaceful past.

They aren't warlike. They're pacifists. We'll just flex our muscles.

Those were the mantras, I'm certain. They didn't want the Algonquans taking a harder look at the territories staked out by the monkey men who evolved on the third rock out from Sol. They were territories that could potentially yield extremely lucrative mineral deposits. Multiple mining conglomerates had been sending out survey teams before investing any money or political flex to get them annexed.

In other words, the Terrans rolled the dice and fired a few shots over the bow of an unarmed Algonquan exploration ship and expected the Algonquans to back off.

The plan backfired.

Badly.

The same said nameless bureaucrat also got their intel wrong when they said the Algonquans were a slowly reproducing race with relatively low population numbers.

They lied. Rather, they failed to take into account the Algonquans' deep desire to survive as a species.

Before all this started, the Algonquans had never done anything to us. They'd even tried diplomatic channels, willing to share the resources they'd discovered there.

The Terrans, however, have never been known for their ability to share well with others. Especially when greedy corporate interests stick their fingers into the mix and heavily lobby for shock and awe to benefit their bottom line.

And now, here I was, stuck fighting a war technically as old as me, even though the bulk of the heaviest fighting had only been taking place over the past fifteen years.

They yanked men from universities and non-essential non-military jobs, and passed marriage and breeding bans, so only certain people could actually tie the knot, thus preserving healthy young males for military duty on the ass-end of the galaxy. Rich people could usually swing exemptions for themselves or their sons.

And as the war progressed, the breeding program started.

I was straight and twenty, and the only women I'd been allowed to fuck were the three breeding partners selected for me before I'd been shipped out across the galaxy.

To do my duty and help pass along my genes.

The thirty-minute sessions with the women, whose names I wasn't allowed to know, were about as romantic as a root canal. I have no idea if I've fathered any children with them, or through the deposits I also made.

I actually enjoyed the sperm donation sessions more than the in-person fucks. I made my required two deposits a week, every week, from when I turned eighteen until I shipped out, just me and twenty-four other guys in a room with jars.

Just in case we didn't come home, they'd still have something to remember us by and help repopulate the species.

I was already starting to think that might not be a great idea. Maybe we would be better off dying out as a species.

At least during the donation sessions I could close my eyes and immerse myself in a fantasy, instead of staring at the face of a woman who obviously would rather be somewhere else and who needed half a tube of lube so I didn't hurt her while we did it.

Finally, however, the Terran coalition government had a cause to unite the disparate and frequently hostile Terran races, and get people firmly behind supporting a common goal.

Survival of our species.

What the fuck ever. Honestly? I wasn't even sure we deserved to survive, as miserable as most people appeared to be.

Even three of the alien treaty races, sensing blood in the water, decided to hop on the bandwagon. Whether to mop up what was left of the Terrans should they get their asses thoroughly handed to them, or to help the Terrans mop up whatever remained of the Algonquans and reap those rewards when all was said and done, who's to say?

It wasn't enough.

Not nearly enough.

I was stationed on the *Washington Franklin*, a battle troop transport cruiser, heavily armed and deadly. We carried fifty buzzer bees, fast two-man fighters that could fly in space or atmosphere, and a total of seven hundred and thirty-two souls on board — buzzer crews, flight maintenance, ship's crew, and bushwhacking grunts.

Lucky me, I'd drawn an assignment to flight maintenance, meaning I didn't have to carry a fucking gun and storm the beach heads or jungles or whatever the fuck terrain our grunts got dropped into.

I could stay on the ship and pray I made it home alive. Not that I had a home, since they drafted me in as an A-1 classification. Meaning this was my home until I died or they finally decided to let me out of the fucking military. My parents had died soon after I shipped out, in a reactor explosion at the plant where they worked.

At least I'd *had* parents and not just a breeder code tattooed on my arm. My mother and father had been married for ten years before my birth. I grew up a happy, well-loved, and fairy well-adjusted resident of the Ganymede colony.

I was born three years before marriage bans kicked in.

Seven years before breeder laws.

How "human" were we Terrans anymore, really?

The government was great at spinning it so people took their dog shit and lapped it up like fine caviar. People my age and older could remember some semblance of freedom. People a few years younger than me accepted without question that we were doing our duty to preserve our species.

I tuned out the morning propaganda bullshit, officially called the morning briefing, or MB. Techs had to sit in as command staff briefed the crews on their missions and reminded us all about the "Algonquan menace." No one, officially, had ever returned after capture over the decades the war had raged.

Were they killed? Turned into slaves? Tortured?

Eaten?

No one knew. An estimated twenty thousand men, give or take.

Never heard from again.

I suspected more missing than that, knowing our government's penchant for not releasing all the facts.

That didn't stop the government from scaring the everlovin' crap out of us by trying to fill us full of their bullshit. Kill or be killed...or worse.

I remember a lot about that morning. All of it, actually. Starting from when I decided to take an extra ten minutes to sleep in instead of going to the wank closet, as the crew called it. We were required to visit it a minimum of three times a week, probably to keep us from getting too rowdy, and I'd already been twice. I could skip a day. I remembered mess, the MB, pre-flight checks on the five BBs I was assigned to as senior tech, the flight crews busting our balls as usual.

"Bye, pussies," one of the BB pilots teased us. "We're off to keep you safe and save the species." His co-pilot brayed with laughter and slapped him on the shoulder.

Yeah, whatever.

I remember passing the BBs off to the launch crews, who lined them up in formation to shoot out of the cruiser's belly like the deadly insects of war they were.

I remember turning to Billy Akins, a year younger than me, a good ol' boy from the Alabama territory back on Earth. This was his first trip ever into space. Being from Ganymede, I'd seen space plenty of times before this fucking fiasco. I remember the look of fear on his face as he stared at the radar monitors used by the launch crew to keep track of fighter squadron distances so they didn't launch too soon.

"Dale, what the *fuck* is *that*?"

I turned and spotted the huge shape on the monitor, looking more like a planet than any ship's radar signature I'd ever seen, and heading straight for us.

And that's all I remember.

CHAPTER TWO

The next thing I remembered, I didn't believe, at first.

My vision slowly cleared as consciousness returned. I laid upright at an angle, not quite vertical but not under my own steam. Some sort of energy manacles on my wrists held them pinned to the sides of the shoulder-high frame I was attached to.

Attached in more ways than one.

As my mind slowly re-engaged with my body, I discovered I wasn't alone. I learned more about my predicament based upon what I saw around me. The huge facility struck me as some sort of warehouse, but then I heard a faint rumble in the distance that immediately brought to mind a ship's engine.

As far as the eye could see, we were immobilized in circular racks of twenty men each, all of us facing the center of the device. We were all gagged. I tested the soft ball in my mouth. It gave and changed shape, but despite not being painfully tight, the strap holding it in place had no slack, and I couldn't dislodge it.

The other men in my rack looked as wide-eyed and dazed as I felt. I didn't recognize any of them, which didn't mean anything because I didn't socialize much when not on duty. I barely knew the flight crews whose BBs I maintained. I slept, ate, wanked, and worked. That comprised my usual day. I existed, barely, to make it through another day.

If it wasn't for my mind-numbing fear, I might have found my situation interesting, something to break the monotony of my pitiful existence.

We'd all been stripped naked. Our ankles bore similar manacles as our wrists, pinning our legs to the frame, keeping them spread apart but not uncomfortably so. I tried and could not move.

Angled slightly forward, I could take my weight off my feet if I leaned against the frame and let it hold me. It wasn't uncomfortable, but it wasn't my choice of accommodations, that's for damn sure.

In the center of the rack, a dome-shaped housing held what I guessed could only be described as a pump. From it, twenty hoses emerged, with an attachment on the end of each one.

Attached to our cocks. Sort of like the pictures of old-fashioned cattle milkers I'd seen in schoolbooks and vids.

I wasn't in any pain. In fact, once I fought back my panic and tried to relax, I realized it didn't feel too terribly bad. Not like I could fight the woody the constant suction from the device gave me anyway.

In the distance, I spotted movement. Blue-garbed figures worked around another rack full of men like ours. I didn't know how many of us there were in this room, or vessel, or warehouse, but I counted at least twenty other racks, and suspected many beyond those, outside my field of vision.

As the figures drew closer to our rack, I occasionally heard muffled grunts from my fellow captives. It wasn't until they reached the rack next to ours that I realized what they were doing.

Photographs of the Algonquans were never shown, even though I knew we had a prisoner complex near Alpha Centauri. I'd heard rumors that the most agonizing of tortures wouldn't get Algonquans to give up information. Again, that little fact didn't stop the government from building them up in our heads as horrible, mutant, insectoid creatures.

If these were Algonquans, then the government had — no shocker there — badly and brazenly lied to us about them.

It also left me praying the Algonquans treated their prisoners better than we did.

Close to eight feet tall by my best guess, they had smooth, golden bronze-colored skin, their black hair falling past their shoulders and tied in a braid. They had four long but thick fingers, although they seemed to favor the first two fingers like a clasper grip. Their large brown eyes were set over a flattened nose with a long, oval face.

They weren't Terran beautiful, but they weren't the ferocious creatures we'd been told about, either.

They didn't talk to any of the Terran men in English, although I was situated close enough that I noticed if one of my fellow captives made a loud noise through their gag, one of the Algonquans would stroke his naked back and make soothing, chirruping noises at him, like you would a child.

Or a pet.

The Algonquans methodically worked around each rack. It was only as they drew within my line of sight that I realized they had a hover cart of some sort, loaded with supplies. Each man was given three injections in the left ass cheek, a metal collar was placed around his neck, and a tag on the collar scanned into a hand-held device.

Next, they donned some sort of mitts and, working from the face down, they rubbed each man, front and back, armpits and groin, all the way down to their feet. As they stepped back to check their work, sometimes going over an area again if necessary, I realized it was a hair-removal process. They left eyebrows, lashes, and hair on the head, but everything else, including facial hair, was removed.

Apparently, they had this process down to a science. The next step, seemingly the one that produced noises in my fellow captives, was squirting a very viscous goo onto a probe that went...well, up the ass. Not just a probe, but hooked to a cord, which they then plugged into a small control panel on the frame each man was attached to.

This is when it got interesting.

As one technician punched in settings, the man's body would tense, squirm, and that's usually when they'd moan around their gag. Their noises didn't sound pained. It finally struck me the butt plug must be inflating because the second tech would soothe the distressed man as the first tech continued making adjustments, until they were happy with the setting. A quick tug on the wire to make sure it wasn't going anywhere, and usually the man received a pat on the ass as the first technician straightened to move to the next prisoner.

I was fifth in line in our rack for the treatment, now able to closely watch the faces of the men taken care of before me. Each one, as the probe was inserted, attempted to struggle briefly when the plug inflated. Then futility set in again and they closed their eyes as they tried to get used to the sensation.

No wonder they gagged us. A whole facility of us moaning and groaning and begging and pleading would have only panicked the others, even if we weren't being tortured.

They turned out to be smarter than our government claimed.

When they reached me, I closed my eyes and patiently waited. Far as I could tell, no one before me had died from the treatment, so I figured if I didn't fight, it might go faster. The injections stung, but nothing worse than I'd dealt with from the military before I was shipped out. The collar wasn't loose enough to get off, but it wasn't tight enough to choke or chafe, either. I suspected the lightweight, rounded metal rod was some sort of unbreakable alloy. The ends appeared fused together once put on and I had no idea how it came off after being attached.

Their hands felt gentle but firm on my flesh as they scrubbed me with the mitts and removed every last bit of my body and facial hair.

They weren't cruel because the lube they used felt warm. Although it didn't numb my rectum when the probe went in, I didn't feel any pain, either. Sure enough, after they plugged it in it started inflating. I couldn't help but moan as it grew in size to feeling like it filled half my abdominal cavity, even though it didn't hurt. It did, however, press against my prostate. I tried to suppress another grunt as I reflexively climaxed from the sensation.

I have to admit, that felt pretty good.

It also earned me a pat on the ass from one of the techs. They slightly deflated the device and then I felt a tug on the cord as they ensured it was securely in.

I noticed they talked to each other, but I couldn't begin deciphering their language. I'd heard we had some linguists who could speak it and understand them. To me, the complex mix of sounds made no sense, although I could almost picture two Terran med techs discussing their day as they went about their normal rounds.

To the Algonquans, perhaps this was a normal day.

I have no idea how long they held us there. I had a feeling probably three days, but it could have been two or four. Every few hours, a tech would come around with some sort of clear liquid that wasn't water, but it didn't taste objectionable. They'd poke a tube through the small opening in the gag and patiently wait for us to drink as much as we wanted. If they didn't feel we drank enough, they'd keep it there until we took a little more, all while they made encouraging-sounding noises at us. There was enough give to the ball gag we could swallow without choking.

Going to the bathroom, apparently, was done through the tube. We all discovered this early on when it became impossible to hold it any longer. Maybe the anal probe took care of business on that end because I didn't have an urge to go. I didn't miss that some of my fellow captives occasionally fidgeted in their bonds, wiggling their asses, then their breathing quickened. Invariably, I'd see a stream of white fluid disappear down the tube.

I quit counting how many climaxes the damn thing pulled out of me. I figured why fight it? At least it felt good.

We could sleep, and we did so by resting our heads on the top of our individual frames. It was either that, or stare at each other across the racks. None of us seemed inclined to do that because we could see our helpless fellow captives and know that's exactly how we were trussed.

Then a group of techs, working quickly and efficiently, moved through the cargo hold. I was inclined to believe a ship at that point simply because we occasionally heard chimes that might have marked shift changes, accompanied by the steady, underlying drone of engines. The techs withdrew straps from our frames, passed them over our asses, and hooked them to the other side of the frame, tightening them securely but not painfully. Not exactly a standard seatbelt, but it added credence to the ship theory. Perhaps we were coming in to land.

The sound of engines grew louder, strained, then slowly eased off again as we felt a tremor pass through the ship, followed by another, then a third, and finally a harder, not quite jarring thud. Everything went still as the engine sounds faded.

Within minutes, more chimes sounded followed by an announcement. None of us could understand the language, of course.

More techs swarmed what, yes, turned out to be a cargo bay.

We were the cargo.

With two techs to a rack, they unfastened our straps, deactivated latches holding the racks securely in place, activated a hover setting, and moved our racks toward an open cargo hatch where they pushed us down a ramp.

I didn't know if this planet was Algonquan. The planet's sun either neared or hovered just past its zenith in a crystalline blue sky without a hint of pollution. We sat in a field with beautiful, lush, emerald green grass beneath us. I looked back and saw the ship was at least five times larger than the transport I'd been on, plus it stretched out into the distance.

I wondered how many of my fellow captives were from my ship or others in our fleet.

I had yet to see anyone I knew.

Because of the way they'd configured us in the racks, I couldn't look around too much. I guessed we were in a smaller town because I didn't see traces of pollution or skyscrapers. Our racks hovered a few inches above the grass as they pushed us in a line across the field and into a large building. Clean, light, airy. This wasn't some rank, dirty torture hole our government swore we'd end up in. It reminded me of a shopping complex because, lining the far wall, sat a row of what were obviously storefronts selling completely unfamiliar merchandise.

With all our racks unloaded and secured in this new place, more waiting began. The tech numbers reduced. Someone again made sure we were fed or watered, or maybe whatever they gave us was both. I never felt hungry or thirsty.

Just…perpetually aroused. Not that I could help it, and the milking device hooked to my cock made resisting the sensation an impossibility. I'd grown used to the fullness in my ass within the first hour or two of having the probe there. Not like I could do anything about it anyway. When I tried to push it out, like passing a bowel movement, I felt a slightly unpleasant buzzing, a borderline electrical sensation. Not a shock, but not something I felt brave enough to test the limits of, either. When I stopped resisting the sensation immediately went away, replaced by a pleasant vibration that instantly made me come again.

When I tried it again later, I received the same result. When I experimented by tightening my ass muscles around the probe, as if to ensure it stayed in, the pleasant vibration happened again, only stronger, making me come immediately.

I was rewarded for not resisting.

Interesting.

I did that more than a few times during our journey, to take my mind off my troubles. It wouldn't surprise me if some of my fellow captives did, too. We were, after all, pretty virile men. It wasn't like we could read or do crossword puzzles or talk to pass the time.

Sure as hell beat the wank closet.

What did that say about the Algonquans, that they used positive reinforcement on their prisoners?

And what did they have in mind to create such a pleasant sensation, anyway?

I had an unpleasant suspicion, but I'd give the Algonquans the benefit of the doubt. I wasn't dead, I wasn't in pain or any real discomfort other than being immobilized, and if this was their idea of torture, hell yeah, keep me signed on. I might get bored to death, but I found that preferable to some of the inhumanities we'd been told they would inflict upon us if captured.

More waiting. Then, the first trickle of what I guessed were civilians appeared. Their appearance was similar to the techs, but they weren't dressed in the blue uniforms and instead wore tunics in a variety of colors and styles. I finally realized they all struck me as male, as were the techs. Or masculine, at the very least. Maybe my perceptions were skewed by my Terran upbringing, but that was my impression.

The civilians browsed our racks and talked to techs. Sometimes, they had questions and would point to one captive or another. They would stroke hair, check skin, look at eyes. When asses were pointed at, the tech would make an adjustment to the console that usually resulted in the captive's body tensing in a now all-too-familiar reaction.

Orgasm.

Shoppers selected captives. When this happened, the techs scanned the tag on the captive's collar and shot an ear tag into their right ear lobe. That was also scanned. Then the shopper gave the tech a card to scan, apparently matching the captive to their new owner and completing the transaction.

Who knew? They used credit cards.

How Terran of them.

Now with the captive purchased, the techs detached the individual frame from the rack, unhooked the milker hose from the captive's cock, and took the captive away in the frame, followed by the purchaser.

Throughout the day, as more captives were purchased, frames would be brought over from other racks to replace them and fill in the gaps, consolidating our numbers. I nearly laughed at the thought of the merchandising going on in this literal meat market.

That's when a horrific thought struck me.

They weren't going to *eat* us, were they?

Keep us calm and relatively happy by subduing us like this?

Not struggling so the meat wouldn't become tough?

I closed my eyes and prayed I was wrong and tried not to think of pampered Kobe cattle back on Earth.

I was looked at a few times in passing but not selected until late in the day. A shopper wearing a finer-looking tunic than many of the previous customers examined me. His hands felt gentle as he took my face and studied me, turning me as if examining a prized hound.

When his gaze met mine, I silently pleaded that, if he did buy me, to please not hurt me.

I forced myself to relax and didn't fight his grip, let him turn me how he wanted.

This was the closest I'd been to one of them who actually paid me attention. I swear it felt like he tried to read my mind, sense my thoughts. His large brown eyes were filled with small gold flecks, and I sensed not some rabid, vicious alien, but a sensitive, intelligent soul.

Or, maybe that was just wishful thinking on my part.

Then again, from what I'd experienced so far, they were obviously intelligent. Far more intelligent than humans.

Please, don't hurt me. I'll be good.

Without breaking eye contact with me, he asked the tech a few questions. The tech leaned over and did something to my control panel.

My eyes dropped closed as the probe swelled and buzzed, making me climax. I moaned at the sensation. No way to avoid it, either, because my climax hit me too hard and fast to prepare for it.

The tech changed the setting, and the probe shrank back to its previous size but left me breathless.

He bought me.

Even getting the tag through my ear wasn't too bad, just a mild pinch. A quick antiseptic swab they used on my ear lobe also apparently contained a topical anesthetic. Once it wore off it ached, but not painfully. I'd felt worse in basic training.

They disconnected my cock from the milker hose. I couldn't see my poor, abused member, but it felt swollen from the constant suction.

Part of me sort of hoped it'd stay that size.

I tried to stay calm. If they planned to eat us, they wouldn't collar and tag us, would they?

I was taken by the techs to a small, private room where my new owner stood to the side and waited for the techs to finish with me. They gave me three more injections, this time in my right ass cheek. They brought in a different kind of frame, similar to the one I was hooked to, but smaller and configured so I had to lie down on it.

A tech hooked an energy leash to my collar. I felt a low-level hum through the connection, a distinct warning to behave myself if I ever felt one. The tech waited for another to join him and together they disconnected first my ankles, then the cord hooking the butt plug to the frame. My wrists were unfastened last, but before they did, I felt all slack tighten in the leash.

Once they released my wrists, I waited for them to signal me to move. No way in hell would I try for bravery. If they were going to eat me, so far they hadn't done anything to hurt me. I figured maybe they'd be into humane euthanasia, too.

One of the techs caught my left wrist and carefully guided me backward, giving me time to step away from the frame, steadying me with a palm to my back.

Then pressure on my back indicated I was to move to the other frame.

No use fighting, so I complied.

I didn't miss how one of the techs said something favorable-sounding to my new owner, who nodded as he watched me. I got the distinct impression they were discussing me. Hopefully they were discussing how well-behaved I acted. My owner's gaze met mine as I continued silently pleading for mercy.

I'm not a grunt. I'm not into fighting to the death. I wasn't into fighting at all. I just wanted whatever next happened to me to be over with as soon as possible and to experience as little discomfort as possible in the process.

The two techs guided me into position on the frame, so I straddled it, almost crouched over it, but able to truly lie down for the first time since my capture.

This was okay. Padded and comfortable, I could actually go to sleep like this if I needed to.

My wrists and ankles were attached to this frame. I felt them connect the butt plug wire as well. Another milker hose, as I'd come to think of it, was attached to my cock.

I immediately grew hard inside it.

I was somewhat surprised Terran governments hadn't thought of an arrangement like this to keep troops under control during transport.

Unlike the other frame, I felt a tether hook my collar to the structure. I could lift and move my head, but not much. I wouldn't get cramped like this though.

Before I could contemplate it, a tech removed my gag and immediately replaced it with another, different kind. Smaller in size but a flat wedge more than a ball. More comfortable, for sure. I felt another hole in it where they could give me the nutrients I'd been fed.

Once the techs checked my bonds, my new owner shook hands with them, then reached down and petted my head. I think he smiled at me. I sensed affection as his eyes studied mine.

He wouldn't eat a pet, would he?

I prayed not.

He said something in his language as he grazed his nails along my scalp.

Then one of the techs gave me another shot, this time in the upper arm, and blackness took me.

CHAPTER THREE

The Algonquans had apparently mastered the art of immobilizing the male human form. I awoke attached to a different frame. The room I found myself in reminded me of a house I'd seen in an old-fashioned vid I'd once watched, set on Earth. High ceilings, brightly colored wall hangings decorated cream-stuccoed walls, with comfortable pillows stacked in one corner. If the dim light in the window could be used as any indication, it was evening. That was all I could see.

The plug had been removed from my ass. That much was different. They still had my cock encased in one of those devious milkers, however.

I couldn't turn my head because my collar was tethered to the frame. I froze when I heard a soft male voice from somewhere behind me say, "It's okay. You're safe."

Still gagged, I couldn't respond. I tried to turn to see him, but I couldn't.

"Just relax. It's okay. They'll be back shortly."

I wished I could see him. He spoke Terran Standard English without any other language accent. Definitely human.

I did the only thing I could do—I relaxed.

I was bent over, my legs spread far wider than they had been before, my ass open and exposed. By now that shouldn't bother me, but it left me feeling even more vulnerable than I had before.

Maybe I wasn't going to be eaten, or kept as a pet. Maybe I was now a sex slave.

When faced with the idea of being a main course, sex slave had a definite upside I could easily dig.

I heard a door slide open and could turn my head enough to spot my new owner enter with someone else. The person with him wore a plain brown tunic. They talked, not paying me any attention even as they walked over to me. My owner placed his hand on my back, still talking to the other man. He didn't do anything except talk.

The absurd image came to mind of an ancient cowboy leaning against his horse while chatting to another cowboy.

I choked back anxious laughter that bordered on hysteria. Waiting was the worst part.

Perhaps sensing my tension, my owner patted my back as if to soothe me, but he didn't stop his conversation. Finally, his hand disappeared.

The unseen Terran male said, "Just relax. He won't hurt you, I promise. Please don't fight them, or they won't release you yet." He sounded borderline desperate, pleading.

I had to trust that voice. I was damned tired of not being able to move.

I heard a noise, like something being moved into position, and then sensed someone sit behind me. I jumped when hands stroked my ass. When I forced myself to relax, that earned me a pleased-sounding noise from my owner.

He examined my balls, gently, obviously not trying to hurt me. Then he placed his warm palms against my ass cheeks and I felt his thumbs carefully press against my rim for entrance.

I took a deep breath and relaxed further. This earned me another pleased sound as his thumbs slid in and massaged my rim, pulling, as if testing how large I could open.

I sensed what might be coming and decided that, no matter what, I'd take it.

I mean, I wasn't gay. Other than medical stuff, I had no experience with...this. I had never been fucked up the ass before, but again, the whole being a chuck roast versus having a fucked ass argument made it a no-brainer, to me.

My owner talked to the other man, followed by more discussion as his thumbs disappeared. I heard a rustle of clothing before something hot and wet pressed against my rim.

His tongue, I suspected.

Holy crap, were they part anteater? It snaked inside me, hardening my cock and making me moan in a good way. He made a chuckling sound as his tongue disappeared, leaving me empty once again and, frankly, leaving me wanting more of *that*.

He patted me on the ass, and then I felt something warm and large press against my hole.

I relaxed.

Well, tried to.

What I guessed was his dick pushed through my rim, making me wince, but I now suspected I understood the reason for the anal plugs. He slid what felt like an impossibly large cock inside me and held still for a moment, stroking my flanks, murmuring soft, soothing sounds at me even as he continued his conversation with the other man.

Then he started fucking me.

I couldn't help it. I flexed my hips in time with his thrusts, helping him, encouraging him to use me. It felt damn good. Combined with the pull of the milker on my cock, I came fairly fast.

Yeah, I enjoyed it.

That earned me the equivalent of what I suspected meant "good boy." He then fucked me harder, holding on to my hips, making me grunt around my gag and hardening my cock again before I heard him let out a gasp. Warmth flooded me as his cock grew impossibly large, and I came again as it pressed against my prostate.

Oh yeah, the anal plug's purpose was quite obvious now.

He caught his breath for a moment before he started talking again to the other man. Laughing, chatting. After a few minutes, his cock shrank, and when he withdrew I felt liquid pour down my inner thighs. I wasn't in any pain, so I hoped it wasn't my own blood.

He lightly swatted me on the ass, not painfully, but playfully. Then he walked around to my head and ruffled my hair, smiling at me.

He made that sound again. The "good boy" sound. One more pat on the head and they left the room.

I closed my eyes and tried to catch my breath. If that was the worst this got, okay, I could deal with that. Maybe not the bravest course of action, but goddamn, it beat the hell out of the wank closet.

The other man didn't speak, and I couldn't speak, so I just waited.

I was getting pretty good at that.

A few minutes later, the door opened again and a different Algonquan entered. He seemed to be the designated clean-up crew and drew a basin of warm water from the sink. Fetching a cloth, he first bathed my upper body before he worked his way down, cleaning up everything else. He detached my cock from the milker and washed me there, too, leaving me detached.

After he dried me off he said something in Algonquan. The Terran man responded in their language. They conversed for a moment before the Terran said, "He'll move you to the bed, if you want. If you promise not to fight him."

I nodded. A bed sounded good.

The Algonquan put the basin away. Walking over to a cabinet, he opened it and withdrew an energy leash, shackles, and a blindfold. After clipping the leash to my collar, he blindfolded me before he unhooked my ankles. I held still while he connected the shackles to my ankle manacles. When he unhooked my wrists, I waited for him to give me a cue to move. He hooked one end of the shackle to my left wrist before he prompted me to sit up on my knees, and then connected the right wrist. He hooked my wrists together in front of me. With no slack in the leash, he held my arms, steadying me as I carefully got to my feet. I let him lead me across the room and kept my motions slow and careful.

We stopped, and he said something.

"Carefully kneel," the Terran male said. "The bed is right in front of you. Your knees will hit it."

I did, slowly.

That earned me a pat on the head.

I couldn't help it. The fact that I was being treated with relatively kind actions gave me confidence I wasn't going to be tortured. I felt myself start to choke up, fighting back the prickle of relieved tears.

The leash was gently tugged and I followed it until my handler hooked it to something. Then he removed the ankle shackles before he freed my wrists last. I still wore the manacles.

I felt the bed move as the handler stepped away and said something.

"You can take the blindfold off now," the Terran told me. "That's just a precaution they use at first, to make sure you're gentle. They'll stop using it if you don't fight them."

I moved slowly and deliberately and worked it off my head, offering it up.

The handler took it from me, pointed at my gag, and nodded.

"You can take that off, too," the Terran said.

I was too focused on my handler to look at my fellow captive. With my fingers, I worked my way around the strap by feel until I located the buckle in back, unfastened it, and offered it up.

The handler smiled, nodded, and exited through a door after turning off the room's main lights, leaving us only with a dim corner lamp.

I finally turned my attention to the other man. Shaggy brown hair, blue eyes. Devoid of any hair on his face or body. A firm military body, although not chiseled like many grunts who spend all their free time doing PT. He sat against the wall, his posture one of ease, relaxation.

He also wore manacles at the wrists and ankles, a collar, and a tag in his right ear. His collar had been hooked with an energy tether to a socket in the wall behind him. Enough slack he could stand up, lie down, and move around a little, but as was I, not enough room we could touch. The bed was a huge, comfortable pallet in one corner of the room, with clean, crisp sheets, soft pillows, and loosely woven afghans for extra warmth. But the room felt comfortable temperature-wise.

Like me, he was naked.

I worked my jaw, the first time I'd not had my mouth filled since before my capture, except for the brief moment when they'd swapped the gags at my purchase.

"Where are we?" I asked, keeping my voice low.

He playfully smirked. "It's okay. We're allowed to talk to each other. That's why he bought you. Well, one of the reasons."

"Answer my question. Where are we?"

"We're on Algonquan. I would think that's obvious."

"We're..." *Holy fuck.* My ship had been five quadrants from Algonquan. That was a six-month trip, even with a jump. How long had I been unconscious, anyway?

He sensed my confusion. "Their jump drive technology puts ours to shame. What takes us months to travel, they literally can jump in a couple of days. Hours, even."

That sucked the wind out of me and I needed a moment to process that news. There'd been absolutely no hint of that info in my training. Not even in the wildest rumors I'd heard.

"How long have you been here?" I asked.

"I don't know, for sure. When were you taken? What's the last date you remember?"

I told him, and he smiled. "Two years then, since I arrived here. At least. Give or take."

He seemed overly relaxed about the situation. I looked around. "Is there any way to escape?"

He shrugged. "Where would you go, naked and alone on a foreign world and unable to speak their language? I've never tried to escape. Please don't tell me you're one of those macho grunt kinds. He had to take the last two back because they wouldn't settle down. I'm really tired of being alone. It'd be nice to have some company."

I suddenly felt badly for the guy. "I'm Dale."

"Mark. Nice to meet you." He waved. "I'd shake your hand, but…" He pointed at the energy tether holding him on that end of the bed.

"Will we always stay tied up like this?"

"No. Usually, I'm allowed free run of the house and backyard."

"Why are you tied up now? What'd you do wrong?"

He laughed. "Dude, I didn't do anything wrong. They wanted me here to talk to you in case you got upset. To help keep you calm. They did this to *protect* me."

"Protect you? From what?"

He pointed at me. "They didn't want me able to get near you in case you reacted badly and tried to hurt me, or if you tried to fight them. They wanted me safely out of the way, but they didn't want to have to hover and make you nervous until you get more used to everything. If you just keep doing what you're doing and don't fight them, they'll let us both loose pretty soon. Once they can trust you." His expression grew grim. "The last guy almost choked me to death."

"Algonquan?"

"No. Stupid asshole grunt from the Texas territory. He bought him because he thought he'd be a good one, huge guy, but still too much fight in him. Too much macho bullshit. He had to return him. That was last week." He tipped his head back and pointed to his throat. I spotted the healing bruises around his neck, even in the dim light.

"Oh. He who? You keep saying he."

"I can't really pronounce his name in Algonquan, so I just call him Master. He seems to like it."

My mind felt too disjointed to make sense of anything without shattering my sanity, so I decided to focus on basics. "Do they torture you?"

He snorted. "No. They've been nothing but nice to me."

"Except for the ass fucking."

He shrugged. "Would you rather get shot at or tortured?"

He had me there. "Not really." I studied him. He seemed at peace with his fate. "So, we're, what? Sex toys?"

He smirked. "Not exactly." He stretched out, hands behind his head, as if getting ready to go to sleep.

"Well what, exactly, are we?"

He looked at me. "Promise you won't freak out?"

"No."

"Ah. I don't want to tell you then."

Horror filled me. "Jesus, I knew it. We're cattle. They're going to eat us."

He burst out laughing, hard and long. I felt my tension grow.

"Will you please tell me what's so funny?" I heard the hysteria in my voice.

"I've been here *two* years," he finally choked out as he laughed. "They would have eaten me long before now." He pulled himself together. "I'll tell you, but you need to promise me you'll stay calm. Seriously. If you freak out, they'll put you back in that again." He waved at the frame.

I looked at it. I didn't want to be over there. I wanted to be here, in a bed that felt a damn sight softer than the crappy bunk I'd had on the ship, and able to talk to this guy. "Okay, fine. I'll stay calm."

I hoped.

Mark looked me squarely in the eye. "We're not going to be eaten. We're breeders."

CHAPTER FOUR

He gave me a few moments to digest that.

"Breeders?"

He nodded.

I needed a few more moments with that. "So, what he just did—"

Mark shook his head. "No. That time, he only fucked you. Getting you used to him. He does that a lot." He smirked again. "As you yourself felt, there are far worse things than having an Algonquan tongue or cock up your ass."

I felt my face heat. "One small problem—I'm not gay."

Mark shrugged. "So? Neither am I. I'm also well past the point of trying to deny I enjoy it. Considering the things I know for a fact our government's secretly done to Algonquans they've taken captive, I think we're being treated a damn sight better than we treat them."

"Breeders?" I felt a little ill.

He nodded. "Yep." He lay back and looked at me. "Seriously, don't freak out. It's okay. You'll enjoy it."

My jaw was probably in my lap at the absurdity of that statement. "Don't freak out?"

He smiled. "Do you see me freaking out?"

I looked at him. Actually studied him. Then I realized his cock, while flaccid, looked unusually large. Larger than mine.

He followed my eyes. "Yeah, nice side effect of spending most of the past two years on the milker. I'm sure yours will grow, too."

I snorted.

"What?" he asked.

"That's what I've been calling it in my head. A milker."

"Well, it fits, right? Ingenious, if you ask me."

I wasn't sure I wanted to know. "Can I ask about the logistics of...breeding?" Not like I was getting out of this situation. I might as well know as much as possible about what lay ahead of me.

"How many details do you want right now?"

"Start with the basics and let's see how I do."

"Algonquans are unisex. Maybe that's not the right word, but I'm not a med tech. They have a penis, as you experienced, but they also have a bodily orifice to carry an egg. Before the war broke out, they would reproduce by partnering with someone and implanting their egg in them. The partner is only a hatcher. The egg totally comes from the one depositing it. I don't know how they obtain genetic variety, but obviously they've thrived as a species. Like Terrans, Algonquans are a species of various races. Depending on which race of Algonquan they are, the egg grows to full size in two to four weeks, approximately. The partner delivers it, then it's cared for until it hatches.

"Unfortunately, they have a high egg mortality rate. But once an egg hatches, they reach maturity in a fraction of the time of a Terran. By the time they're around seven Terran years old, they're full-grown adult Algonquans and ready to start their reproductive cycles. They have long lives, and a hundred or more Terran years is on the short end of the scale, for them.

"Before this stupid war started, they carefully regulated their population. They didn't have to reproduce frequently because they wanted to keep their population stable. Once the war started, they realized they'd be forced to build their numbers quickly, if they wanted to preserve their species.

"The best I can ascertain, they didn't plan to use Terrans as breeders, but see, they have a cycle. When they're with a partner, it's usually under control and doesn't naturally happen very often. They can also take medicine to trigger it. Sometimes, actions like getting in a fight can trigger it. Strong emotions, right? And when they're in a cycle to produce an egg, they must implant it, or it literally will kill them. They get egg bound or something.

"From what I understand, how humans ended up in the picture is that at some point someone was desperate to implant an egg because they didn't have a partner, but they had a Terran prisoner, and decided what the hell, why not? It was better to risk that than dying. *Voilà*. I guess neither the human nor the Algonquan found the process objectionable, so they did some research and came up with humane logistics to scale it up to a mass production process."

The ramifications staggered me. "So all those missing guys…" Which I now stupidly realized included me, at this point.

He nodded. "We aren't missing. Some are dead, yeah, but not murdered. I'm sure some of them died fighting, or trying to escape. Most of us are breeders being used by the Algonquans to rapidly replenish their population and win the war. Under normal circumstances, two Algonquan partners deliberately reproduce only once or twice every few decades if that, and with no guarantee the eggs will survive. Using us as breeders, they can lay a new egg every few days, if they trigger their cycle." He laughed. "Ironic, huh? We're helping them build their ranks."

I tried to digest that. "How many times have you…" I couldn't say it.

He shrugged again. "Master doesn't want to wear me out, I guess. He's only bred me about twelve times or so, including this time. I quit counting. I think it's twelve. Could be thirteen."

"*This* time?"

He nodded. "Two weeks ago. Usually, the eggs drop around four weeks with him." He grinned. "In a few more days, I'll be so fucking horny I can't see straight, once it gets big enough. That's one of the best parts."

I couldn't see anything different about him. "So where...is it?"

He arched an eyebrow at me. "Isn't it obvious? That's the reason for the butt plugs. The bigger the plug can be made, the bigger the guy is, that means they can comfortably hold a larger egg. When they put you out for sale, that's what the prospective buyers want to know, how big you are and how hard you can come. When you climax, ass muscles clench, and that helps pull the egg in. Also helps with the delivery of the egg. That, and if you're well behaved, of course."

I didn't know what to ask next. Logistical questions came to mind, but I didn't know if I really wanted those answers or not.

Mark sensed my confusion. "Whatever they feed us, it apparently doesn't pass through our intestines anymore. I mean, not like it used to. We do eat solid food. They'll start you on it in a few days, once your body has fully adjusted. Yes, the egg is up my ass. That's what you want to know, isn't it?"

I nodded. No use denying it.

"It goes in small and comes out big. The last two weeks, it's pretty much at its final size, and in the last several days it constantly rubs against your prostate. Meaning you will willingly spend a lot of time on *that*." He pointed at the frame again.

"Willingly?" My throat felt dry.

"If he's got us both knocked up at the same time, he might need to invest in a second one. It feels better being connected to the milker and it's more comfortable lying on the frame, once you hit that point. Every time you move, you come."

He grinned. "There are far worse tortures. I suspect whatever they feed us has amped up our sex drives. I once tried to keep track how many times I climaxed in a day when I was early in my egg cycle, and I quit counting at fifty. The last few days of a cycle, before I drop, I'm constantly hard, even right after I've come. If I have to choose being a human kept as an Algonquan breeder, or an Algonquan kept as a human prisoner, I'll stay right here, thank you very much."

"How did you learn so much? How'd you learn their language?"

"I was a linguist with the military. I thought I was pretty good with their language, until I got captured. Then I realized what our government doesn't know about the Algonquan language and culture would fill a dozen libraries. I don't understand a lot of what they say. I don't understand many of Master's friends, either. There are different accents and dialects, just like in Terran languages. I understand enough, learned enough, that I can communicate with Master and the few others I interact with on a regular basis."

That's when the shakes hit as the full ramifications of my situation slammed into me. My teeth chattered as I realized how thoroughly—literally—screwed I was.

I reached for one of the afghans and pulled it around me as I curled into a ball on my side.

Mark sat up, his expression looking concerned. "Hey, it's okay. Don't worry, please? It's all right. As you can see, they haven't hurt me. Other humans I've had contact with, they're happy, too. This is a good life! Beats the hell out of getting shot at, or dying in space."

I couldn't respond. I felt tears rolling down my cheeks and I didn't even care. I rocked myself, even wishing I could curl up with Mark for comfort.

He looked worried. "Dale, please, it's all right. Please don't be frightened."

I'd had enough. I was ready to check out for the night, so I closed my eyes.

* * * *

I woke up to what felt like early morning in our room. The corner lamp was on, but the light through the window had brightened.

Mark was sitting up, staring at me. "You okay?"

I nodded. I sat up and wrapped the afghan around myself.

I didn't miss that his cock looked hard and engorged, standing straight out from his body, clear pre-cum leaking from the end.

"They'll be in soon," he said. "For our morning routines."

He no sooner said that than the door opened. The Algonquan man who put me to bed last night flipped on the ceiling light and smiled at us, then said something cheerful sounding.

Mark smiled and responded, making the Algonquan laugh. He immediately walked over to Mark, who lowered his head so the Algonquan could detach the energy tether from his collar. As soon as he was free, Mark jumped up and raced for the frame. I watched as he grabbed the milker hose, stuck it on his cock with a relieved sigh, then climbed up onto the frame and laid his head down. His hips gyrated as his fists clenched around handles built into it.

The Algonquan shook his head and laughed as he walked over to Mark and patted his ass. I wondered if he'd tether him to it, but apparently Mark was a well-trained and trusted pet. He spent the better part of a half-hour on it, during which I heard him come at least five or six times. Our caretaker moved about the room, tidying things up, smiling at me in what I guessed was supposed to be a comforting way. He checked on Mark every so often, asked him a question, usually getting an answer in a moaning voice, which made the Algonquan laugh every time and earned Mark another gentle pat on the ass.

My own cock slowly inflated.

Finally, the caretaker walked over to him and rubbed his head, saying something to him. Mark made a negative sound in reply. The Algonquan laughed and chided him. Mark groaned, but sat up. I didn't miss how his expression looked content and glazed. Sated.

The caretaker removed the milker and offered him a steadying hand getting off the frame and helped him over to the bed. He started to attach Mark's tether but then paused and asked him a question.

Mark shook his head.

The caretaker warily eyed me as asked Mark something else, as if confirming Mark's answer.

Mark closed his eyes and shook his head.

The caretaker shrugged and turned to me.

"He said he won't shackle you if you promise to behave," Mark said. "If you don't behave, or if he thinks you're going to try to hurt me, he can and will shock you with the leash. He doesn't want to do that, so behaving is easiest for everyone." He sounded like...well, like a guy who'd just gotten well-laid.

My cock throbbed harder. "I'll behave," I said.

Mark nodded and said something to the caretaker, who smiled and nodded as he reached for my tether.

I also had to pee. "How do I tell him I need to use the facilities? Is there someplace else?" I'd used the milker last night while I was on the frame.

"You use the milker. Just like you did while transported in the frame, before you were brought here. It's a multi-tasker."

I waited for the slack to be taken up in my leash before I slowly got to my feet and let him lead me to the frame. I climbed on, but he hooked my wrist and ankle manacles to it before he attached my cock.

I immediately relieved myself, and then another need took over. I didn't bother trying to stay quiet when the first and second orgasms hit me in quick succession. The third was smaller and, after, I laid there with my eyes closed, simply enjoying it.

As Mark had said, there were far worse things.

The caretaker patted me on the ass and left me there.

That was fine with me. I didn't want to go anywhere, quite frankly.

"He's going to fix breakfast for us," Mark said.

"What's his name?" I mumbled.

"That's Qhan. He's one of the few whose names I can say. He's the one who will normally take care of us. He's nice, easy to get along with. He likes to sneak me extra treats when Master isn't looking. He can't afford a breeder pet of his own, but he's got a partner. They live here with Master. His partner, I call him Mack, is Master's driver and assistant. He's the guy from last night."

Pets. We were pets.

Then another orgasm hit me, and I laid there and enjoyed it.

A few minutes later, the door opened. Qhan returned, followed by Master. Master walked around and smiled at me, patted my head, and asked Qhan a few questions. Then he stepped behind me again and repeated the previous night's encounter. Warm hands, thumbs opening me, exploring my ass with his tongue.

I rocked my hips against him, wanting more than that.

Pride? What pride? Pride didn't get me laid.

Master chuckled and stroked my butt. In another moment, he withdrew his tongue and replaced it with his cock.

He held me still with his large hands on my hips, giving me time to get used to him before he started fucking me.

"He's not in his cycle," Mark said, sounding more normal now. "He enjoys a morning fuck like any other man. He hasn't been able to fuck me for two weeks because of the egg."

I laid there and enjoyed it, earning more praise when I climaxed twice more before my spent cock decided it'd had enough for now. I knew it'd probably be a while before my drained balls could recover from that.

Master finished, talking to Qhan as he waited for his cock to recede before withdrawing. I opened my eyes when he walked around the frame to stand in front of me. He stroked my hair, my cheeks, then brushed his fingers along my lips and gently pressed.

I opened my mouth and sucked on his finger. He stroked my hair with his other hand as he softly talked to me. I couldn't understand a word he said.

"He likes you," Mark said. "He's telling you how happy he is that you're settling right in. Letting you suck his finger is really good. He's trusting you not to bite him. It's a gesture of faith with them."

I didn't reply. I simply laid there and waited and sucked his finger as I felt my cock impossibly twitch inside the milker.

He finally finished with me. Qhan cleaned me up and released me before helping me back to the bed on my shaky legs. Master had knelt behind Mark, who'd gotten on his hands and knees. Master was examining him, apparently, his tongue already buried inside Mark's ass. Mark had his eyes closed and seemed to be enjoying the experience.

Qhan attached my energy leash to the bed again but with more slack than I'd had before. When Master finished, he sat up and patted Mark's ass before climbing out of the bed and leaving us.

Qhan handed Mark a bottle of clear liquid, a dish of food, and a spoon. The food reminded me of oatmeal, except it had a bluish tinge. Qhan handed me a bottle of clear, pinkish liquid, although it was in a different kind of bottle, like he'd had to mix it, whereas the bottle Mark drank from had a label, as if store-bought.

"Go ahead and drink it," Mark said. "It's food and drink, for now. If you're hungry, he'll bring you more. Drink as much as you want. They don't want you to be hungry or uncomfortable. Anytime you need something, just ask for it. Food, drink, the milker—anything."

I took it and nodded to Qhan. He smiled and patted me on the head, making the now-familiar chirruping noise.

"That's their equivalent of 'good boy,' if you haven't guessed yet," Mark said as he opened his bottle and took a long drink.

Qhan exited the room, but he left the door standing open. From where I sat, I could only see the opposite wall of the hallway the door opened onto. Mark quickly finished his breakfast and drink and carried his bowl over to a small table near the sink. When he returned to the bed, he took my empty bottle from me and also put it with his dishes. Then he sat, cross-legged, in front of me on the bed.

"No chores. No work. No morning wake-up, no mandatory lights out. No goddamned wank closets. No PT. No danger. Nothing to do but literally eat, sleep, and fuck around. It's not a bad life." He grinned. "Then again, I don't know about you, but I hated the military. I didn't want to be there. They drafted my ass."

"Neither did I," I admitted. "Like it, that is. I was drafted, too."

His grin widened as he stuck out his hand. I shook with him. "Then you're perfect. Usually, I sleep with Master in his bed, except for the last couple of days before I drop an egg. Then I'm usually sleeping on that." He pointed to the frame. "I'm so horny I hate being away from the milker."

I wondered if this was some sort of whacked out dream. That maybe I was actually lying unconscious on the flight deck after having hit my head or something and I was dreaming all of this. Now that Mark was closer, I realized he had no morning stubble on his face despite not having shaved. It would seem the hair removal was permanent.

"Why do they shave us when we're captured?"

He ran a hand up his smooth, hairless arm. "Whatever it is they do, it's permanent. I think our hair itches them. They have very sensitive skin. If you'll notice, they have no body hair, just hair on their head." He ran a hand through his scruffy hair and looked at my still regulation-short cut. "Master doesn't like long hair on me, but he likes it shaggy. Qhan usually trims it for me about once a month. Master will let yours grow out about the same as mine."

"We're never going home again, are we?" I softly asked, my situation finally sinking in.

He frowned. "I *am* home. This *is* my home. I have no family except Master. My parents died when I was a kid, and I was raised in a foster warehouse. I wasn't eligible to get married, and I didn't have any money. Fuck Terrans! *This* is my home, and Master is my family."

He almost seemed angry with me.

"I'm sorry." I don't know why I felt the need to apologize.

His expression softened. "It's okay. I'm sorry, but when I think about the lies the government told us about them, and what I know they do to Algonquan prisoners..." He chewed on his lower lip. "As you can see, the government lied to us about what kind of race they are. They're humanoid, and while yes, they are different from us, I personally think they're more 'human' than we are."

I laughed.

"What's so funny?" he asked.

"I sort of had a thought like that before he bought me. That they were more human, and humane, than we were in some ways. I was afraid I would be eaten."

He grinned. "They're not barbaric, trust me. I think they eat seafood, but I've never seen anything I would call meat. Fruits, vegetables, things I can't identify that are some sort of protein, but never anything resembling beef or pork or chicken. They don't shit like we do. Their elimination is all liquid. They don't even have facilities like we do. They have bathrooms, washrooms, but you'll see little receptacles all over the place where they pee. You can use those if you have to go and you're not near the milker."

I thought about how Master, as I realized I had no problem thinking of him, seemed comfortable talking to the other man while fucking me. "They're pretty open, huh? During sex?"

"Yeah. With each other. They don't hump each other in public like that, but..." I sensed him wording his next statement carefully, probably so as not to upset me. "Let's be honest. We're breeders. Pets. Animals. Because when I'm brutally honest about it, comparing technology and civilization, Terrans aren't a fraction as advanced as they are. We're treated well, here. Pampered, even. They obviously know we are reasonably intelligent and feel emotions. Still, it's not uncommon to see a human get fucked in public if the urge strikes them."

He glanced down at where his hands lay in his lap. "And sometimes, Master might let one of his friends fuck you. Never breed you, but fuck you. We're possessions." He looked up at me. "Let me tell you something, though—I feel loved. For the first time since my parents died, it honestly feels like someone gives a damn about me. Loves me, even. Master is my life, and he's all I need. I was terrified when I first arrived, wondering what they were going to do. Qhan and Master were always very patient with me, soothing me, and after the first week, I realized I wasn't going to die. And Qhan never fucks us," he clarified. "He only cares for us."

I noticed he included me in that. *Us*. "Does it hurt?" I quietly asked.

"Does what hurt?"

I pointed at his stomach.

He smiled. "Not hurt so much, but the first time, both when he bred me and when I dropped, it scared the hell out of me because I didn't know what to expect or what would happen. There's a little bit of discomfort sometimes, but as you'll soon find out, the pleasure you'll also feel completely overwhelms that and makes it amazing."

My stomach growled and Mark heard it. "Are you still hungry?"

"Yeah."

He rolled his eyes. "Seriously, Dale," he said, standing and walking over to grab my empty bottle. "If you need more, say so." He left the room. When he disappeared down the hall, a brief skitter of fear trilled through me.

I was absolutely alone.

Mark returned a few minutes later with another full bottle. I was damned happy to see him, too, and not just because of the bottle.

He sat on the bed and handed it to me. "See? Easy."

I mumbled my thanks and took it, quickly finishing the contents. That seemed to fill me up, and I even burped.

He laughed. "Qhan said he'll be in as soon as he's finished with his breakfast. We get to shower with Master this morning."

I noticed his cock had already inflated again. He stood and walked over to the frame, hooked himself to the milker, and climbed on. That's where he was when Qhan returned.

Our caretaker laughed and patted Mark on the ass, saying something to him. Mark moaned but stood and detached himself. Qhan walked over to me and I felt guilty that he looked at me warily. I lowered my head, as I'd seen Mark do, and docilely waited.

What good would it do to fight if they weren't going to hurt me?

What, fight for my pride? What fucking pride?

If that made me a pussy in some people's eyes, so be it. Because what Mark had said about no one else loving him resonated deeply within me.

I was alone in the universe, before now, although I'd been fortunate enough to have my parents longer than he had.

If I was being treated well and had been given a new family of sorts...why not enjoy it?

My gesture seemed to please Qhan. I earned another *good boy* and he unclipped my leash from the wall. He gently tugged on the leash, prompting me to my feet. Mark waited for us by the door and, together, the three of us left the room.

CHAPTER FIVE

I finally got my first look at more of my new home. Now the sun was well up, but it still felt comfortably cool in the house despite the bright sunlight slanting through the tall windows. Green tiles lined the floors and the walls were smoothly stuccoed in different muted colors, depending on the room. As we walked down the hall I glimpsed rooms down other halls. The house felt enormous.

Three rooms down, we were led into a sitting room, then into a bedroom. From there, into a gigantic bathroom.

Master stood at the sink, naked, his back to us as he brushed his teeth.

Not much different than a Terran male preparing for his day.

Mark immediately stepped into a large alcove I recognized as their version of a shower. Qhan asked Master something, received his answer, and led me in. My leash was tethered to a connector on the shower wall.

"Don't worry," Mark assured me. "The leash can get wet and it won't shock you."

I hadn't worried until he said that, but it was nice to hear.

After he finished, Master joined us. Now I got my first look at Master's cock. It wasn't just huge, it looked like it would rip a human apart. I honestly couldn't see how it fit inside me at all if it was that large when flaccid. He didn't appear to have an external ball sac.

He grabbed Mark and kissed him before turning on the water. I stood there and waited. Not like I could do anything anyway.

Mark dropped to his knees and licked and sucked the head of Master's cock. It inflated slightly, as did Mark's. Master stood there, eyes closed, and ran his hands through Mark's hair. After a few minutes of this he tapped Mark on the head, prompting him to stand.

Master stepped over to me. He examined my cock, which started to harden in his hands, pleasing him. He brushed his fingers over my nipples, then turned me around and nudged my feet apart. I braced my hands against the wall and waited.

He slowly ran his hands over my back, down my spine, to my ass. His touch felt sensuous, loving. Then he pressed a finger deep inside me, making me moan as my cock throbbed even harder.

When he dropped to his knees behind me, I rested my forehead against the wall and waited.

Anticipated.

His tongue pressed through my rim and swept my insides, caressing my gland and making me shoot jets of cum against the tile wall.

"There he blows," Mark joked.

My cock remained hard though, and Master didn't withdraw his tongue. Now that he'd found that sweet spot, he kept working it with his tongue, caressing it, until he forced another orgasm out of me.

Then he withdrew and stood. I wondered if he'd fuck me again, but he didn't. He turned me around and said something to Mark. Mark handed him a washcloth and soap, and Master moved me to stand under the spray. Getting my hair wet and starting at my head, he worked his way down my body, thoroughly washing me, but gently.

Is it weird that it felt even more intimate than anything I'd already endured?

After satisfied I was clean, Master rinsed the soap from me and nudged me to stand out of the way.

He washed Mark, who stood there with his eyes closed, obviously enjoying it. His cock was already hard again.

Master gently flicked it with his fingers and laughed. Not as if mocking it, but like he was happy to see the reaction. Then he inserted a finger inside Mark and grabbed Mark's cock with his other hand, quickly making him shoot his load. Mark leaned against him to catch his breath.

He tenderly nuzzled Mark's forehead and a brief wave of jealousy washed through me, startling me. It was obvious he cared for Mark.

Would he ever come to care for me like that?

As if reading my thoughts, Master looked at me and smiled before stepping over to me and kissing me. I'd never been kissed by a guy before, but I enjoyed it. When Master stepped away, he winked at me.

I felt an unexpected warm heat flood my insides.

I was pretty sure he liked me.

* * * *

After our shower, we were towel-dried and Qhan led us back to our room. Mark immediately headed for the milker while Qhan stood there, holding my leash and waiting. Truth be told, I was getting pretty horny again myself. I didn't know if it was the situation, what they fed me, or what. After Mark spent a few minutes on the frame, he climbed off without prompting and Qhan tugged my leash.

I didn't need to be told twice. Qhan hooked my wrists but not my ankles before he attached the milker. I closed my eyes and let it work its magic.

I don't know how much time passed before Qhan disconnected it and removed me from the frame. I thought he'd take me back to bed, but then I realized Mark had, at some point, left the room.

Qhan led me through the house, which was even larger than I first thought. He took me through a room I suspected was the kitchen, out a back door, and I found myself in a large, fenced-in yard.

Mark lay in the middle, face-up in the soft grass, with his eyes closed and a smile lighting his features.

Qhan led me over to him, drove a stake into the ground, and hooked my leash to it. Then he retreated to the shaded patio and sat reading a hand-held computer device.

Mark didn't open his eyes. "This is my idea of heaven. Did you ever have a yard?"

I sat in the grass next to him. "No yards on Ganymede." I snorted. "No grass on Ganymede, either."

I closed my eyes and tipped my face to the sky, enjoying the feel of the warm sunlight on my pale body. I realized how tan Mark's skin was compared to my pasty white flesh. Being outside, for me, was a rarity. In my life, the only times I'd been "outside" on a planet were my two trips to Earth in the military.

Admittedly, there were far worse places to be held in captivity.

"They won't keep us out here too long," Mark said. "Or else they'll move us to the shade for a while." He waved in the direction of a few trees off to one side, including one that bore pinkish fruit.

I lay back next to Mark. When I felt his fingers brush mine, I didn't pull away.

Apparently realizing I didn't object to the contact, he loosely curled his fingers around mine.

After a few minutes, he softly spoke.

"'Love has earth to which she clings
With hills and circling arms about —
Wall within wall to shut fear out.
But Thought has need of no such things,
For Thought has a pair of dauntless wings.'"

He looked at me. "That's the old Earth poet, Robert Frost. Ever hear of him?"

"No."

As he continued reciting, I realized I enjoyed the sound of his voice. Soothing, warm, rich. How long had it been since he'd been able to freely talk with another human in his native language?

"'On snow and sand and turf, I see
Where Love has left a printed trace
With straining in the world's embrace.
And such is Love and glad to be.
But Thought has shaken his ankles free.'"

He chuckled. "That's not the whole poem. I used to love his works. I remember quite a few of them."

I felt him roll to his side toward me, not releasing my hand. "Please don't fight them," he whispered. "Please, don't do anything to make them send you away. I've been so lonely. When he started looking for another pet for me, I thought *finally*, I wouldn't be alone. But the first two he picked were grunts who needed a lot of re-training and gentling to fit in. They were beyond angry at me for accepting my fate. They didn't understand." He sniffled. "Like I said, the last one nearly killed me."

I opened my eyes and saw him near tears. I didn't have any friends on board the ship. I wondered what happened to Billy Akins and felt a brief moment of sadness for that kid, who was probably scared witless wherever he'd ended up. Mark wasn't just alone on an alien world—he was lonely.

I had a choice to make. I could accept this, enjoy it, and take each day as it came, or I could make myself and Mark miserable by wishing things were different and trying to uphold "principles" I didn't even believe in.

I rolled onto my side and propped myself up on one elbow. I laced my fingers through his and squeezed. "Screw the military. I never liked the damned military anyway."

He laughed before blinking away his tears. "Thank you, Dale. I can't tell you how grateful I am."

His cock had inflated again.

"Jesus, will I get like that, too?"

He looked down and laughed before rolling onto his back again. He let go of my hand and started stroking himself. "Yeah. You'll find when you're carrying, toward the end, you're only really satisfied if you're hooked to the milker. You can jerk off, but it's not nearly as strong."

He proceeded to do just that, his hand slicking pre-cum over the purple, engorged head, quickly bringing himself to climax, but his cock barely softened.

I watched, my own cock now hard.

When I heard Master's voice, we both looked. He stood on the patio next to Qhan, talking with him. They watched us, their body language indicating how pleased they were that the pets got along so well.

The other man, the one who talked with Master when he fucked me the first time after I was brought home, walked out onto the patio, carrying something about the size of a small duffel bag. Mark sat up, his eyes lighting.

"What?"

He grinned. "Master bought us a new toy. That's Mack, Qhan's partner. He works for Master."

Qhan took the item, and as he carried it over to us, he laughed when he spotted Mark's happy expression. When I saw the two hoses attached to it, I realized it was, in fact, a smaller, portable version of the milker. Setting it on the ground near us, he uncoiled the first hose. He attached it to Mark, who immediately let out a happy moan and fell back in the grass as his hips thrust in the air.

Qhan held up the second one to me, asking me something in a teasing, playful tone.

Immediately, my mind flashed to a human teasing a dog with a toy, asking the dog if it wanted it.

I nodded and lay down in the grass, my palms flat on the ground.

He laughed and made the good boy noise before he attached the hose to my cock.

I closed my eyes and groaned. I didn't care that the three Algonquans stood on the patio and watched the pump sucking off the human pets.

All I cared about were the three orgasms I experienced in quick succession, wringing the energy from my body.

At some point, they decided we'd had enough sun, yet they didn't want to take us inside. Qhan didn't unhook us from the milker. He pulled up the stake holding my leash, waited for us to get to our feet, and led us into the shade. Then he restaked me and set the pump down. He gave Mark and me pats on the head before returning to his previous post to watch over us.

"This is great," Mark mumbled. "*Fuck* those damn grunts. Who *wouldn't* love this life?"

I had to admit, Mark made an excellent point.

CHAPTER SIX

Qhan brought our lunch to us out in the backyard. By this point, I felt sane enough, and Mark had enough relief, to talk again. We were still connected to the portable milker. I felt no rush to unhook myself, either.

I kind of hoped they'd just leave us out in the backyard all day.

As far as I was concerned, they didn't need to stake my leash in place to keep me there. I'd stay right with that damn pump.

"I think they want you to get sunlight," Mark said. "They know we don't get enough natural sunlight stuck in ships. Normally, I can come and go out here as I want to, but the first few weeks I was here, they used the stake and leash on me, too, just to make sure I didn't escape." He chuckled. "Once I got the hang of the routine, I did everything in my power to prove to them there was no way in hell I was going to try to escape."

He looked over at me. "Any questions?"

Tons. "How do you know if you're being bred versus if he's just fucking you?" I nervously asked.

Mark snacked on a piece of fruit. "You'll know. First of all, his cock starts out really hard and rigid. Then he swells up even bigger than normal right off the bat, to hold you in place." He held up one hand, his fingers hooked into a claw. "When he's laying, he's got this small appendage that comes out of the end of his cock, and it has these little tiny barbs in it."

I must have looked pale because he laughed. "It doesn't hurt bad. It's sort of a pinchy king of sensation, but not like ripping your guts out. It doesn't last long, either." He reached over and pinched my inner arm. I winced. "Like that."

I rubbed my arm. "What does that do?"

"It grabs on to you, to ensure you're in place. Don't worry, they'll have you hooked to the milker and horny as hell. The first couple of times, they gave me something to drink beforehand, and it had me so horny I could barely see straight. You'll feel the egg passing through as it enters you, and then it emerges from him and he'll stay connected to you for a long time, until it's securely implanted in you.

"How long it takes isn't predictable. Sometimes, it's only an hour or two, sometimes a couple of hours. One time, it was like six hours. Then the barbs let go, his cock eventually goes down, and he pulls out. They'll put a plug in you for a day or so and make you stay mostly in bed, just to make sure it takes. Then the vet—"

"Vet?"

He laughed. "That's what I call their doctor. I guess if I'm a pet, that would make him my vet, right?"

I nodded.

He continued. "The vet will come in and examine you to make sure everything took okay, and then you can go back to normal activities after that. Except Master won't fuck you from that point on, until after you drop."

I needed to hear it all. "What's that like? Dropping?"

"Well, that's a different experience. Remember the anal plug, how if you pushed, you almost got shocked?"

"Yeah."

"Well, get over that. You have to push when they tell you to get it out. You'll start feeling crampy, some pains. That's the process starting. The eggs are hard when they're first laid, then before you drop they soften. They'll start stretching your ass again a few days early with massage and possibly a plug, to help relax it. Once the actual drop starts, Master will sit there with you to catch it."

I didn't miss the frown that passed his face. "That, sometimes, can be difficult. I know from what I've seen that Master's eggs aren't the largest, but they're big. They use the milker, of course, to help ease you through it, but sometimes it's a little rough."

"How big?"

He held up his fist and used his other hand to indicate how much bigger it was than that.

Now I felt scared again.

He spotted my worry. "Seriously, don't stress. It's okay. After it's over, you get pampered for the next couple of days like you wouldn't believe."

"And then it starts all over again."

He nodded. "Eventually."

"You never see the...children?"

"Nope. I don't know what happens once Master takes the eggs. I guess he's got someone to take care of them for him. Or maybe they get sent off to the government to raise. I don't know. I do know they use the extra eggs for troops." He shrugged. "We're just the breeder. There's none of our DNA in the eggs. If they could replicate a mechanical breeder, I'm sure they would."

After we finished eating, Qhan walked over with a basin in his hand. I couldn't see what was in it, but he made a hand gesture to me that clearly meant "roll over."

I looked at Mark. He laid back in the grass and enjoyed the pump, his eyes closed.

I swallowed and rolled over, careful not to dislodge the milker hose as I did.

Qhan patted the back of my thighs, and I realized he wanted my ass in the air, so I obeyed.

I closed my eyes, hands clenched in the grass as he rubbed something on my rim. When I felt him slide something in me, I grunted. It then grew in size, stretching my ass almost to the point of me asking for him to stop. It also inflated deeper inside me. When he was satisfied, he patted my ass and left me there.

There went my cock again. I couldn't help it, the new device was rubbing against my prostate.

I flopped onto my side and moaned as another orgasm hit me.

Mark opened one eye. "What?"

I couldn't talk. I just rolled over, ass facing him, so he could see.

He laughed. "Oh, sorry. Forgot to tell you about that. They usually don't do that to me anymore. Before the first few times they bred me, they did it. Probably to open you up, make sure you're nice and loose. They don't want to hurt you."

"Thanks for the warning."

He shrugged and closed his eyes again. "You'll enjoy it. I do. The first time, like I said, that was a little scary, because I didn't know what the hell was going on exactly." He opened one eye and looked at me. "Look at it this way, at least you know what's going to happen. I'll be there with you to talk you through it. All you have to do is enjoy it as much as you can."

By that evening, I still had the butt plug in. Qhan had adjusted it several more times throughout the afternoon, making it uncomfortably large, to the point that if I moved wrong—or would that be right?—I orgasmed. Mark talked them into taking the leash off me and letting him show me around the house, although I walked funny and he fought the urge to run back to the milker.

He pointed to a group of comfortable pillows in one corner of the living room where a darkened vid screen filled one wall. There was a large, comfortable looking couch in front of the screen. "At night, when Master's watching vids, he'll bring me in here with him. Sometimes, he has me sit with him. Sometimes, I just lie in the corner. Depends on if he's got company or not, or what kind of mood he's in."

"Sit with him?"

Mark smirked. "Yes, sometimes with his cock inside me."

"Ah. He doesn't have a...partner?"

Mark looked sad. "I don't know the whole story, but from what I heard, I think his mate was killed by Terrans in the war. He doesn't like to talk about it."

I stopped, in shock. "And he doesn't hate us?"

The anger I'd seen in Mark's face before returned. "They're not like Terrans. They're *better* than Terrans. They didn't want this war. They're only holding a line to protect their territory until the Terrans finally give up. They have no desire to take over the whole universe. They could be at Earth in three fucking days with their jump technology. You don't think they could take over Earth any time they want? They're just waiting on the Terran government to give up and leave them alone."

He waved his arm, indicating the house. "They could have fucking killed us, blown us out of airlocks. Destroyed our ships. Or tortured us, dumped us all on some shithouse planet with crappy atmosphere, and let us fend for ourselves. Or they could be torturing us and forcing us into labor camps. Do you think Terrans treat Algonquans this well? I can assure you that they don't."

I swallowed hard. "I'm sorry."

He took a deep breath to calm himself. "I'm sorry. But I love Master. I love my life here. Is it what I planned for myself? Of course not. In a lot of ways, it's a hell of a lot better. I don't regret a thing, except I wish they'd captured me sooner."

We heard a whistle from somewhere in the house, followed by Qhan's voice calling out.

"That's us. Dinner time." Mark led me back to our room, where sure enough, Qhan waited for us with Mark's food and more of the drink for me. He pointed Mark to the bed in the corner, where he'd left the portable milker and Mark's food. Mark rushed over to the bed and hooked the milker to himself with a happy moan before he started eating.

Qhan patted the frame. My cock was stiff again and I willingly climbed aboard. This time, Qhan left my hands and ankles free and handed me the bottle of drink after attaching the milker. He patted me on the ass and left us alone for a while. When he returned, he checked me, took the empty bottle, then connected my wrist restraints to the frame.

I tried not to worry, but since I'd been trusted free most of the afternoon, I wondered what he was about to do that would make him truss me like that.

I worried even more when he connected my ankles.

Mark walked over. "He's just removing the plug. It's okay. At first, they're still going to restrain you to do certain things. Don't let it spook you. I promise you, he won't hurt you."

I tried to relax. After Qhan shrank and removed the plug, I felt him massaging a salve on me. It felt like he worked his whole fist inside me, and my face heated when I realized I was rocking my hips in time with his movements.

He murmured something positive.

Mark confirmed that. "He's glad you're enjoying it." Mark leaned against the frame and watched. Qhan touched my sweet spot again, triggering another orgasm.

That prompted a laugh from Qhan, and a comment.

"He said he's glad Master picked a smart one, a fast learner this time instead of one of those stupid grunts." Mark walked around me and sat on the floor so he could look up into my face. "They had to keep the first one gagged for three days, hooked to the frame the entire time. He'd scream and bite. Finally, they gave up on him and sent him back. Master never could get him settled enough to breed him."

"The second?" I mumbled, feeling too good to care how whacked this was.

"He played possum. He fooled us, doing just enough to sucker us all in to get free from the frame, then he attacked me. Tried to use me as a hostage. When I fought him, he choked me. They had to use a stunner on him. He went back before he could be bred, too."

I studied Mark's face. If my hands were free, I would have reached down and stroked his hair. "Well, like you said, I hated the military. No great loss if I'm not in it anymore."

Mark translated my comment to Qhan, who grunted approvingly. I wondered how much of his arm was now inside me. He continued massaging and stroking me, pulling out and getting more of whatever it was he used on me before pushing his hand inside me again.

"What is he doing to me?" I mumbled.

Mark reached up and stroked my hair. "I don't know what it is, but it's something they use to prep us before breeding. The massaging helps loosen you up."

My eyes opened. "They're going to do it now?"

He asked Qhan, who answered.

Mark's eyes met mine.

"Well?"

He nodded. "He said Master came into his cycle this afternoon. I thought they were going to wait a day or two at least, to give you more time to settle in."

Fear threatened to take me. Apparently, both Mark and Qhan sensed this. Qhan must have felt my body tense because he stopped his movements inside me and patted my ass with his free hand, soothing me. Mark crouched in front of me, cradling my cheeks in his hands.

"Please, just relax, Dale." His voice sounded as anxious as I felt. "I promise, they won't make me leave you. I'll stay here with you. Please, don't fight them."

Left unsaid, but painted across his face, was the plea for me to behave so they didn't take me back, too.

I wanted to be brave. If Mark had handled all of this totally alone and in the dark, I could handle it, too.

"Will they let you hold my hand?"

He smiled and asked Qhan, who after a pause replied.

"One hand free. Hold on." He dragged the portable milker and a soft pillow over. Then he sat and hooked himself up. He released my left wrist manacle from the frame, lacing his fingers through mine and holding my hand against his cheek. "I'm here. I won't leave you, I promise."

CHAPTER SEVEN

Qhan finished whatever he was doing and inserted another, larger plug to keep me open. Mark didn't leave me. He sat there holding my hand and reciting Robert Frost's poetry to me. I focused on his blue eyes and tried to keep my breathing steady. I wondered if my sanity had slipped, accepting this situation so readily. As he'd said, fighting wouldn't do any good.

If I didn't fight, I made them happy.

I made Mark happy.

And it all felt good, so far.

Qhan brought a bottle of a pinkish-colored fluid and handed it to Mark, who held the straw up to my lips. "Drink this."

I didn't bother questioning what it was, assuming it was the stuff he'd told me about earlier. I obediently finished it. Within a minute, my cock started to inflate even more. My balls tightened and swelled, as if filling directly from what I'd drank.

He set the empty bottle aside and we didn't have to wait long until Master entered the room. He spoke to Qhan before he leaned in and ruffled Mark's hair. He made eye contact with me and said something.

Mark answered him. "He wanted to know if you know what's about to happen, and I told him yes."

Master reached out and stroked my hair, then hesitated and touched my lips.

Obediently, I opened my mouth.

He smiled, let me suck his finger for a minute before withdrawing it, and kissed me. I laid my head down on the padded frame and focused on Mark again as the effects of the drink they gave me raged through my system.

"You feel it?" he asked.

I nodded, unable to talk.

Mark smiled. "The second time he bred me, I was literally begging for him to do it, I was so horned up, once I knew what was happening."

Master walked around behind me and talked with Qhan. I felt him step into position behind me, more movement, then his hands stroked my ass.

"Qhan's going to take the plug out."

I wished I could come again. Desire had built inside me to a fever pitch, yet now I couldn't make it over the edge. I had a feeling whatever they gave me was designed to help me hold back until I really needed the distraction of the release. I didn't even flinch when they removed the plug.

Master made the good boy noise again. He pressed the thick head of his cock against me, breeching and feeling much harder than the other times. He waited a moment to ensure I was okay before pressing forward. I closed my eyes and squeezed Mark's hand as the cock inside me ballooned to what felt like almost impossible proportions.

I also thanked the gods for the preparation Qhan gave me.

My first orgasm hit me hard and fast and Master stroked my back, praising me. He didn't fuck me the way he had before. This time, he pressed in deep, bottoming out and making me groan at the sensation of him hitting a wall somewhere inside me.

That's when I felt it.

My eyes popped open. Mark carefully rose to his knees, not dislodging his own milker hose. He pressed his forehead to mine and whispered to me. "It's okay. If you need to cry out. Go ahead."

I felt the claws penetrate. There was a second of jabbing pain before it faded into a strong, uncomfortable pinch. It hurt, yes. Not as bad as the broken arm I got in basic training, but it hurt.

I let out a pained groan, but then another orgasm of equal intensity slammed into me, taking the edge off the pain and earning me more praise.

"That's it," Mark said. "You'll start coming harder now. It's the way the process works."

"How long does this last?" I gasped through my cycle of pain and pleasure.

"A while."

I felt Master shift position behind me a little. "Qhan just brought him a stool to sit on. Sometimes, it goes quickly. Sometimes, it takes longer. He can't control how long it takes. The more and harder you come, the faster it sometimes goes, like your body helps massage it out."

After a while, I adjusted to the pain, punctuated by harder orgasms that made me cry out and left me breathless. Then I felt something, even more pressure against my ass, making slow and steady progress.

I gasped. "I think I feel something."

Mark said something to Master. He grunted a monosyllabic reply.

"The egg's moving."

It felt like an hour or more passed as the pressure increased on my already impossibly stretched ass. Then something entered me and slowly worked its way deeper inside. My orgasms built in waves, almost predictably after a while, wringing the strength from me.

I felt the pinch turn to a deeper burn that forced another pained groan from me. "It hurts," I gasped.

He stroked my head. "It won't for long. That means it's attaching. Then it'll ease up, and you just wait for it to finish."

Another orgasm hit me. If it wasn't for that, it wouldn't be tolerable. I could see how terrified Mark would have been by this process.

A hand gripped my balls, gently massaging. Took me a moment to realize it belonged to Mark. My eyes opened and I stared at him.

"This sometimes helps," he said, his forehead nuzzling mine. "Just focus on what feels good and the pain will go away soon."

It did help. He squeezed and tugged, intensifying the strength of my orgasms and earning me more pleased comments from Master.

I don't know how long it lasted, but eventually the pain did ease, until, suddenly, the pinch totally disappeared.

Another orgasm hit me, hard, punctuating my pleasure. I cried out as my back rounded, and I clamped down on Mark's hand.

Mark stroked my hair again. I was aware of him kissing my sweaty forehead. "It's okay, Dale," he whispered. "You did it. You did well. The worst is over. It's all downhill from here."

I closed my eyes and shivered with each wave of pleasure forced from my body. Never in my life would I have imagined I would want to stop coming, but I was exhausted. All I wanted to do was sleep. Outside, the light had faded to black and I had the impression we'd been there for a while.

More time passed, and I think I drifted in and out of consciousness. I was covered with sweat, and every time I faded in again, Mark still held my hand. I rose back to awareness as I felt the cock in my ass begin to slowly shrink, finally enough that it could withdraw, leaving me feeling like I gaped open except for a sensation of fullness, as if I had a bowel movement to pass and couldn't.

Qhan spoke with Master. The two of them worked to do something back there. I felt a plug slide in my ass, but compared to what I'd just gone through, it was no big deal. They caressed my ass and lower back, talking to me.

Mark kissed my forehead again. "You made him happy. He's telling you how good you did, how proud of you he is."

Warmth filled me, and I squeezed his hand, too tired to respond.

He squeezed back.

Master walked around the front of the frame and stroked my hair. Qhan used a cloth and basin of warm water to bathe the sweat from my body before he released my wrist and ankles and unhooked me from the milker. Mark unhooked himself from the portable milker and didn't let go of my hand as Qhan and Master carefully lifted me from the frame and moved me to the bed. I rolled to my side where Mark curled along my back and held me.

At that point, I welcomed the comfort.

Master sat next to us, speaking with Mark, stroking my hair, brushing his fingers down my arm. I felt hands between my legs and realized Qhan had moved the portable milker over to the bed and hooked both of us up to it.

Mark protectively cradled me against him. "He wants me to tell you tomorrow night we can start sleeping with him again, but he doesn't want to move you again tonight. He wants you to rest."

I felt the effects of the concoction they gave me earlier fading from my system, leaving me weak and woozy in its wake. "Okay."

Master leaned in and kissed me, kissed Mark, and left us alone. Qhan turned down the lights, leaving only the dim corner lamp on to see by. I could tell from the shadows on the wall that he left the door to our room open.

I closed my eyes, and while Mark whispered soothing words to me, I crashed into sleep.

I awoke the next morning to dim grey light and the feel of Mark's body still cradling mine.

How had I reached this point? It seemed a lifetime away since I stood on the launch deck, even though in reality it was probably less than a week, depending on how long I'd been unconscious after my capture.

I had never before spent the night in intimate contact with another human. It didn't matter to me that Mark was another man. In him I found comfort, affection. He was solid and there and willing to hold me so I wasn't alone.

How many nights of his two years here had Mark slept alone? Had Master or Qhan held him after his breedings? I shivered when I thought about the drops, if he'd been alone after those.

Mark smoothed his hand down my stomach, his arm draped over my waist. "Good morning." He kissed the back of my neck. "Are you okay?"

"I think so." My ass felt achy and stretched, and I still had that feeling of fullness, but I thought I'd survive.

"You sleep all right?"

"I slept like a log." I closed my eyes and let my bladder empty into the milker. That was getting easier to deal with. Then my cock immediately hardened. I couldn't help it, I pressed my body against his as I quickly had my first orgasm of the day. His arms tightened around me, whispering to me as I recovered.

"Feels good, doesn't it?" he asked.

"How the hell does that happen?"

"Don't know, don't care." He laughed. "Just wait a couple of weeks. You think you're horny now, you won't want to leave the bed."

I tipped my head back so I could look at him. "What happened after your first time? When he did this to you?"

He smiled. "Master spent the night with me. Don't worry, I wasn't alone." I must have looked shocked because he laughed. "No, I didn't read your mind. I just think you and I tend to think alike."

"Thank you."

"For what?"

"For welcoming me like this."

"Dude, he bought you for me so I wouldn't be alone. You have no idea how glad I am to have someone. I feel sorry for the guys who can't speak any of their language. They're flying blind, at first."

I laughed. "I wonder what happens to the grunts like that asshole who attacked you."

"I asked Qhan. He said they usually end up shipping them out to egg farms in the distant colonies. The really bad ones go to the troops for ship use."

"What?"

"They give their troops a medication that makes them lay sterile eggs. But they still like to fuck." He grinned. "And since they're fighters, they're used to dealing with grunts. It's the smart ones like us, who know a good thing when we see it and take advantage of it, we're the ones who have a good life."

"Do I want to know what an egg farm is?"

"To buy your own breeder pet, you have to be really wealthy and approved. When I first got here, there was some dude in a blue tunic coming over several times a week to check on me, make sure I wasn't mistreated. They've got egg farms though, run by the government, where people who can't afford their own can go and breed."

I shuddered, glad I'd missed out on that experience. "That sounds horrible."

"I've talked to guys who started out there before they were bought. They're not bad. Better than some people have it in the Terran military, that's for fucking sure. Not personal like this though. They're clean and comfortable, and guys who get to know each other, they'll let them bunk together, if they want. So they aren't alone, at least."

I snuggled tighter against him. "You're not alone now."

He sounded hoarse. "Thank you."

I looked into his eyes, and without thinking about it, I reached up, pulled his face down to mine, and kissed him.

That's when Qhan decided to walk in. His pleased laugh startled us.

I don't know why I felt embarrassed, but when I tried to sit up, Mark held me until I looked at him again and he kissed me. I heard him moan as his body tensed, the machine pulling an orgasm out of him.

Breathless, he rested his forehead against mine. "This is a nice way to wake up every morning."

I couldn't have agreed more.

CHAPTER EIGHT

I wondered if they'd get me up and move me to the frame, but apparently that was the last thing on their mind. I had actually forgotten about the large plug still in my ass until I went to scratch and felt it there. That's how used to it I'd become.

Mark sat up and spoke to Qhan for a moment before Qhan left again. "He's going to try you on a little solid food this morning, but if you don't like it, or if you don't think your stomach will tolerate it yet, he's still going to give you the liquid supplement."

"Okay." I tried to sit up but Mark shook his head and placed a gentle hand on my chest.

"Don't. Seriously, you'll freak them out. They want you on bed rest for today, until they know for sure if it took or not."

"I'm stuck in here all day?"

He smiled. "I'll be here with you. I won't leave you, I promise."

"Okay."

Qhan returned with our breakfast. They went as far as Qhan insisting on helping feed me as if I were a baby.

"Just sit back and enjoy it," Mark recommended. "Keep thinking, 'pampered pets.'"

The blue stuff had a mildly fruity taste, not too sweet, and certainly not objectionable. I finished a bowl of that and some of the liquid. Then Qhan gave us both a sponge bath and was doing that when Master walked in. He wore a beaming smile and sat at the end of the bed, talking with Mark and watching Qhan take care of us.

Mark patted me on the arm. "He wanted to know how you felt, how you slept, if you were in any pain this morning. I told him you were okay. He said he's happy you're feeling good, and he's glad he didn't hurt you. He also said he's looking forward to having us both in bed tonight because he's lonely."

I met Master's gaze, and he smiled. He stood to go, leaning in and patting us both on the head before he did. He said something to Qhan, who responded, then something else to Mark, who also responded.

"He's going to work. Said he'll see us later tonight."

"Where does he work?"

"For the government. He's got a high-ranking job of some sort." He grinned. "We're not just pampered pets, we're *privileged* pampered pets. Best of the best for us."

After Qhan finished and left us alone, Mark and I sat there talking, my head in his lap. Mostly I asked him questions about Algonquan and his life here, how he was captured, things he'd learned and seen.

He was twenty-six, and had been raised on Mars before being drafted at eighteen. His parents died in an influenza outbreak when he was younger and he hated the foster warehouses.

The story of his capture sounded similar to mine.

"I was like you. I was standing on the bridge of my ship one minute when the alarm klaxon sounding red alert went off. The next thing I knew, I was naked in a rack with some of my shipmates."

He smirked. "I don't know what you did, but I was in command crew because I was intel, being a linguist. I was a non-commissioned officer, so I used to catch holy hell from my shipmates because I wasn't a grunt or flight crew. They called me a geek. So I'm in a rack with several of the guys I know who razzed me, and these macho men are so terrified that they're shaking. They fought like hell when they stuck the butt plugs in, screaming against their gags, trying to fight. Here was me, the guy they picked on, taking it like a man, so to speak."

His left hand absently stroked my arm. I didn't mind. "Never saw them again after Master bought me. I thought for sure I'd be one of the last ones bought, but I picked up on some of what the techs were saying during the journey here. I damn sure enjoyed making myself come with the plug. I think when they looked at my chart, because they track that after they put the plugs in, Master was impressed at how smart I was and picked me."

"The geek shall inherit the universe."

He laughed. "Yep."

"Do you ever get to go anywhere?"

"I've traveled with Master a few times, when he thought something might trigger his cycle and he didn't want to risk being away from me."

"Naked?"

He shrugged. "I got over that after the first week or so."

"What's the weather like here?"

"Pretty much this. There's a mild rainy season, and an autumnal season of sorts, but where we are is very temperate. I think we're close to the equator here, although I don't know for sure."

"What was that like, traveling?"

"Qhan stays here and takes care of the house. He's Master's majordomo, for lack of a better term. Mack travels with Master, so I basically stayed on a leash with them and followed them around and kept my mouth shut unless I was asked a direct question. It sucked not being home."

"Why?"

"No milker. They had one at the hotel room, but I went around half the time horny as hell, and while they don't punish a pet for whacking off, it's sort of distracting in a meeting. They discouraged me from doing that." His face clouded. "Sucks getting bred away from home, too."

"Did it hurt?"

"No, but I get used to doing it a certain way, and mentally it fucks with me when it's different."

"How often does he share you?" I didn't know if I wanted to hear that answer.

His hand didn't stop stroking my arm. "Not all the time, not like that. And only if I'm not carrying. He doesn't loan me out to others, if that's what you're worried about. It's only guests he has here, so don't panic." He closed his eyes for a moment, took a deep breath, and I felt his body tense as an orgasm washed through him. When he opened his eyes again he looked down at me and smiled. "You know, this is good for you because you get to see what a drop is like. Won't be so scary for you. You can help get me ready."

"How?"

"A few days before, you can help them keep me stretched. Help rub my back when the cramps hit." He grinned. "The first day after is mostly spent sleeping and being totally spoiled rotten. Then you start to get your wind back, and I don't know if it's hormones or what, but I'm even hornier than I was before the drop for about the next two days or so. I feel like I could hump anything. There were a couple of times they had to strap me down in the frame and keep a vibrating butt plug up me to keep me happy. I wanted to be fucked hard and constantly."

That nearly pulled another orgasm out of me. "Really?"

"Yeah. I've wondered if it's like a prime time for him to breed me then, like showing I'm ready or something, but I don't know. Even though our bodies handle the eggs fine, there's still differences. They don't get the horniness like we do in the last part of the cycle. There's some parts of it that are unique to humans dealing with it. I think some of the shots they give us when we're captured make changes in our body chemistry or something."

We talked all morning. Qhan checked on us occasionally, sometimes just sticking his head in the door to make sure we were okay and making sure that I was staying in bed, sometimes coming in to ask Mark if we needed anything.

Nope. We had our milker and a soft, comfortable bed. Check and check, we were good to go.

Since I tolerated the blue stuff at breakfast, they didn't want to press their luck. My lunch was more of that, with the liquid. Mark had plenty of fruit and something resembling cheese.

He grinned. "I'm eating for two. Once they know how your system will react, they'll give you more of the solid stuff."

"That just doesn't seem healthy, that we don't...you *know*...anymore."

"What, crap?"

I nodded.

He shrugged. "Two years or so, and I'm still alive. I'm not complaining. Considering how they go through great pains to ensure we're healthy, I can't believe they'd do something that would harm us, or without making sure it was completely safe first."

He had a point.

Master returned later that day, after we'd had dinner. Qhan unhooked me from the milker and handed it to Mark— still attached, lucky bastard—while Master bent over and picked me up in his arms as if I weighed nothing.

"Did you tell him my legs work fine?" I quipped.

Mark laughed and translated, and Master replied, making Mark laugh again.

"He said get used to it, because he likes indulging his pets."

"I feel a little silly being carried, Mark. I can walk."

Master carried me out of the room, with Mark and Qhan close on his heels. "He knows, but especially since this is your first time, they aren't taking any chances. After the first two days, they'll let you back up again because they'll know for sure everything's all right."

Master carried me into his luxurious bedroom. The bed, very tall, up past my waist and more than large enough for several Algonquans to stretch out in, was very soft and comfortable. He carefully laid me on it as he and Qhan fussed over me. Qhan made Mark unplug himself from the milker long enough for Master to playfully boost him into the bed, then they hooked us both up.

It finally struck me the device was totally silent. I didn't know what they did with what it collected, or perhaps it took care of that. I never saw them empty it.

Qhan seemed to look around for the best place to set the device. Master pointed at a chair in the corner. Qhan set the milker on the bed for a moment, brought the chair over to the foot of the bed, then placed the milker there. We had plenty of hose to move around with.

Those logistics now handled, Master turned on a vid screen on the far wall and Qhan left us alone.

I didn't know what to expect. First thing Master did after stripping off his clothes was to pat Mark's ass. Mark rolled over and stuck it in the air as Master leaned in and I finally got to see that tongue up close and personal. The sight of it sliding inside Mark allowed the milker to pull another orgasm out of me.

Once Master was satisfied at whatever he needed to check, he carefully got into bed between us, cradling both of us to him.

I thought about trying to watch the vid, but I felt really sleepy and noticed Mark had rolled onto his side, clinging to the huge man.

I did the same on my side. Master placed a kiss on the tops of our heads, and before I drifted to sleep, Mark reached across his chest and laced his fingers through mine.

The last thing I remember before going to sleep was hearing Master's pleased chuckle and the good boy sound.

CHAPTER NINE

I awoke early the next morning wrapped in Mark's arms. We were alone in the bed, and it surprised me when I realized I felt a little sad Master hadn't woke us up to say good-bye.

Then I closed my eyes as the first orgasm of the day hit me.

Okay, bonus, no giving up sleeping late to visit the wank closet. Or having to go pee.

"He'll be back," Mark sleepily mumbled, nuzzling his head against mine. "He sometimes goes out to exercise early."

"Oh." I felt better about that. After all, why would you wake a pet to tell them you were going jogging?

Mark reached back to a shelf on the headboard and found a remote control for the vid screen.

I couldn't do anything but cuddle with him and watch. He listened, translating for me. It was a news and information program, very much like what I was used to seeing back on the ship. There was no rah-rah pro-Algonquan propaganda about the war, just stated facts and reminders to all citizens who hadn't yet done their duty to make sure they visited their local egg farm if they didn't have a private breeder or partner. They had to hold the line until the Terrans gave up and left them alone.

Qhan heard that we were awake and came to check on us. Mark was admonished to make sure I stayed in bed until the vet arrived later to check me.

Then my nervousness returned.

Mark sensed it. "He's a nice guy, if it's the same guy Master usually uses."

Master returned a little before Qhan brought us our breakfast. Master wore loose shorts and dripped with sweat. He leaned in, kissed both of us, then went to take his shower before eating his breakfast.

Apparently, pets were allowed the leeway of eating in bed, but Master sat at his desk and watched the vid screen as he ate once he finished his shower.

I didn't miss how he kept looking over at me. With fondness.

Or maybe with hope.

They moved me, Master again carrying me, when the vet arrived. I'd dozed off in bed and liked sleeping there even better than in our room, but apparently the vet wanted me on the frame. He even insisted on my wrists and ankles being connected.

Mark was allowed to stand by my head, his hands holding mine, to keep me calm. "It's okay," he said. "Once he's seen you a few times, he'll trust you and won't insist on restraints any longer."

"Do they ever take the manacles off?"

"Nope. I woke up captive with them on, and they've been on ever since. I don't even know how they come off. Never tried to take them off."

Qhan removed the butt plug and quickly washed me down. Mark told me what they were doing.

"The vet's going to check you."

I winced as I felt a large, slicked hand press inside me. Both Qhan and Master put their hands on my back and soothed me while I waited for the milker to work its magic on me.

The guy felt around inside me, then he withdrew his hand and said something that brought relieved, happy sighs from Master and Qhan.

Mark kissed my forehead. "It took. Everything looks fine."

The vet washed his hands. Master shook hands with him and showed him out while Qhan quickly unhooked me and helped me sit up.

We were allowed outside, but Master still wanted me to take it easy today. I felt good that he worried about me. Cared about me.

We lay outside in the sun, holding hands, with Mark reciting Robert Frost to me until Qhan called us in for lunch. Of course we had our friend the milker with us. Damn, I was already addicted to that thing. Instead of going to our room we were allowed to eat in the dining room, where Master sat at the large table, a portable work terminal set up by his place. Both Mark and I cast a wistful glance at Qhan as he carried our beloved friend off to another room. We'd have to tough this meal out, even though I already felt my cock twitch.

Master's black hair flowed loose around his shoulders and, frankly, I wanted to walk over to him and run my hands through it. All the Algonquans I'd seen so far looked similar, but I'd know him amongst the sea of others.

I was *his*.

After we finished eating, Master pushed his chair back and patted his lap and Mark and I walked over to him. He pulled us both up, one on each leg, and talked with Mark for a while before kissing us.

Mark rested his head against Master's shoulder. "He says he's very proud of us, and of you especially, for how well you did today. The vet told him we're the two best-behaved Terrans he's ever dealt with, and he wishes all his patients were as easy as we are."

I felt a flush of pride over that.

"He also said until it's time for me to drop, we're sleeping in bed with him every night, so we have permission to go in there whenever we want and get in his bed."

Frankly, I could use a nap right then. I was wicked tired and wondered if that was an effect of the breeding.

"Please tell him I said thank you. For everything. For picking me and being kind."

Mark smiled as he told him.

Master gently turned my face to his and kissed me again. His beautiful brown eyes stared into mine as he said something.

Mark translated. "He said instead of going for big this time, he went specifically looking for someone who reminded him of me. Someone smart."

Master looked down at our laps, where both of us had grown hard. Mark was worse off than me, his cock thickly engorged and dark with blood. I was just hard. Master gently stroked me, then Mark. He patted us both on our backs and helped us out of his lap before he returned to his work.

We were excused.

Mark grabbed my hand and led me back to Master's bedroom, where Qhan had set up the portable machine for us next to the bed. We both climbed up and, a minute later, we held hands and blissfully sighed as the machine milked our cocks, giving us relief.

I dozed off. When I awoke, the light in the room had dimmed. I found I'd rolled over to Mark in my sleep. He lay there awake, watching a show on the vid screen, one arm around me, my head in the crook of his shoulder.

"Sleep good?" He looked down at me with a content smile.

"Yeah. Is that normal?"

He nodded. "First few days, you'll want to nap a lot."

Master must have heard us talking. He walked in and stripped, then joined us in bed. He said something to me and then patted Mark on his ass.

Mark grinned as he assumed the position. "He wants you to watch what he does, so you're not scared. Trust me, this doesn't hurt."

Master's tongue breached Mark's rim, quickly bringing him to orgasm. Once Master had checked whatever it was he was checking, he sat up and patted Mark on the ass again. Algonquans had muscular, flexible tongues capable of extending several inches from their mouth.

Mark rolled over, a happy smile on his face. "He does that deliberately, too, by the way. He knows about the prostate and deliberately makes you come like that. He checks the way the egg is connected, and the size, and if it's still hard or getting soft. He likes to do it because, obviously, it's clean up there since nothing's coming out, and he feels it's less dangerous than probing around with a finger."

"And it's more fun for the one being probed."

Mark laughed. "I'm damn sure not complaining."

I assumed the position without waiting for the command, making Master laugh. I felt him move behind me followed by his warm breath on my ass, then that fantastic tongue slithering inside me. He immediately nailed my prostate and I didn't bother holding back my happy moan as my hands fisted in the covers. What I really wanted was a good, hard fucking, but knew that wouldn't happen for a few weeks now.

He took his time, making me come twice more before he sat back and patted my ass. When I rolled over, ready to go back to sleep, I spotted his playful smile.

He moved up the bed, kneeling over me.

Mark propped himself up on one arm. "Open up."

I did, and got my first taste of any cock, not just Algonquan. It was musky and sweet and tangy at the same time. Reminded me of cantaloupe in a way. Far too large for me to deep throat, I focused on the head and stroked the shaft with both hands. He leaned forward, bracing himself on the headboard, and closed his eyes as he softly moaned.

"He likes it. You're doing fine."

I fought the urge to close my eyes. If I was giving my first blow job ever, I wanted to watch him. In a few minutes he threw his head back and let out a cry as his load hit the back of my throat, filling my mouth almost as fast as I could swallow.

Of course I came, too. Thank you, milker.

He carefully climbed off me and settled on the bed between us after kissing me, swirling that nifty tongue around in my mouth and tasting himself on me.

I curled up next to him and promptly fell asleep.

Mark gently awoke me some time later. "You want dinner?"

Qhan had brought our food. Master sat at the desk, eating there. I sleepily nodded and sat up. After dinner, Mark and I took our shower in Master's bathroom while he took care of something for work. Qhan brought me what passed for their version of a toothbrush, which I gratefully used. I was dozing again when Master returned to bed.

As night fell and the house grew quiet, I realized I felt, as strange as it sounded even to my own ears, happier and more contented than I had ever been in my adult life.

* * * *

We had an unexpected visitor the next morning. Master had left for work after breakfast. Mark and I lay in Master's bed, me dozing and Mark watching vids, when a chime disturbed my nap.

When Qhan entered the room a few minutes later, followed by one of the blue-garbed techs, I panicked.

I shrank away from the tech, afraid they were going to take me away. I clung to Mark, knowing I was babbling incoherently but unable to control my panic. It took Mark a minute to calm me down and talk with the tech to get me to understand it was just a random, routine welfare check.

I still didn't want to let go of Mark and realized how much I'd come to rely on him. He had the benefit of being able to speak their language. He could reasonably communicate with many of them.

I only had him.

The tech kindly smiled, made a comment, and noted something on a hand-held device. Both Mark and Qhan laughed. When I asked what was so funny, he looked down at me and smiled. "He said it's obvious you had no trouble whatsoever bonding with the household."

Even I had to laugh at that. No lies detected.

Reassured by the tech that I wasn't being taken away, and in fact had probably just cemented the fact that I shouldn't be removed from Master's care, Qhan led the tech out of the room.

I burst into tears I didn't understand.

Mark held me, soothing me, rocking me. "It's okay. You're not going anywhere."

"I just freaked out. I was afraid he would take me away."

"*Shh.* No. Never." He flicked my ear tag. I'd noticed his bore the same code as mine when we compared them in the mirror before our shower. We did look very similar. Hair almost the same color, and while he was a little taller than me, we were built similarly. Neither of us stacked and ripped like the ground grunts, but we both had trim, muscled bodies from military training and years of required PT every day. Captivity hadn't softened him any. Wide shoulders tapering to narrow waists. Tight asses, if I do say so myself. Muscular legs. Flat stomachs. He had blue eyes, while mine were a hazel bordering on green.

"This marks us as his. He would have to do something spectacularly, colossally horrible, like abuse us, for them to take us away from him at this point."

"God, if you felt a fraction like that before I got here, I feel horrible you were alone."

"I wasn't technically alone. I had Master and Qhan, but yeah, it's a lot better with you here."

I looked up into those blue eyes and realized I was in love.

And I didn't care.

I kissed him. He kissed me back, and we were happily enmeshed in each other's arms, letting the milker pull as many orgasms from us as it could while we kissed, when we heard Qhan clear his throat.

We looked up. He stood in the doorway, the bemused-looking tech with him. The tech made a comment, and they both laughed before they turned and left.

Mark roared with laughter. When he finally composed himself, he translated.

"They must be happy because they're the most naturally horniest Terrans I've ever seen."

CHAPTER TEN

Our days merged together. I felt the egg growing larger inside me and enjoyed Master's status checks. I also grew increasingly horny. Qhan was frequently forced to carry the portable milker outside to the backyard, making us follow our beloved device, just to get us out of bed and into the fresh air and sunlight.

I had taken over the role Mark had with me in the first days, holding him, talking with him, trying to distract him. When awake, he spent most of his time trying not to move and aggravate his constant, incessant urge. His nights grew restless, and more than once Master would wake up and try to soothe him by using his tongue on him.

Mark got to where he could barely move without feeling like his cock would explode. Sure, it beat the hell out of being tortured, but it was incapacitating nonetheless. A couple of days before Mark's estimated drop date, Qhan made us go to our room and helped Mark up onto the frame, where he happily collapsed while the milker took care of him. The erotic friction of the egg against his prostate put him into a nearly constant state of orgasm when made to move.

I guess I had that to look forward to.

Qhan took me by the hand and pulled me behind Mark, where he handed me a glass jar of something. Mark could barely talk by this point, too overcome by the nearly constant stimulation to form coherent sentences or translate for me.

Qhan opened the jar, put the lid on a small table he'd brought over, and pointed at Mark's ass. He mimed scooping some of the white goo out, and I did. He grabbed my hand, dipped my fingers back into the goo, and like that showed me I hadn't gotten nearly enough.

He took the jar from me and with his hand over mine, he pressed my fingers against Mark's rim, which already looked a little swollen and distended.

Mark groaned, but I assumed a happy groan because Qhan nodded at me and mimed a gentle back and forth motion.

Ah. I thought I understood.

I tentatively started massaging the ointment into him. Qhan nodded again, indicated I could and should press in a little more, so I did. After a few minutes I understood what it was I should do, and Qhan handed me the jar again, pointing at Mark.

"More!" Mark gasped.

Qhan brought me a stool to sit on. I spent at least an hour there, eventually working up to using both hands and helping relax him. When Qhan felt I'd done enough, he brought an anal plug, much shorter than the others but very large in diameter, and carefully inserted it before inflating it.

Mark loudly groaned as his body shuddered through another orgasm.

Qhan left Mark there because he'd drifted to sleep and desperately needed the rest. He mimed me washing my hands and pointed to the sink. I did, and then he waved at me to follow him.

He led me to the kitchen where he prepared my dinner for me and pointed at the small breakfast table for me to sit and eat. I was eating nearly all the things Mark could now, but they'd pulled Mark back to a lighter diet as his drop date approached. In fact, once I finished, Qhan handed me a bottle full of the clear liquid preparation I'd lived off of at first and waved at me to return to our room.

"Pol," he said, pointing at the bottle and waving me off again. That was Master's name for Mark. I was "Kal." I didn't

know if it was because he couldn't say our English names or if
Master preferred to name his pets what he wanted.

Mark still slept and I didn't want to wake him. Now I
understood why he said he practically lived on the frame the
last couple of days of his cycle. It held him in the perfect
position to allow him some uninterrupted rest. I dragged a
couple of the large pillows over to the front of the frame,
much as he had for me that day almost two weeks earlier, and
I hooked myself to the second hose now coming from the
main milker. Another of Master's investments for his beloved
pets.

I stared up at his peaceful face and waited for him to wake
up. Qhan checked on us frequently, sticking his head in the
open door, also not wanting to wake Mark.

At one point Qhan walked in to look at him closely. He
reached over and patted me on the head, letting his fingers
linger along my ear before gently chucking my chin and
leaving.

He really liked me, too. I fit into the household, all right.

As I waited for Mark to awaken, I drifted into my
thoughts. The tech had come back one more time. Despite
everyone reassuring me I was staying, I couldn't help but
cling to Mark as he laughed and stroked my hair.

How had I gotten to this point? I'd once been a fairly
confident man, survived military training, held my own in a
few bar fights. Now I clung to my fellow naked captive and
prayed they wouldn't take me away from him.

I hadn't yet met any of Master's friends. Mark said Master
wanted to wait so I wasn't overwhelmed this close to my first
drop. Normally, it wasn't unusual for Master to have dinner
parties.

I both looked forward to those, to see what others of the
species were like, and dreaded them in case I had to put up
with someone other than Master touching me.

The vet had checked me again as well, said I was doing
fine, and didn't insist on ankle restraints although he wanted
my wrists secured. He also checked Mark while he was there,

and apparently everything was on track with him. Mark slept right through it.

Mark finally awoke, his face looking weary. I got up on my knees and held the bottle for him. He took a few sips before shaking his head. "I'm done. Thank you."

"You didn't drink much."

He shook his head and collapsed again, his body trembling as another orgasm wracked him.

Worried, I found Qhan in the kitchen and showed him the bottle, indicating with my fingers how little he drank. Qhan wiped his hands on a dishtowel and looked concerned as he took the bottle from me. Leading the way, he returned to our room and knelt in front of Mark, gently shaking his shoulder and saying something to him.

Mark groaned and shook his head.

Qhan sounded like he was pleading, wheedling. Mark shook his head again.

Qhan nodded and patted his shoulder, then set the bottle on the floor next to the frame and mimed for me to stay there and watch him.

Like hell I'd leave him.

Master returned home shortly after, and Qhan updated him. Master stroked Mark's head lovingly. I'd only gotten Mark to take another couple of sips since the last time.

Master talked with Qhan again, and I heard the vet mentioned. Mark had started teaching me their language, and I was far from an expert, but the vet's name was a distinctive sound I could pick out from their usual words.

Master went to take a shower while Qhan took up a chair in our room and kept himself busy reading. I sat at Mark's head and waited.

Later in the evening, Qhan left the room for a while. Mark awoke groaning, but not in a pleasurable "oooh, coming yet again" way. It sounded pained.

I stood and stroked his hair. He grabbed my hand and squeezed hard as he moaned again, and his body tensed. I heard him gasp something before finally realizing he felt the cramps.

Forgetting the few words I knew in Algonquan, I yelled for assistance. "Help! Qhan! Master!"

They came running immediately. They removed the butt plug and checked him. Master smiled and patted him on the ass, and Qhan hooked his manacles, ankles and wrists, to the frame.

I felt helpless seeing him like that, restrained, and I had no idea what to do. I held his hand as he let out a louder groan, and his whole body strained against his bonds.

"Back," he whispered. "Rub my back, Dale. Please."

I reached over his head and did that as Master sat behind him and murmured calming words to him while Qhan helped him.

In a few minutes, another wave hit him, and I did my best. When he caught his breath, he called me. "Dale."

I leaned in close.

"Remember how I massaged your balls?"

"Yeah?"

"Do that with me. Please. It helps."

His hands tightly fisted around the built-in handles by the restraint points and he let out another loud cry. I reached under him, found his sac, and started gently tugging on it.

His pained groan turned pleasurable at the end. Master nodded at me that I did well.

Throughout the night it continued, each round getting more intense, but with longer intervals of calm between. It felt contrary to me, but obviously that's how it was happening. Finally, a little before dawn, Master inserted his hand to check him when another wave hit. Mark cried out, and Master gave him a stern command I didn't understand.

Mark's back rounded as he lifted off the frame, a pained cry bursting from him that finally ended in a happy gasp as Master let out a happy shout of his own.

Panting and exhausted, poor Mark limply collapsed, too weak to move. I smoothed the hair from his forehead as

Master handed off a large, greenish brown egg to Qhan. He took it from the room while Master stayed, still doing something back there to Mark.

I kissed Mark's forehead and held one of his restrained hands. "It's over, buddy. You're okay."

He weakly nodded. I offered him something to drink, and he finally sipped nearly half the bottle. He was bathed in sweat, so I ran a basin of warm water and started washing him down, drying him as I worked so he wouldn't get a chill.

When I finished everywhere else on him, Master called me around to his ass. He held a small, egg-shaped wad of gauze and inserted it in Mark. Then he took my hand and placed it inside him, holding the gauze in place and gave me a wait signal. He returned a moment later with a different kind of butt plug, gave me the okay to let go, and inserted it, inflating it to hold the gauze in place. After I finished bathing Mark, Master released his bonds and gently carried him to our bed, where he held him cradled in his arms.

I felt a little jealous. I wanted to be the one holding Mark, like he'd held me. I satisfied myself by laying on his other side, his hand in mine.

Master softly murmured to him, Mark occasionally nodding but not opening his eyes. Then he leaned in and kissed Mark, nuzzling his nose, so much blatant love in the gesture that it nearly broke my heart.

Would he hold me like that, too?

I hoped so.

Qhan returned, brought the portable machine over for me and hooked me up, hooked Mark up, and turned off the overhead light. Just the three of us like that, I tried to sleep and not think about what was ahead of me.

CHAPTER ELEVEN

I awoke the next morning horny as hell and stared at Master. He still held Mark, who slept. Master offered me a smile before his focus returned to Mark.

I felt better now, knowing if this was how Master cared for Mark from the beginning, then even if Mark had been scared at least he hadn't been alone and lacking in comfort.

In my adult life, there had been no romantic love. We were genetically hardwired to seek a mate, to crave love and affection. Unfortunately, the Terran military machine married us to it and did everything in its power to discourage us from forming intimate connections with others of the opposite sex, much less each other. We worked and lived in close proximity to each other on board, and yet I couldn't have told you half the names of the other nineteen guys whose bunks were in the same room as mine.

Most of them probably didn't know mine, either.

We were serial numbers, impersonal, forced to sleep and wank alone.

I didn't want to be alone. I wanted…someone. Anyone. I needed that missing piece inside my soul, and I'd reached the point that I didn't care who supplied it.

How lucky was I to land in this home? I thought of the egg farms and wondered if those men received even a fraction of the kind treatment we did. At least they could form relationships with each other.

Mark awoke and rolled toward Master, burying his face against his chest and mumbling something to him in Algonquan. Master laughed and stroked his back, kissing the top of his head. Then he carefully untangled himself and left the bed.

Mark rolled over to me and I felt my heart swell as he let me hold him. "You okay?" I asked.

"Yeah. Tired. First good sleep I've had in days." He tipped his head back to look at me. "Are you okay?"

"You went through that and ask me if I'm okay?"

"I mean are you freaked out?"

"I'm not going to lie and say I'm looking forward to it, but if you could survive it, I'm sure I can."

He smiled and closed his eyes again, slinging his arm around my waist. "It's not nearly as bad as it looks. It wears you out because you're almost always coming until it's over." I didn't miss how his hips slowly started rocking, humping against my thigh, the hose from the milker rubbing against me.

Qhan chose that moment to walk in and made a clicking noise at him that I'd learned was a warning tone. Like getting a dog's attention when you think they're contemplating doing something you know they shouldn't. Mark kissed me, deep tongue and passion that startled me at first and triggered another orgasm in me.

I wasn't sure if that part of this situation was a blessing or a curse. Not that it mattered, I supposed. I enjoyed it either way.

Qhan set a tray down on the table by the sink and called to Mark again, a little more sharply. He whined his reply but finally unplugged his cock and dragged himself out of bed and over to the frame. Once on it, his hips once again flexed, humping the air as the milker tried to take the edge off his need.

Qhan removed the plug and the gauze and was apparently happy with what he found because he didn't replace either.

He slapped Mark on the ass and smiled at him as he pointed to our bed.

Mark quickly returned to me. Before I knew it, he had me pinned down on the bed, kissing me. He hadn't bothered to hook himself back to the milker, and in fact I felt him disconnect me.

"What—"

"Shh." He kissed me again, silencing both of us. Then he rolled off me, onto his stomach, wiggling his ass at me. "Please," he begged. "Fuck me."

I froze. I'd never fucked a guy before. My cock, which had already started protesting being disconnected from the milker as the egg rubbed inside me, made the decision easy. I ignored the fact that Qhan laughed as I rolled on top of Mark and plunged home inside him. No lube necessary, whatever they used on him provided plenty of lubrication for me. I wasn't a fraction as large as Master, but Mark didn't care. He buried his face against the mattress, ass hiked in the air, slamming back to meet every thrust.

"Hard," he begged. "As hard as you can. Please!"

I had no trouble obliging him there. By now my cock was screaming for release, and my first climax hit me as I filled him.

"More!" His hands fisted the covers. "Please, more!"

I didn't pull out, waiting for a moment and, sure enough, I grew hard again. Between the egg bouncing inside me and whatever effects of carrying it played on my body, I had a feeling we could sit here all day fucking. Qhan let us play for a while before he walked over and made me pull out. When Mark and I tried to get together again, he made that warning click and grabbed the milker hoses, hooking us both up. Then he snapped his first two fingers together and pointed at our collars.

The warning was clear. We'd better stop, or he'd tether us.

We ate breakfast, Mark back to his normal diet. Then Master came in. Mark threw himself at him when he stood by our bed, wrapping his arms around his legs and begging him.

I didn't have to understand the language to guess what he wanted.

Master chuckled and scratched his head. I heard the vet's name mentioned again after the doorbell chime sounded. Master patted Mark's head while Qhan left the room. He returned a minute later with the vet.

Master pointed at me and the bed, and his meaning was clear. *Stay.* Mark eagerly went to the frame, where the vet checked him out. Apparently satisfied, the vet talked with Master for a moment before leaving.

Mark begged, pleaded, whined. Chuckling, Master stepped behind him and fucked him, hard. That's what he'd craved, and his happy moans had me falling over on the mattress and orgasming just from watching them.

When Master finished with him, he returned to me and gave me my morning exam. I closed my eyes and surrendered to my body's now insatiable sexual appetite as his tongue coaxed two orgasms out of me.

Yes, the Algonquans were far smarter than Terrans. How could even the most obnoxious, macho grunt not turn into a begging, drooling, puddle of compliant pet feeling like this? I'd do anything they wanted me to at this point.

When Mark returned to the bed and tried to coerce me into fucking him again, Master smacked his ass and pointed to the frame. Sulking, Mark went and climbed on. Then Master patted me on the head again, smiling. I got the impression Master didn't want Mark wearing me out.

Qhan attached Mark's wrists to the frame but left his ankles free. He inserted a different butt plug than I'd seen before — they seemed to have one for every occasion — and only after he finished and Mark started loudly moaning did I realize it must have a built-in vibrator.

It apparently cycled because he would have periods of relaxing, happily sated, followed by frantic moans and humping as it built up again.

Master left us for the day. Once I felt a little strength return to my limbs, I dragged myself and a pillow over to the frame, plopped down again, and hooked myself to the milker.

Even that much walking proved almost unbearably erotic, the egg a constant aggravation at that point.

I stared up at Mark's face, and he finally cracked open a blue eye to look at me. "It's automatic. It has a variable setting. I can't predict when it'll go off."

"I wondered if it was."

He closed his eyes and nodded. "It's not as good as the real thing, but it helps."

"You don't mind being restrained?"

He slowly shook his head, tired. "It makes it better, in a way. All I can do is lie here and enjoy it. I think they're worried I might try to fuck your ass right now. Qhan has stuff he has to do. He can't spend all day watching me."

"Would you?"

He smiled but didn't open his eyes. "Quite possibly. Just wait. You'll see. This first day or two, it's a constant craving. It's different than before the egg drops, that's a constant physical stimulation. This is a need. It gets better in a couple of days, though."

Qhan let him loose for lunch, keeping the plug in him as we both moved to the bed to eat, but moving his own chair next to the bed, sitting there and reading.

I also noticed he'd brought an energy leash, looped over the arm of the chair.

"He's not taking chances with you, is he?" I asked.

Mark shook his head and rolled onto his side, his back pressed against my chest. When the vibrator kicked on, I felt it through his body. My arms tightened around him as he succumbed to the sensation.

Qhan carefully watched us. Satisfied I wasn't being unduly molested by Mark, he went back to reading.

Too bad the Terran government hadn't figured this angle out. They could have had a waiting list for people volunteering to join the military if they'd institute a program like this and give everyone a milker for their bunk.

Then again, they might not be able to get the guys out of their bunks if they did that.

Qhan let us take a nap together after lunch. Then he ordered Mark back to the frame and attached his wrists again. After carrying pillows over to the frame for me and helping me over to them, he patted me on the head and left to take care of whatever it was he had to do.

I lay on my side, how I'd basically landed when I flopped over, and tried not to move. It was a strange combination of overwhelming pleasure, yet exhausting. Definitely wouldn't call it torture, because yes, I had to admit I loved it. But I found myself longing to be able to walk across a room without doubling over from an orgasm every other step. Standing upright for more than a minute or two was out of the question because the egg seemed to press directly on my prostate when I did. Now I understood why trying to get Mark to move had been a chore over the past few days. There were times Qhan just picked him up and carried him, rather than arguing with him for several minutes. Despite Mark being six-three and three inches taller than me, the Algonquan was two feet taller than him and could pick us up as if we weighed nothing.

Mark smiled down at me. "I hope he holds off breeding me again until after you drop."

"Why?"

"Because I'd love a chance to be able to roll around with you without them interrupting us."

I laughed, and the mental image his words conjured triggered another orgasm. I I just laid there and moaned.

CHAPTER TWELVE

Master returned home later that night after dinner. Mark, released from the frame, went to take a shower with him while Qhan gave me a sponge bath on the frame.

I was happy to just lie there and enjoy it. I felt beyond caring at that point.

I asked Mark earlier why he hadn't seemed this disabled by the egg when I first got there.

"The first time was the worst, relatively speaking. The more you get used to it, the easier it gets. My first time I was like you—I could barely walk the last two weeks. By the third or fourth time, it was only the last week that was the worst."

I must have dozed off and I awoke as Qhan carried me out to the living room. Master sat on the sofa, watching the vid screen with Mark happily impaled on his lap. Qhan laid me on the couch next to them and brought me a pillow for my head. Master reached over and stroked my hair, laying his hand on my head. I closed my eyes and dozed. Mark laced his fingers through mine, and like that, we spent a family evening together.

Until I had a horrific nightmare. In my dreams this whole experience had itself been a dream. I'd gotten knocked in the head while on the flight deck and awoke in sick bay, still in the military. Ordered to take a shift off by the doc to recover, I remembered lying in my bunk and thinking about Mark and Master and Qhan and crying at how lonely I felt. Alone.

Cold and emotionless. Wishing I was back in captivity and loved and cared for.

And no longer alone.

I awoke being gently shaken, Master looking down at me with concern. Mark had climbed off his lap and knelt in front of me, stroking my hair.

Realizing the nightmare was just that, I threw my arms around him and sobbed. "You're real. Oh, thank the gods, you're real!"

"Um, yeah, buddy. Course I am." He carefully held me, not rocking me, probably aware of what that would do to my body, the chain reaction of orgasms it'd set off. "I'm real, and I'm right here."

I finally sobbed out what had terrified me, and he kissed me tenderly. "I had some dreams like that, too. We're trained to hate and fight and defend our species, when the truth is, you and me, we've found a family we never had anywhere else. Not like this. We can't have this with the Terrans. Frankly, even if they gave me a chance to go back, I wouldn't. If they attacked us here, I'd take up arms with the Algonquans to defend my home."

He sat back and cradled my face in his hands, his voice soft. "*This* is my home. I know it's whacked, and I don't care. It's not Stockholm Syndrome because I'm happy here. Happier than I've been since I was a kid. If you want total honesty, I was sort of relieved when I realized I didn't have to fight the good fight anymore. Maybe if things were different, if I had something or someone to give a shit about, or who gave a shit about me, yeah, maybe it'd be different. Let me tell you something, a fucking principle isn't any reason, in my book, to leave here." He smiled. "Besides, I love him, and I love you. I've got all I need."

I sniffled. "I love you, too." I knew it was the truth as soon as I spoke it. I loved him. I think I loved Master, too, by that point.

They were my family.

And as Mark had said, I felt happier here than I'd been since I was a kid. I had more freedom and less responsibility now than I did in the fucking military.

"Good." He hugged me again and explained to our anxious Master what had scared me. Once reassured I was okay, Master also kissed me and said something, punctuated several times by a word I'd heard before, especially during Mark's drop when Master talked to him, but I didn't know what it meant. It sounded like a purr, a sweet, gentle sound.

"What does that mean?" I asked Mark. I tried to replicate the word.

Mark smiled. "That's their word for love. He's telling you he loves you, too."

Master smiled at me and nodded. "Love," he tried to say, a little garbled, but understandable. "Love Kal."

* * * *

Mark returned to normal two days later. He didn't even use the milker that much, only a couple of times a day. I, on the other hand, could barely think, much less move. I whined every time they had to separate me from my beloved milker for more than a few minutes.

I had no pride. I could not have cared less.

Master didn't breed Mark, although, lucky bastard, he did get fucked morning and night. Mark helped Qhan take care of me and they tried to move me as little as possible. We spent most of our time in Master's bed, Mark holding me and reciting poetry or translating the Algonquan vids for me.

Time blurred. By the end of week three, I'd become one large, throbbing erection. Mark learned how to climb in and out of bed without disturbing me because although I craved the comforting contact of his body around me, jostling me usually triggered a series of explosive orgasms that left me barely conscious.

The vet examined me. Our good behavior earned me the ability to stay curled on my side in the bed, Mark restraining me by holding my wrists to appease the man while I was quickly examined. Not like I could have moved if I wanted to. A brief three-way discussion took place between Mark, Qhan, and the vet before the vet left. Master had gone away overnight, apparently on business, but was expected back late that evening.

"Time to start stretching you, baby," Mark told me. He'd started calling me that a few days earlier. I liked the way it made me feel.

Loved. Protected.

But right now, I didn't think I could stand being moved. I groaned, trying to protest. "Don't move me. Please, for the love of the universe, just let me lie here." I wasn't in pain, that was the bitch of it. I felt pleasure so pure and aching, the likes of which I'd never experienced before. While I couldn't wait for it to go away, I suspected that as soon as I healed from dropping, I'd be craving it again.

Yeah, it was that worth it.

He chuckled. "I warned you it was good, didn't I?"

I groaned.

They didn't make me move. Qhan carefully slid some towels under me and handed Mark a jar of the same goo we'd used on him, along with a butt plug. Moving slowly so as not to jostle me, he lay down behind me and started working the stuff in.

It felt good. I'd progressed well past any squeamish reactions about touching another man, or having one touch me. What he applied to me felt nearly as good as the incessant pleasure torturing me. Cool and soothing, almost like it had a minty herb in it. Just the slightest bit of numbing effect, as well, although when I'd applied it to him I didn't notice any of those sensations on my skin. Maybe it was specially formulated to react only with our most sensitive tissue, I don't know.

Didn't care.

All I knew was that he started with one gentle finger, working slowly, and by several hours later he had his whole fist in me and put the plug in, expanding it a little to keep me loose. That completed, he washed his hands and returned to bed. Qhan brought his dinner and my drink in and examined Mark's handiwork. He nodded approvingly and patted Mark on the head before leaving us alone again.

Mark held the bottle for me. I couldn't drink very much before I was full. They'd given up on trying to get me to eat the day before.

I drifted in and out of sleep, catching a few undisturbed minutes here and there until I awoke to the sound of Master's soft voice talking with Mark. They disappeared for a few minutes, and I assumed Mark was getting fucked from the happy sounds I heard down the hall.

Lucky bastard.

I closed my eyes and forced myself to lie still. I was dying to feel that again, yet just the thought of moving nearly sent me into another spasm of climaxes.

They returned a while later, and Mark repeated the massage. Master watched, approving and discussing things with Mark. I tried to go to sleep. This time Mark almost had two full hands inside me by the time he stopped, and the butt plug was sized a little larger when he reinserted it.

Master laid down beside me and let Mark hold me. It felt good being securely in the middle like that. Comfort from both sides.

As we all settled in, they to sleep as I tried to get what little sleep I could, Master kissed me. "Love Kal," he said.

I managed an exhausted smile. "Love Master," I said.

* * * *

It was five days before my estimated drop date, and I wasn't sure I'd survive. I couldn't sleep, I couldn't move under my own power. I could barely talk.

But damn, what a fucking fantastic way to go.

Whatever exact combination of things were happening inside my body, it was like someone had mainlined an electrical connection to the pleasure center of my brain, flipped the switch, and walked away. If the damn grunt that tried to choke Mark had experienced this, he no doubt would have been a happy camper.

I know I sure was, as long as they didn't try to make me move.

Or take away my milker.

Master was very careful during the checks, trying not to move me any more than necessary, and very gentle despite me practically being in tears from the overwhelming pleasure that swept through me.

Mark had spent two years doing this? Lucky fucking bastard. I'd spent the last two years miserable in the military.

Master left for work after his morning routine of exercising, fucking Mark, and taking a shower. He would be gone overnight on business. I just lay there. It was all I could do. The house could have caught fire and I probably would have died because I couldn't walk without crumpling to the floor in an orgasming puddle.

Mark checked on me, went through the stretching process with me, and then left me there so he could help Qhan somewhere in the house. He left the vid on for me, more for noise than anything. At this point I understood why moving to the frame and staying there was a pretty damn spiffy option. I was about ready to ask for that, except I'd miss the physical contact with Mark, and I craved that almost as much as the overwhelming pleasure assaulting my body.

I still laid there a few hours later, not quite lunch time, when I felt something wrong. A sharp, cramping pain hit me, low and deep in my bowels. I would have cried out except it triggered an even stronger orgasm in counterpoint that left me writhing on the bed, unable to catch my breath. Recovering from that, I tried to take a few breaths to pull enough air into my lungs to call out when another, even sharper pain hit.

Of course, followed by an orgasm.

I would have laughed at my situation if I could have spared the breath for it. Whatever the Algonquans did to our bodies, they were fucking tricky bastards. If Terran women felt like this during labor, they'd always want to stay pregnant, and there would be no need for the breeder laws ensuring the population kept growing to feed the Terran military machine.

Hell, most of the *men* would want to be pregnant, too.

Maybe the Algonquans could conquer Terrans by developing just such a system and selling it to them.

I nearly laughed again, except yet another, even stronger pain hit me. This wasn't like a cramp, this felt sharp and raw, almost like a tearing sensation, and it scared me despite the counterpoint pleasure.

I cried, feeling helpless and weak. Mark had gone through this with so much more bravery than I. Fighting through it, I managed to cry out his name, but I think it came out louder in my mind than from my mouth.

Another wave of pain, dizzying, and the pleasure. I think I passed out briefly. As soon as I came to, I screamed for him.

That one they heard. Mark, Qhan on his heels, raced into the bedroom. I couldn't speak to tell him what was wrong, just grabbed his hand and squeezed hard, hoping he could understand.

"Oh…shit! You're dropping early." He spoke rapid-fire Algonquan to Qhan and detached me from the milker. Peeling my hand from his, he moved out of the way as I cried, wanting him back. Qhan stepped in, gently picking me up from the bed and carrying me into our room where Mark helped position me on the frame. Mark connected my manacles, wrists and ankles. Qhan plugged me into the milker, and I checked out from sanity for a few minutes as I screamed from the pain and pleasure of the next wave hitting me.

I came back on the downside of the climax to find Mark kneeling in front of me, his forehead touching mine, his hands buried in my hair and trying to get me to look at him.

"It's okay," he kept telling me. "It's okay. They'll start spacing out after a while, longer between them, it'll be okay."

It wasn't okay. It felt like my guts were being ripped out and put back in between bursts of pleasure I thought I'd never experience and survive. Every time I thought one of them was the most powerful climax I'd ever had, the next one would blow that one out of the water.

At one point, I realized the vet had arrived, but Master still wasn't there. Mark rubbed my back, massaged my balls, but the contractions stayed close together, and even in my tortured state I recognized the tone of conversation didn't sound good.

"What's...wrong?" I managed to gasp during one brief break.

"You're okay," Mark insisted. "It's okay. It's just a little early. That's not uncommon the first time. It's not as soft as it should be."

"Master?"

"They're trying to get in touch with him. He was out at one of the military installations in meetings. He'll be here as soon as he can. We didn't expect you to drop this soon, and he was trying to take care of some stuff before his time off to be home with you."

I know I cried, and again with the whole no pride, not caring thing. I wanted him there, the way he'd been there for Mark, assuring me everything was okay, and his strength there to comfort me.

The evening progressed, the vet and Qhan and Mark talking and Mark deliberately not translating everything for me. During one break in the agony-ecstasy dynamic, I caught Mark's eye. "Tell me," I gasped.

He looked worried, and I didn't like that. "This isn't uncommon, Dale. It's okay."

I stared at him, pleading with my eyes because I couldn't spare another breath.

He took a deep breath and leaned in, his lips by my ear. "You're okay. Remember, I told you they have a very high egg mortality. Four of mine either came too early or weren't viable when delivered. I was the exception, not the rule, that my first time went perfectly. It's okay." He stroked my head and kissed me. "You'll be okay. They have to wait for the connective tissue between the egg and you to either let go on its own or lengthen and thin enough from the drop process that you can push the egg out and they can sever it."

The hours passed as my sanity slipped. There were never more than a few minutes of respite as my body struggled to deal with the situation. What little lucid time I had was spent crying or screaming while Mark did his best to soothe me.

All I wanted was Master.

What tiny little bit of reason remained within me understood why Mark had picked Master over me the night of his drop because I wanted Master, his strength, his comfort. I knew Mark was doing his best and understood my agony, but it wasn't enough.

I needed Master.

It was late in the night, or maybe early morning, when a heated argument between Mark, the vet, and Qhan erupted. Whatever it was, apparently Mark and even Qhan stood fast against the vet. Mark started to yell when I heard the front door open and slam and Master frantically calling out for us.

I sobbed with relief. He'd fix everything. Whatever it was that the vet wanted to do and Mark objected to, Master would fix it.

Voices hushed as the three men updated Master. He knelt in front of me, and all I could do was cry with relief that he was there. He kissed me, making those soothing noises to me, and whispered, "Love Kal. Dolmo. Dolmo."

Mark knelt beside him. "That means sorry. He's sorry he didn't get here sooner."

Mark had a hurried, hushed conversation with Master, fast, desperation threading through Mark's tone. Pleading. Master went quiet, then nodded and said something firm-sounding to the vet.

Mark moved behind me as Qhan brought Master a chair so he could sit at my head. He held my manacled left hand and rested his head beside me on the frame, whispering to me in Algonquan. I didn't understand a word of it, but his tone comforted me.

I felt Mark's gentle hands doing something, pressing, easing against my ass, but I was such a bundle of raw nerve endings I didn't know what for sure he was doing. "Okay, Dale, baby, I need you to push for me. Hard."

"I can't," I gasped. I was too exhausted, wrung out.

"You have to." His tone turned stern. "You need to do it for me, baby. You have to push. You can do it."

I cried as another wave of pain hit me. When I came back out of it, he yelled at me. "Now, Dale! You have to help me. Push, goddammit!"

I took a deep breath and tried, but I couldn't manage much before another wave of pain hit. When the pleasure faded, the pain still lingered, a background curtain distorting my world.

"Again. Push, hard as you can." I thought I felt something, maybe his hand slip inside me. I cried out at the different kind of pain.

"That's good," he said. "That was real good, baby. Just hold on. I'm going to fix this for you." I realized both his hands were inside me. I could feel them working, doing something.

The vet's voice had changed from his previous know-it-all tone to amazed. He asked Mark something. Mark snapped back at him, silencing the vet.

A sudden, sharp pain sent my vision red and made me scream, followed immediately by...the most blissful lack of sensation. No pain, no orgasm. Then reality slammed into me. The pain was still there, but had suddenly retreated to a completely manageable level of discomfort.

Mark removed one hand from me. "Okay, baby. Push for me."

Without the agony robbing me of breath, I could. I felt immense relief as I stretched, huge, then...

His other hand and the egg both slid out of me. It was heaven. I closed my eyes and basked in the feeling of the cycle of pain and pleasure ending. I felt practically numb from exhaustion, but I had a suspicion in a few minutes I'd be crashing into my best sleep in a while.

Master, Qhan, and the vet all happily cried out.

Mark went to the sink and cleaned up before coming over to me. "You're okay," he murmured, kissing me, stroking my forehead. "You're okay. I made it all better for you, baby. I fixed it. You're okay."

Master left him with me, and I felt him, or maybe it was the vet, checking me, doing something to me, and then releasing my manacles.

I closed my eyes and Master carried me not to our bed in the corner, but back to his room. He waited for Qhan to put down some towels, and then he cradled me in his arms as Mark crawled in next to us and held my hand.

"Dolmo, Kal," Master whispered. "Love Kal."

That was the last thing I remembered that night, and for that I was grateful.

CHAPTER THIRTEEN

When I awoke late the next morning, Master and Mark were still in bed with me, holding me between them.

My ass hurt like a motherfucker. But for the first time in weeks, my first thought of the day wasn't *oh, goody, orgasm.*

Mark stroked my forehead. What parts of the previous night's activities my sanity had retained came to mind. "What happened?" I asked. "What did the vet want to do to me?"

He smiled. "I figured you were too out of it to hear that."

"That's not answering the question."

Master lay there, holding me and listening to us, but not interrupting.

Mark sighed. "He wanted to take you into town, to the clinic, and operate on you. Normally when this happens to an Algonquan and it won't detach, they can go in and cut the connection. But Algonquan asses are, as you can guess, larger than ours, so their hands can get up in there. They also have special muscles down there, they can open their asses much wider than we can. Humans are a lot smaller. With a full-sized egg in there, there's no room to get their hands in there to do it. They'd rip a human apart. I kept arguing that my hands were smaller than theirs and I could get up in there and sever it without hurting you."

"You were afraid. I heard it."

He finally nodded. "They're good, and they try their best, but I didn't want to see you sliced open if I could fix it." He stroked my forehead. "I'm sorry it went so bad for you. I've had rough ones but nothing like that."

I felt a prickle of tears in my eyes again. "It didn't survive, did it?"

He shook his head a little. "It was too early. If the egg hasn't gotten fully soft yet, it can't survive. It's okay, baby. I told you, they're happy if one out of five is viable and makes it."

I finally looked up at Master. "I'm sorry," I said. "I'm sorry it didn't make it."

Now how totally fucked up was that? After what I went through, I felt guilty that I hadn't performed as expected. I worried I'd let him down.

Even Mark teared up. He translated. Master shook his head and kissed me. "Dolmo," he said, followed by a lot of other stuff I couldn't understand. "Dolmo."

"He said he's the one who's sorry, that he wasn't here for you. He says you have nothing to be sorry for, that you did nothing wrong, and that he's very proud of you. He's the one who is sorry."

"Love Kal," Master said, kissing me again. "Love Kal." He looked at Mark. "Love Pol."

* * * *

We spent the morning in bed. I was sore and achy, but even through that I felt the first twinges of the heavenly backside of the previous night's hell.

Master left us alone for a little while late in the day to take care of some work issues, but he worked from the dining room and left Mark strict instructions to call him if I needed him. Qhan brought the milker in for Mark, and that's when my cock decided it'd had a long enough break.

Need flooded my system. Where before I couldn't stop coming if I tried, now I'd chew through my left arm to have an orgasm.

Mark looked at my face and laughed before he called for Master. "I think you're recovering," he joked with me.

Oh, I could walk again! Under my own steam, we all moved to our room, and they put me on the frame, checked me out, and inserted the vibrating butt plug. Mark hooked my wrists to the frame, and I couldn't move.

I moaned, happy. "Oh...fuck. Now I understand." My memory of the previous night's pain evaporated as pleasure washed through me, sating my urge. I didn't understand why, but for some reason not being able to move made it feel that much sweeter.

He grinned. "I cannot wait until the vet clears you to play."

That happened later that evening. Mark translated. "He's amazed you've healed so well, and he apologized to me for not listening sooner." The vet said something else that had Mark and Master laughing. "He also said he should have known his favorite patient would know what was best for his second-favorite patient."

Master fucked me, hard and fast, and I loved every second of it. I begged him not to stop, tried to buck my hips against him to make him go harder and faster, but I think he held back a little. I sensed him afraid to go too far after the ordeal I'd been through. Mark said he would hold off breeding either of us for a while.

I also thought he still felt guilty for not being there for me. I didn't hold it against him. They hadn't expected it, and he had planned to take the time off when they thought I would drop.

He loved us. We were cherished pets, not just egg production captives.

The next afternoon I actually felt...almost normal. I could be away from the milker and not feel panicked. They tried me without the butt plug, and after lunch Qhan and Master waved us out into the backyard.

I didn't miss the evil gleam in Mark's eyes, and an impromptu game of tag started. Except he tackled me, rolling on top of me and pinning me to the ground. He kissed me, grinding his cock into mine and leaving me ready to fuck. He lifted his head. "Tag, you're it." Like that, he was off me and laughing, racing across the yard.

I gave pursuit, caught him, and we rolled around on the grass. I'd never had so much fun. No cares, no worries, no concerns. We did that for a while, amping up the excitement every time but not quite taking it over the edge to making the other climax. We were working up a good sweat. I enjoyed like hell the ability to move and think at the same time again. I'd totally forgotten about Master and Qhan because they'd been inside.

I was it. Giving a war whoop, I chased Mark across the yard, catching him with a flying leap that tumbled us both into the shade under the trees. I pinned him to the ground, on his back, arms over his head, and was leaning in to kiss him. All of a sudden, Mark's eyes went wide, and he started screaming something in Algonquan.

I went flying. It felt like a troop transport hit me. Stunned, I slammed hard against the base of another tree, and as I lay there gasping for breath, Mark scrambled around Master, racing to put himself between us.

Master looked ready to kill me.

Terrified, I clung to Mark, crying and wondering what the fuck happened as I became aware of the pain of cracked ribs.

Mark screamed at Master and had his arms spread wide, shielding me from him.

Master suddenly stopped a few feet away as horror filled his expression.

Silence descended over the yard. Well, silence except for my hysterical sobbing. What the *fuck*? Why had he attacked me? I suspected he'd kicked me.

Master asked Mark something, and Mark nodded, affirming.

Master started for us again, this time his face back to love, with more than a hint of grief.

I screamed as he moved toward us, scared shitless, quite honestly.

If I could shit, that was.

He froze again, his face a vision of agony.

Mark managed to turn in my death grip and forced me to look at him when I wouldn't take my eyes off Master. "He thought you were attacking me. He didn't realize we were playing. He saw you tackle me, and he assumed you were trying to hurt me. He was thinking about the guy who tried to choke me."

Behind him, Master reached out for me, but I cringed away from him, trying to keep Mark between us. Okay, not the most manly of actions, but the fucker had two feet and over a hundred pounds on me, and I was the one he'd attacked, not Mark.

"Dolmo, Kal," Master whispered. "Love Kal. Dolmo." He sat back on his ass and closed his eyes, his head in his hands. "Dolmo."

Mark managed to shift me in his arms, not letting go of me, still trying to reassure me. "He's sorry. He thought he was protecting me."

That might be fine and dandy, but who the fuck would protect *me* if the fucker mistook rough sex for hurting Mark? And holy gods, my ribs felt like they were on fire. I'd taken shots like that before in bar fights, but usually I knew it was coming and could tense up.

Oh, hey, look, something could take away my woody. Finally. Getting sucker punched by the man I thought would always take care of me.

Terrific.

When Master raised his head and looked at me, I froze.

He was crying. He started talking, pausing so Mark could translate every sentence for me, word for word.

"I'm so sorry, Kal. I thought he was in danger, and I didn't stop to think. I worried for him. And I felt so angry because my first thought was of the one who tried to hurt him. And I felt angry because I love and trusted you and thought you betrayed that. I'm so sorry, Kal. I understand if you don't forgive me, but please, I'm sorry. I would never intentionally hurt you. I didn't know. Please forgive me. I love you."

Okay, fuck me. Now I was crying. I could see that. It made sense. If I was in his position, I might have freaked out, too. He'd never seen us playing before because we never had a chance to play like this until today. Either one or both of us were too fucking horny to do anything but lie there and come.

Only I hadn't been in his position, I'd been in mine, and on the receiving end of one hell of an ass whooping.

I nodded. Then Mark shifted position again, but one of his hands accidentally hit my cracked ribs and I passed out from the pain.

* * * *

What a fucking pussy I am.

I survived nearly having my insides ripped out and recovered from that just fine, then something as stupid as fractured ribs puts me on my ass.

As I gathered my wits around me, I panicked. I looked up at the ceiling and realized I was not in Master's house. From the exam lights above me, I guessed it was some sort of clinic.

I lay on my back, strapped down, including my head, to a cold metal table. Totally immobilized, I couldn't move.

I started crying and thrashing, screaming for Mark and for Master. Immediately, Mark appeared on my right side, holding my hand, soothing me.

I relaxed as my fingers clamped around his. I had Mark. I figured I could handle anything if I had him.

"Where are we?" I croaked. Breathing hurt, and it felt like maybe my ribs were now bandaged.

He started to unfasten the strap holding my head steady when an unfamiliar voice barked an order at him. He shot back with what I suspected was the Algonquan equivalent of "fuck you" and continued. When I sensed someone stepping over to stop him, another familiar body appeared there on my other side, blocking them from interfering.

Master.

His eyes, red from crying, didn't leave me. He nodded to Mark to continue. I didn't flinch when Master reached down and carefully unfastened my left hand. He looked like he wanted to hold it but was afraid to. He stroked the back of my hand with one finger, and I turned my hand palm up and grabbed him.

That earned me a tentative, sad smile.

"Dolmo," he hoarsely whispered again. "Love Kal."

I nodded. "Love Master."

He cried again and leaned in to kiss me. He quickly removed the rest of my restraints and helped me sit up, taking over from Mark.

We were in a clinic of some sort. Another irony, medical facilities appeared pretty similar despite the species. Our vet and an unfamiliar man wearing the same kind of tunic stood there.

I also noticed two dour-faced, blue-garbed techs glaring at Master.

Okay, bad. Verrry bad.

I clung to Master. "Please don't let them take me!" I shrieked. I looked at Mark. "Please, tell them what happened! Tell them it was an accident!" If I could have burrowed inside Master's tunic to hide, I would have. I tried to get off the table and climb behind Master, but he wouldn't let me down. I had to settle for letting him hold me.

Apparently, my reaction soothed some of the techs' doubts. Both of their faces relaxed.

Before Mark could translate what I said, a third tech entered the room, and I recognized him as the one who'd been to the house and visited me there. Everyone but me was then talking in Algonquan and I felt near tears.

"Mark!" I cried. "How do I fucking say, 'Don't take me away from him!'"

Everyone fell silent and looked at me.

He smiled. "Bautu dal golan pauchan."

I screamed it, tears streaming down my face.

No pride…check.

The three techs looked at me, considering. I said it again, and again, begging, pleading.

Screaming

Mark rounded the table and stood there with Master, talking to the techs. Master kissed the top of my head and I think I had a death grip on his arm. If they tried to take me, they'd have to drug me or forcibly peel me off his body.

I wouldn't go willingly. They wanted to see a feisty Terran? They'd have a panicked one on their hands if they tried to take me from Master and Mark.

Our vet got into the action, apparently testifying to Master's level of love and care for us. I closed my eyes and rested my head against Master's chest, praying, muttering my mantra over and over.

Bautu dal golan pauchan.

When Mark grabbed one of my hands, I held on to him, too.

The tech from the home visit stepped forward and said something.

I felt Master and Mark both tense.

"What? *What?*" Yeah, girlie shriek in fine voice…check there, too.

Mark took a deep breath. I wouldn't like this, regardless. "They want to talk to you without Master here."

"*NO!*" I went beyond girlie shriek, skipped right over screaming my lungs out, and dove into full-blown tantrum mode. "No!" I shook my head, panic setting in. "No!" If they separated me from Master, I might not ever see him again. Or Mark.

"It's okay, I'll stay with you, and so will our vet. They want to make sure you're saying this of your own free will and not because you're scared of Master."

I actually trembled.

The tech's voice softened as he talked to Mark and Master. Then Master made the decision for me. He gently peeled me off him and put my arms around Mark.

"Calpa."

I knew that word. *Stay.*

Master leaned in and kissed Mark, then me. "Love Kal," he whispered. "Love Pol."

When he walked out of the room, the vet had to help Mark hold me down when I tried to go after him despite the pain in my ribs, which were, yep, bandaged.

From the smug look on the other vet's face, I supposed he was the one who hadn't wanted me released from my restraints. I think he was enjoying his "see, I told you so" moment.

"Dale, *please*, calm down," Mark begged. "The sooner you calm down, the sooner we can answer their questions, and the sooner we can go the fuck home."

With tears streaming down my face, I forced myself to stare into his beautiful blue eyes. Finally, I nodded.

He kissed me and carefully pulled me close to hold me, mindful of my ribs.

Even the vet stayed beside me and kept a gentle hand on my shoulder, petting me, stroking my hair. Hell, we *were* his two favorite patients, after all.

They didn't question us for long. Apparently, one of the other two techs knew enough English to verify Mark's translation of my account, and that I was definitely adamant about staying with Master. After what felt like forever, Master was allowed to return to the room, and I threw my arms around him and proceeded to try to climb him like a tree. It only took a few more minutes before they finally signed off on me being released back to Master's custody.

What a helluva way to get my first view of Algonquan outside of our sanctuary. And frankly, that's how I thought of it — a sanctuary. I'd never been one prone to wandering. If it wasn't for the military, I would have been happy right there on Ganymede, in my tiny apartment not even as large as Master's bathroom.

They brought something resembling a wheelchair and Master himself carefully pushed me through the complex while Mark walked beside me, holding my hand.

We passed rooms where humans lay in beds while their Algonquan owners sat with them. In other rooms, which were little more than comfortable cells, some humans lay, usually restrained, on soft beds. Twenty rooms in all, by my best guess.

Outside it was now late in the day, and my stomach rumbled. Mack was there, waiting with a vehicle the likes of which I'd never seen. The same kind of hover technology that powered the carts the techs had used in the ship we rode in, and that the racks themselves utilized when they moved them. I saw no roads, just flat, grassy lanes, although they did have what appeared to be sidewalks.

Mark squeezed my shoulder. "Your chariot, sir."

Master helped me in, fussing over me, making sure I was comfortable before he let Mack drive us away from there.

Mark smiled as he watched me watching the landscape. "Cool, isn't it?"

I nodded, stunned.

It was beautiful.

Ganymede, being an artificial colony without a natural atmosphere that wouldn't kill you, was constructed of metal, domes, and artificial lighting. I'd been to Earth twice while in the military, and while a few natural preserves remained there, it looked nothing like this.

This reminded me of vids of old Earth hundreds of years ago, when it still had plenty of open, natural spaces people could enjoy.

We cruised a few feet off the ground, over the grassy lane. Other vehicles did the same. Made sense, a vehicle that didn't have to touch the ground didn't need pavement. We passed buildings, but they were either artfully camouflaged by plants so as to be barely visible, or they were made in such a way as to appear part of the landscape. I'd been wrong when I thought we'd landed in a small town. Where we lived was apparently one of the larger, well-populated cities on the planet.

They were just a lot fucking smarter than Terrans in how they built their cities.

I'd never see so much grass or so many plants in my life. We passed a park where Algonquan handlers exercised their human charges. The humans all looked happy.

Like Mark and I felt.

Before coming here, I'd never seen Terrans look this happy, either while I was in the military or before.

It took us about fifteen minutes to get home, giving me my first look at the front of our home.

Our home.

It was as beautiful as the rest of the city. We had a gated driveway, and our front yard was even larger than the back. I'd never seen past the ten-foot-tall privacy fence that separated us from the rest of the world. Lots of large, beautiful shade trees, lush grass.

I longed to be back there.

At home, Master insisted on helping me out of the vehicle and made me hold on to his arm all the way inside. I nearly cried with relief when I walked through that front door for, technically, the first time.

Well, the first time I actually walked through it and was conscious when I did so.

We headed straight for Master's bed. He helped me climb in and waited for me to get comfortable before he undressed and got in. Mark climbed in on my other side.

I'd willingly kill for the look of love in Master's eyes. I didn't flinch when he stroked my cheek.

"Love Kal," he said. "Dolmo."

I nodded. "I know." I reached up to his face and stroked his cheek. I didn't know if I was breeching protocol or not and, frankly, I didn't care. I brushed my finger against his lips and he smiled, opened his mouth, and sucked my finger in, swirling his wonderful tongue around it.

Aaannnd there went my cock. Okay, so that's all it took to get it hard again.

Cool.

Mark laughed. "You're a smart fucker, and dammit, I love you." He kissed the back of my neck.

"I love you, too," I said, not shifting my gaze from Master. He continued to tease me, noting my cock's reaction to the delicious sensation.

Then Master sat up and carefully moved down the bed, positioning himself so he lay between my legs. He kissed my cock, wickedly grinned, and out came his tongue.

I closed my eyes and moaned as Mark laughed. "Oh, yeah. I forgot to tell you, he gives wicked awesome blow jobs."

His tongue wrapped around my cock, gliding up and down it before releasing it, sucking my balls into his mouth and doing beautifully delicious things to them. Then his tongue slid into my ass, where he teased and tormented me without giving me release. Returning to my balls and cock. Over and over, back and forth, until he focused on my cock and gave me a sweet release I was happy to see satisfied my willful member for a while.

He released me with a kiss on the balls and asked something.

Mark laughed. "Good?"

"How do you say, 'Fuck yeah!'"

Mark laughed and translated my comment and the idiom for Master.

Master also laughed, grinned, and nodded. "Fuh ya."

Mark and I both laughed. "Fuh ya," I said. "I think we just corrupted the Algonquan language."

Mark shook his head, a handsome smirk on his face. "Well, if there's one thing we humans are good at, it is fucking things up."

CHAPTER FOURTEEN

Apparently, they gave me some sort of healing accelerant, because by the next morning my ribs felt nearly normal. As he had with dinner the night before, Master insisted I sit in his lap in bed while he hand-fed me. I tried to protest that I could feed myself, but Mark laughed.

"Dale, he feels guilty as hell. Let him do it."

Resigned, I leaned against his chest and let him pop chunks of food in my mouth. He kept saying that sweet, purring word, over and over again.

Let's see, preparing buzzer bees for launch, or being curled up in an Algonquan's lap and getting hand-fed.

Hmm.

No brainer.

A horrible thought hit me. "What if after the war is over they make us leave and go back?"

Mark frowned. "No. Absolutely not. I won't leave. I'll hide if I have to, but fuck that. I'm not leaving. I'd rather live as a feral Terran here on Algonquan, hiding out in the woods or whatever, than go back to them. Do we have to talk about that? It won't happen."

By that afternoon we were allowed out in the backyard. The vet and one of the techs stopped by to check on me. My chest was unbandaged, and I could breathe normally and without pain. We had to re-enact what happened for the tech, so they could complete their report. Master's face filled with shame when he showed the tech how he raced over and kicked me to get me off Mark.

I threw my arms around him, hugging him. "It's okay. I forgive you. You didn't know."

He hugged me back, rubbing his face in my hair and muttering to me.

Mark stepped in. "He says he'll never assume the worst about you ever again. He'll always remember you'd never hurt me."

The tech wanted to see how we were playing. The vet cleared me to roughhouse, and within a few minutes Mark and I had really gotten into the game, forgetting it was supposed to be a demonstration.

Mark tackled me, and we both went flying, laughing our asses off.

Master called out to Mark. He looked up from where he had me pinned to the ground, probably just seconds from fucking my brains out.

"What?"

Mark looked down at me and smiled. "The tech's convinced. He said he might have reacted in the same way if he'd seen us playing and not realized what we were doing. Especially after I'd nearly been killed once before."

I bumped my hips up into his. "Does that mean we can get down and dirty now?"

He sat up, pushed my legs back, and thrust home, making both of us happily groan.

I was vaguely aware of the sound of Algonquan laughter, then they left us alone.

Mark reached down and pinned my wrists over my head as he fucked me. "You like that, baby? I know my cock's not as big as his, but your ass feels so good."

I tried to kiss him, but he kept just out of reach, teasing me. "Feels damn good. Fuck my brains out."

And that's exactly what we spent the rest of the afternoon doing. By the time Qhan brought us in to clean us up before dinner, we were both a sopping mess of sweat and cum and dirt and grass stains. Nice to know we didn't need the milker when we weren't carrying. I was no expert in giving blow jobs, but Mark coached me, and we didn't bother counting how many times we made each other climax.

I wondered what it was they did to us that made us able to effortlessly fuck as much as we wanted. My cock had indeed increased in size, still not quite as large as Mark's but definitely larger than it had been. I'd never been a pencil dick, but in the showers there'd been grunts who took great pride in having large cocks.

What I had now would put almost all of them to shame.

Another bonus to this situation.

And it didn't grow overly sensitive after climax like it used to, either. I could be ready to go again in just a few moments. It also didn't seem to lose any sensitivity despite everything it had been subjected to. I wondered if all that time using the milker would decrease sensation, but apparently not.

Again, the Algonquans could conquer the humans if they'd just market this technology. Greedy Terrans would pay for this without question. They could easily bankrupt the government by charging for it, then just walk in and take over.

Not that any men would want to give up their new toys long enough to fight back.

Because we were good pets, we were allowed a special treat after dinner. Master apparently had been invited to watch a televised sporting event at a friend's house. Qhan would go with us, and he leashed us and led us outside to where Mack had the vehicle waiting.

Mark had been there before, so he explained the ground rules to me. "You'll see other human pets. This guy has one, his name is Bob, and some of Master's friends will bring theirs, too. Some of the owners won't let their pets play with other pets, some will. So just stay with me. If any of the guys get too frisky with you, just ask them to back off."

I felt nervous. "What if another owner wants to fuck me?"

"Not tonight. The host might offer some of his guests the opportunity to play with Bob if they want, but Master's not about to share us right now after what we just went through."

I relaxed. This could be fun, a chance to see some other humans. I reached out and held Mark's hand. "They won't separate us, will they?"

"Doubtful." He grinned. "Do you honestly think Master's going to risk you going batshit on him?"

I smiled. "I'm sorry. I'm a bad dog. I get separation anxiety."

Mark laughed. When Master and Qhan both wanted to know what was so funny, he told them, and they also laughed.

Master smiled as he shook his head and made the good boy noise.

The house was as large as ours, and the owner had a swimming pool. We'd no sooner walked in the door and Qhan had unclipped our leashes than a human who looked like he was in his forties, not quite my height and with brown eyes and shaggy blond hair, came running up to Mark. He threw his arms around Mark, almost knocking him down.

"Mark! Gods, it's good to see you!"

Mark hugged him and turned to introduce me. I didn't miss the flash of jealousy in the man's eyes. That in turn ignited my own possessiveness. Mark was mine, not his. "Bob, I'd like to introduce you to Dale. Master bought him a little over a month ago."

Bob hesitated, then reached out and shook hands with me. The tag in his ear bore different coding than mine and Mark's, lending credence to the theory that it identified our owner.

"Hi." He turned to Mark, holding his arms and effectively trying to shut me out. "You want to go swimming? The pool's really nice right now." He tried to capture Mark's hand, and I had to hand it to Mark, he was a diplomat.

He gently turned back to me. "Bob, Dale's really new, okay? We need to show him around and introduce him. He had a really rough first drop. They almost had to operate. He's still trying to get settled in. Okay?"

I wished he'd left that part out, but it seemed to open Bob's eyes and he saw me in a new light. "I'm sorry!" He threw his arms around me, hugging me. I didn't miss how Mark winked at me. "I'm just...It's just that I've been here over ten years, and Mark's the only human I know who can speak their language, and—"

"It's okay, Bob," Mark assured him, peeling him off me. "It's all right. Come on, let's show him around."

It looked like I'd finally get past the foyer, but his revelation still had me reeling. *Ten* years. Obviously, Bob seemed to have adjusted. He acted more like a pet than Mark did.

Was that a preview of what I'd become? It didn't shock me to realize the prospect didn't bother me in the least.

Again, the whole "no pride" thing.

The Algonquans, more than thirty of them, had gathered in what looked like a large, comfortable living room. A couple of them had their human pets on leashes. The humans looked at us, one of them waved at Mark and he waved back, but they made no move to escape their owners to join us.

Out back, in a fenced-in yard not quite as large as ours, nine other humans splashed around in a pool under the supervision of two Algonquans. Several of the humans, upon seeing Mark, swam over to the side and greeted him.

My Mark appeared to be very popular.

Their ages ranged from a little younger than me to one man I'd guess was nearly in his sixties. Made sense, if humans had been disappearing for twenty years.

Mark introduced me to them, and they all greeted me warmly. I sat on the edge of the pool, my legs dangling in the water, and tried to absorb this.

Mark stayed close to my side even though he talked with everyone. A couple of the men tried to get him to pair off with them, but he politely declined. No one seemed offended, and the men usually ended up pairing off with another.

I wasn't sure I could get used to that. Then again, give me ten years and it might seem perfectly normal.

Mark leaned back on his arms and smiled at me. "Jealous?" he softly asked.

I felt my face heat. "Yeah." No use lying about it.

He patted me on the thigh. "It's okay. Most of them don't have another human at home." He glanced around and leaned in, whispering in my ear so none of the other men could hear. "Before I had you, I would have been in there with them."

I felt a different kind of heat rise in me. "Yeah?"

"Yeah. I love you, dumbass. I don't want to fuck around with someone else now that I've got you."

"So what if I went out there and played around?" Not that I wanted to, but I was curious to see what his reaction would be.

He grinned. "I'd tell Qhan you weren't playing well with others, and he'd leash you."

"You wouldn't?"

He waggled his eyebrows at me. "Try me. Not like you could tell them I was lying, right?"

I started laughing and hugged him. He stroked my back. "I'm sorry," he said, "but I'm possessive. Master bought you for *me*, not for them." He kissed me. "I don't want them. I only want you."

I leaned against him and he draped his arm across my shoulders. We sat there for a while before Mark led me into the pool. The water felt comfortably warm, and we swam over to an empty corner. He pulled me into his arms, hiking my legs up around his hips and sinking his cock into me. With the water to buoy us, we kissed, my arms wrapped around him as he fucked me.

It felt good. Totally right.

The Terran government hadn't outlawed homosexuality, but they discouraged men hooking up with each other. Stupid in my opinion, because even though I hadn't done it, most men had no other option for companionship other than another man. Many held on to some false hope they'd one day be allowed to marry and have a family. Most women were forced to stay single and lived in protected breeder communities, and only ones in higher positions of authority — or with a lot of money — could petition to get married.

The Terran government saw men as a disposable commodity, raised to fight if born to a breeder, raised to do something to support the government or military machine if born to someone blessed enough to be married, and raised to be in the government hierarchy, usually, if they were fortunate enough to have rich and well-connected parents.

If you survived long enough in the military and rose through the ranks, you could earn a marriage slot. Good luck finding a woman to marry, though. Contact was extremely regulated.

I'd never allowed myself to hope for a wife. I knew the facts. I wasn't rich, I wasn't well-connected, and if they ever gave me a chance to get out of the military, I'd take it in a heartbeat, meaning I'd never advance to a high enough rank to earn a slot.

With the first round of sexual appetites sated, the men lounged around and talked, usually paired off, holding hands, stroking arms, enjoying the feel of another body against them.

Mark assured me I could ask questions, and I did. I was the most recently purchased, and my last remembered date before capture helped them all re-adjust how long they'd been captive. The longest held was the eldest man, Carl. He'd been there seventeen years. No longer used as a breeder, his owner worked underneath Master in the government, and he had no complaints about his life.

"I was a damn grunt," he said. "We'd landed on one of their colony planets, and next thing I know, I'm for sale." He laughed. "I'd never been so fucking scared in my life. After the first month, and surviving my first drop, I realized that was the worst it got and I just enjoyed life."

"Did you ever try to escape?"

He shook his head. "Where the fuck would I go? Maybe if they'd tortured me, sure." We'd been brought something to drink and he sipped his. "No way in hell I'd ever leave now. I produced over a hundred eggs that lived," he proudly boasted. "Including the egg Olco designated his heir. I helped him continue his line. If I want something, Olco has it for me by the end of the day. Like that." He snapped his fingers. "Whatever I want. I lie around and watch vids all day. I get laid." He grinned. "Fuck Terrans."

That seemed to be a common theme. I heard many of the men echo the sentiment. "How much of their language do you speak?"

"Not much. I always sucked at languages. I can't tell their words apart like Mark can. I know basic commands, but Olco put together a chart with pictures. When I need something, I just show him. Or if I see something on the vids I want, I point and he gets it."

Mark laughed. "Or Olco calls Master and they put us on the com together so I can translate."

Carl laughed. "Yeah, that's been nice, having you around." He tipped his drink at me. "You're lucky you've got him."

I met Mark's blue gaze. "I know."

Tomas, unlike the rest of us, started his time as a breeder in an egg farm before he was adopted by his owner. He'd been a captive for more than five years.

"What was that like?" I asked, curious. "Being in an egg farm?"

He shrugged, his face clouding. "I mean, it was weird, at first. I damn sure prefer this to that. The ones that aren't sold after a few days are sent to egg farms to start producing. They didn't abuse us. They fed us, took good care of us, treated us kindly, but they kept some guys on those frames almost all the time, if they wouldn't settle down. Like those fucking grunts Mark's owner tried to tame. Some of the guys who were there a while, who were trusted, they allowed them to move about freely. They talked to us, told us what was going on. Once they trusted us, we could pick someone to bunk with. They'd have one of them with us when we got bred and when we dropped, to talk to us. But for the most part, there wasn't a lot of social interaction with the staff."

"How'd you get adopted?"

This is when he smiled. "I'd already had three drops, and Ylazo lost his partner in the war. There wasn't a current shipment of new arrivals. He came in with the intent of breeding since he'd hit his cycle. By that time I was allowed a little freedom once a day, in a common room with some of the other men who had shown they weren't going to fight or cause trouble. He was looking at us and he said he just fell in love with me. I damn sure wasn't going to argue with leaving there. He took me home that night."

I frowned. "I thought you didn't know the language?"

He looked at Mark with almost as much love in his eyes as he had when talking about Ylazo. "Ylazo took me over there to meet Mark's owner soon after he bought Mark, and Mark translated."

That was another common theme. Some of the men, while they had suspected their owner's feelings for them, hadn't had true confirmation until Mark's arrival. Our owners were a close-knit band of friends. Mark's ability to communicate, even though he couldn't understand all Algonquans, was enough he'd helped forge a deeper bond between the captives and their owners.

I thought about that word. Captive. Maybe true in the beginning, but like these men, I agreed I didn't want another life. I liked this. If circumstances were different in the Terran world, sure, I could see wanting my freedom, but I wasn't captive.

I was loved.

I felt a little overwhelmed, and perhaps Mark sensed that. He kissed me and led me back inside to find Master and Qhan. The sporting event, which resembled Terran rugby, had started. When Master saw us standing in the doorway, he smiled and waved us over to where he sat on the large sofa. I didn't miss how one of his friends eyed me and leaned in to talk with him. I didn't like the look on his face. Almost a hunger.

Master told Mark he could drag over a couple of pillows from a pile in the corner. Apparently, they were the designated pet pillows. While at home we were allowed free run of the house and the furniture, but Bob's owner didn't allow pets on the furniture. Or else he didn't want all the pets doing it. We sat by Master's feet, Mark holding me as we reclined against Master's legs.

The man who'd eyed me said something. Master laughed and patted my head.

I didn't want to know. I couldn't stop it if it happened anyway.

Mark kissed my forehead. "Don't worry, he's telling him we're not for sharing tonight."

"Has he ever fucked you?"

"Once. He doesn't have a pet."

"I don't like him."

"I don't either, but don't worry. Qhan or Master stays with me when that happens, so I'm sure he wouldn't leave you alone, either."

I closed my eyes and tried not to think about it.

CHAPTER FIFTEEN

I enjoyed sleeping with Mark and Master every night. With both of us up to full strength, Master wouldn't bother taking us to our room to fuck us. We'd get hooked up to the portable milker and fucked right there on our hands and knees in his bed. He took turns, one of us in the morning, and one of us in the evening, alternating to be fair. The one who didn't get fucked got one helluva blow job.

One morning he woke up and fucked Mark, blew me, then kissed us both and waved us into the shower. Qhan had entered the room and I guessed they needed to discuss household affairs. Mark and I enjoyed getting started, even though our need took over. By the time Master made it into the shower, I was bent over with Mark's cock plumbing my ass.

Master laughed, let us finish, and we had our shower. He indicated for me to take my turn topping Mark, making us both laugh as Mark got into position. Master loved watching his pets play almost as much as he enjoyed playing with us himself.

When we climbed out of the shower to find Qhan waiting with towels, I caught site of Master taking a pill and wondered what it was for. Before I could ask, Qhan was hustling us to our room where our breakfast awaited. I knew something was up when, after we finished, he ordered Mark up onto the frame and clipped his wrists to it, then hooked up the milker.

He asked Qhan something but didn't translate the answer. Qhan took up position behind him with the same ointment he'd used on me before I was bred. I suspected what was happening.

Walking over to the frame, I watched what Qhan did. It felt weird when my cock inflated, remembering how good the preparation had felt to me. Mark, naturally looser from two years of the procedure, didn't need nearly as much stretching as I did.

I needed the milker. I took up my familiar position in front of the frame and hooked myself up. Mark laid there, eyes closed, hips rocking in time with Qhan's ministrations.

When he heard me lay down, he smiled. "I'm assuming you connected the dots."

"Yeah. It probably explains the pill I saw Master taking after our shower."

Mark nodded. "He's triggering his cycle. Qhan said he'll do it tonight."

A thread of fear ran through me. "What happens if what happened to me happens to you?"

His eyes opened. "It's okay. I trust you. I know you'd do for me what I did for you."

He had more faith in my skills than I did. "How will I know?"

He smirked. "I was flying blind, baby. What, you think I've done that before? All I knew was there's a connector, like an umbilical cord, that holds the egg in. It thins and stretches and usually breaks during the drop. I found it and used my fingernails to pinch it free from the egg."

"Doctor Mark."

He laughed. "Vet extraordinaire."

"When's he going to breed me again?"

Mark closed his eyes and asked Qhan, who replied. "Next week." Qhan said something else, making Mark laugh. "Master wants us as close as possible because he likes watching us fuck."

* * * *

Master arrived home later that evening. Mark had spent half the day on the frame being massaged and stretched and enjoying every second of it.

Lucky bastard.

Qhan gave Mark the liquid supplement for dinner instead of solid food. Master greeted me by kissing me and saying something. Mark, already on the frame, wrists and ankles attached and hooked to the milker, laughed.

"He said don't worry, he'll give you what you want once he's done with me."

Okay, so I enjoyed getting fucked up the ass by that huge cock. So sue me. It felt good, and I never had to touch my own cock anymore for pleasure. I had the milker, Master, and Mark. It was the rare case one or more of those three weren't ready, willing, able, and eager to help.

Well, the milker wasn't eager, but you get my point.

I took up my position at Mark's head again as Master stepped behind him and opened his tunic. His cock looked different, harder, almost pointed at the head, a darker color than usual. He saw my wide eyes and crooked his finger at me, motioning me over. Taking my hand, he pressed my finger to the slit at the end and used one hand to pull back on the head.

I gasped when I felt the tiny barbs. But when I looked, they didn't appear at all menacing.

If his intention was to make me feel better, it worked. Mark translated his comments. "It only comes out when the egg's ready to come out. The egg pushes it out. Normally it's about halfway down, deep inside the penis."

Ingenious.

I returned to Mark's head, and Qhan brought Master a stool and me a chair. I sat, plugged into the milker and with my head resting on the padded frame next to Mark's. He smiled and kissed me. "I have to admit, I love this part," he said.

"You said you love all of it."

"Yeah, well, I do. I can't help it. I like having him buried in my ass and knowing he can't go anywhere." His eyes met mine. "This'll be you next week."

There came my fear again. Not fear of this part because, yeah, in retrospect thinking about it made me hard. But fear of how badly the drop had gone. "You won't leave me, right?"

"Never, babe. You're stuck with me."

Master stroked Mark's ass. Mark closed his eyes again, sighing with contentment as Master talked to him. He positioned his cock and thrust home, hard. Mark let out a hissing sound. "Yes!" he gasped.

That triggered a climax of my own. I kissed him and then watched his face. His lower lip caught under his teeth as he winced a little, and I noticed him trying to press his hips back, against Master, to take him deeper. Master laughed and lightly swatted his ass, making Mark smile when he made a comment.

"He called me greedy," Mark said before he gasped again.

I groped for Mark's hand and he took it, his grip tightening on me as his own orgasm shuddered through him. "He's hooking up," he whispered before he moaned again, his grip growing even tighter before another content sigh hit him. "Fuck, yessss."

Master settled onto the stool and now the waiting began. Mark retreated into a haze of bliss, the discomfort he felt familiar to him and more than overshadowed by the pleasure he also experienced. I didn't let go of his hand, and when I lifted my head to look at Master, I noticed his eyes were closed, his hands slowly stroking Mark's ass. He must have sensed me watching him because he smiled at me, giving me a playful wink.

After an hour or so of Mark repeatedly coming, he let out a soft groan. "There it is. I feel it." I let go so I could look. A bulge in Master's cock was pressing its way into Mark's stretched rim.

I returned to him and kissed his hand. "Yep. I could see it."

He nodded. It didn't take nearly as long with him as it had with me. Within another hour it was implanted, Mark letting out another brief hiss of pain before moaning with pleasure. Master finally withdrew, they inserted a plug, and then released Mark from the frame.

Master ordered me up onto the frame. Qhan stayed with me as Master carried Mark to his bedroom. He returned a minute later and sent Qhan to go stay with Mark. Master didn't hook my restraints, and when I looked over my shoulder I saw a slow, sly grin crease his face. His hands caressed my back, my hips, my ass, before he licked a finger and pressed it inside me.

I didn't understand the low, breathy things he said to me, but they sounded absolutely filthy and sexy in tone, so I went with that and enjoyed the hell out of what he did to me. Not just probing me with a finger, but his delicious tongue, torturing me, making me come, and I finally begged him to fuck me even though he couldn't understand me.

I'm sure my ass wiggle was an indication.

Laughing, he plunged home hard and deep, hesitating as he stroked my back again. Then I felt his lips along my spine, kissing me, and I came right then.

Thank the gods for the milker. I loved that fucker.

My reaction pleased Master. "Love Kal," he whispered as he gripped my hips and started a slow, deep thrusting that turned hard and fast, and he finally gave me that jack-hammering I craved. I thrust my body back, willingly impaling myself on that massive cock and wishing it'd been me up there tonight getting bred.

"Love Master!" I gasped as another climax took away my strength, and I felt him swell inside me before the familiar warm flood of his juices filled my body.

We lay there for a moment, his body pressed against mine as he caught his breath. He nipped my right ear lobe, by the tag.

"Mine," he whispered.

I shivered. He knew a few English words. "Yours!" I agreed.

With a delicious chuckle, he withdrew after his cock softened and he ordered me to stay. He drew a warm basin of water and washed me down, dried me, then pulled me up from the frame and enveloped me in his arms.

I couldn't wait for next week.

We returned to the bedroom where Qhan sat on the bed with Mark, holding his hand. Mark opened his eyes and gave us a sleepy smile when we came in. Qhan moved out of the way, and Master stripped before gathering Mark into his arms and cuddling with him. I crawled in behind Mark, too tired to even hook myself to the milker. Qhan did it for me, and Mark pulled my arm around him as I snuggled my head against him and fell asleep.

* * * *

Mark and I spent the morning snuggled in bed. The vet stopped by to check him, pronounced him carrying, and left us alone again after patting us both on the head.

"Let the games begin," I mumbled.

"Mmhmm," he agreed. "I fucking love this life. I couldn't begin to explain it to someone else, and even though I'm praying for the egg to hurry up and drop by the end of the carry period, I can't wait for it to start all over again. I'm addicted to the way it feels. It's fucking great."

He had a point. With every day that passed, I wanted to feel that constant aggravation again. It's indescribable. There's no pain while carrying, just bone-melting pleasure that never stops. It's a type of bliss, despite the exhaustion in the final few days.

Three days later, Master was hosting his first dinner party since I'd been there. Smaller than the party we'd attended, Mark was able to hear bits and pieces of conversations and ascertain it was more a working dinner than a social occasion. No other pets would come with their owners, and of the ten guests, four worked directly under Master and would be spending the night.

I tried not to worry about the man I'd seen at the other party. Maybe he wouldn't even be there.

At the party we'd attended, Bob had been turned into a party favor later in the evening after some of the guests left. Three men who'd been there without pets were allowed turns with him hooked to a frame similar to the one in our room. Of course, if the sounds Bob made were any indication, he didn't seem to mind in the least. Especially when the last one finished and he frantically begged for someone else to fuck him.

The man who'd eyed me had been one of the men, and I didn't like how he seemed to treat Bob more as a hole than a human. The other two men had fucked him, sure, but they stroked his back, obviously enjoyed the way he reacted to them, liked giving him pleasure as much as they took it. The man with the hungry eyes simply fucked him, hard, and maybe Bob didn't care and enjoyed it, but I felt a little ill watching.

When he'd finished, his eyes landed on me with such a dark and hungry look I had to turn away.

Unfortunately, he showed up at Master's dinner party. I also understood that physically, if he fucked me, my body most likely would respond in a way I could no longer control and would enjoy the hell out of it as long as he didn't hurt me.

That didn't mean I'd like it.

I tried to avoid him all evening, unable to hide in our room because we were told to stay out on the pillows in the living room. Since he was carrying, Mark would obviously not be used by anyone.

I lay there curled up with him, my eyes closed and arms around him as he napped. At one point in the evening we heard raucous laughter, and both of us looked. The party had dwindled down to Master and his four overnight guests gathered around the table and sipping an amber liquid. One of them was the man with the hungry eyes.

"That's like brandy," Mark whispered. "It's an after-dinner drink."

Master laughed about something else, and he rose from the table, followed by the man I didn't want to see and another. Master reached for my hand, and I hated like hell to go with him, but he ordered Mark to stay there and sleep.

With my heart in my throat, Master led me to our room and patted the frame. He and the other two men were talking. I hooked myself to the milker, climbed on, and prayed it wouldn't hurt.

Master clipped my wrists but left my ankles free. I closed my eyes.

Master sat by my head and whispered to me, a faint scent of the drink on his breath. Sweet and spicy. Then he reached under me and started gently massaging my balls.

The man with the hungry eyes stepped up first. I knew that because the other man walked over to the front of the frame to talk with Master. He plunged home, fast, deep, and hard, and immediately started a rhythm that had me shooting right away.

Master's free hand engulfed mine as he continued massaging my balls. His tongue snaked into my mouth, and I softly moaned at the taste of the drink on him.

Orgasm number two.

The man fucked me harder, laughing, and he slapped my ass hard.

Number three.

Despite my body's reaction, I wanted it to be over and I kept my eyes closed, determined I wouldn't embarrass Master, but trying not to cry.

He finally finished as he swelled, hard, shaking the entire frame with his thrusts and pulling another orgasm from me. Once he shrank he pulled out, slapped my ass again, hard, which that time earned him a sharp rebuke from Master. The man muttered something and left the room.

Master kissed me again. "Dolmo, Kal," he whispered.

The other man was tender and gentle by comparison, and I enjoyed it, welcoming the positive energy from him as he stroked my back and ass much like Master did while fucking me. Then he stayed while Master fucked me, and he even reached under me and played with my balls.

Now I understood why Mark didn't mind. If this man wanted to use me, okay, I was cool with that. But I would talk to Mark about asking him if we could ask Master not to let the other man use us anymore. Him I didn't like. At all.

Sated, I sighed when Master and the other man worked together to clean me up. Master released me from the frame and led me back to the living room. As we passed one of the guest rooms, I thought I caught sight of the hungry-eyed man taking a pill, but I could have been wrong.

Master had me return to the pillow. Exhausted, I fell asleep next to Mark, who snuggled against me.

The discussions went on long into the night. I must have slept through everything, because when my eyes popped open, I was alone on the pillow. The living room was dark and silent. A little miffed no one woke me, I stood and started for Master's bedroom. I was passing one of the guest rooms when someone grabbed me and clamped a hand over my mouth, the other around my neck.

I struggled. My assailant made a low, hissing sound in warning and tightened his grip on my neck until I could barely breathe and spots appeared in my vision. Scared, I remained silent and quit fighting. He could have snapped my neck with his huge hand. I smelled the drink on him, oozing through his pores and realized whichever man this was, he was drunk, making him even more dangerous.

He dragged me to our room and without turning on the overhead light, shoved me toward the frame. Okay, if that's what he wanted, fine, but I was damn sure telling Master about this. I hooked myself to the milker and as I tried to get in place, he grabbed my hands and attached my wrists and my ankles to the frame, immobilizing me. I closed my eyes and prayed he wouldn't last long.

I heard him rummaging through the cabinet until he found whatever it was he wanted. He shut the door, and in the dim light from the corner lamp, I recognized him.

Hungry eyes. I think I'd already known, but the dark fire in his gaze scared the crap out of me.

He jammed a large gag into my mouth. Not the wedge I'd arrived in but a thick padded one that filled my mouth and made screaming impossible. He grunted as he tightened the strap, painfully so, the straps cutting into the corners of my mouth.

Now I felt afraid. What the hell was he going to do to me that he wanted me gagged?

The answer soon became obvious when, without further ado, he plunged home and I felt his hard and rigid cock immediately bottom out in me, seeking the farthest recesses of my body.

I screamed, now understanding, as his cock ballooned inside me, trapping me.

He was going to breed me.

No! I begged, screamed through the gag, moaned, tried to fight. I didn't want this man. I'd fuck him if Master said, but no way in hell did I want his egg in me! When I wouldn't settle down he slapped the back of my head hard enough to make me dizzy for a minute.

I sobbed, crying as I felt him hook into me, and he grunted in satisfaction.

My body responded to the painful stimulus in the only way it could, giving me physical pleasure that left me crying even harder in anger and shame.

I didn't want this man.

I tried to mentally check out, ignore the pain and focus on the pleasure and pray it would end soon. It didn't last as long as the first time Master had bred me, but it hurt worse. When he finally finished, he smacked the back of my head again, hard, and I was aware of him stumbling away from the frame as I passed out.

CHAPTER SIXTEEN

I awoke before dawn the next morning, still gagged and attached to the frame, with Mark frantically screaming for Master and Qhan. Fuck, my ass hurt, and not in the good "morning after" bliss kind of way, either. What the hell happened?

Then the night's events slammed back into my brain and I couldn't help the tears.

Mark had turned on the overhead light and Master and Qhan ran into the room.

"Jesus, Dale, baby." Mark gently tried to remove the gag, but I cried out in pain as the straps came free from where they'd cut into the corners of my mouth. "Who did this to you?"

Master looked enraged as he and Qhan hurriedly unhooked my manacles from the frame, and I collapsed onto the floor, sobbing as Master's arms encircled me.

Master looked at Mark, who knelt beside me. "Baby, tell us. Who did this?"

I buried my face against Master's chest as Mark traced the mark of the bruise on my throat where the asshole had grabbed me. "That guy. The one we didn't like. The first one Master let..." I broke down sobbing again as Master tried to soothe me.

Mark sounded ready to kill. He told Master.

Master let out a deadly-sounding growl. He handed me off to Mark and Qhan and ran from the room. We heard the sound of enraged screaming and more voices as the other guests and Mack showed up to see what was going on. The sounds of a struggle followed then, a moment later, Master returned, dragging the son of a bitch by his hair. He threw him to the floor in front of me and pointed at the guy, screaming at him.

"He's the one?" Mark asked.

I trembled in his arms and didn't miss he had a death grip on me, rocking me. I nodded.

The man looked like he'd been asleep in a drunken stupor and weakly tried to hold his hands up in self-defense. Master screamed something else.

Qhan also tried to comfort me, wrapping his arms around both Mark and me. "What'd he do to you?" Mark softly asked. "Did he just rape you?"

I sobbed and shook my head, unable to look at Master. If I'd yelled when he first grabbed me, maybe Mark or Master would have heard him and someone would have stopped him.

Mark forced me to look at him. "Did he breed you?"

I nodded and sobbed again.

Mark tucked my head under his chin and rocked me. "Shh, it's okay, baby. It's okay. You're safe now. I've got you."

Master looked at Mark and asked him something.

I felt Mark nod.

Master roared, enraged. The other guests looked ready to rip the offender limb from limb, including the other man Master had shared me with. Master grabbed the man and, with the help of another, dragged him from the room. We could hear them struggling with him and Master screaming. The front door slammed.

Qhan said something soft to Mark, and Mark let him carry me over to the bed, where he gently rolled me onto my side. I laid my head in Mark's lap, and he stroked my hair and whispered to me, trying to soothe me. Qhan made a *tsking* noise. A moment later he was gently washing my violated ass with warm water. His tender, kind treatment made me cry even harder.

I don't know when the vet was called, but around dawn he arrived and checked me there in the bed, where I'd lain with Mark's comforting arms around me since Qhan put me there. Qhan asked him something. The vet sighed and nodded.

I cried harder. I didn't need a translation.

"Shh, it's okay, baby. You didn't do anything wrong."

"I couldn't fight him. He grabbed me by the neck and dragged me in. He put his hand over my mouth. I thought he was just going to fuck me and then..." I couldn't continue.

Mark translated as the vet looked at my bruises. He had something I guessed was a camera and photographed the bruises.

I wanted Master and told Mark that.

"He'll be back soon. He's taking care of this. He's outside with the law."

A few minutes later, Master did reappear. After a quick consult with the vet, he looked even more upset.

Then he walked over to the bed, and the sad look returned. "Dolmo, Kal," he said, his voice choked. He took me from Mark and cradled me to his chest, kissing my bruised mouth where the straps had left my flesh raw. "Dolmo. Love Kal."

I cried harder, holding on to him.

He picked me up and carried me outside the front door. Mark, the vet, and Qhan followed us. They'd amassed quite a turn-out. The bastard was trussed, bare from the waist up, to the back of an official-looking vehicle. Three stony-faced men in uniforms stood there. From the sidearms they wore, I assumed they were the police.

The man was begging, pleading, struggling against his bonds. One of the officers slugged him, and dazed, he fell still. Master handed me over to Qhan, who cradled me in his arms while Mark still stroked my hair. Master walked over to the officers with the vet and said something.

Mark whispered, "He's demanding immediate justice. For your attack, rape, and breeding."

The officers listened to Master, nodding. One of them injected the perpetrator with something and asked him a question.

He nodded.

"That's like a truth serum," Mark said. "He just confessed."

Master spit on the man and held his hand out to one of the officers. They handed him a wicked-looking implement that must have been like a lash. Master walked over to me, kissing me and murmuring he loved me and how sorry he was. Then he returned to the prisoner and savagely flayed him as the man writhed and screamed. I didn't want to look, but I couldn't help it.

I lost count of the lashes, but when Master finished, he was breathing heavy, sweating, and handed the lash back to the officer and said something else. The man's back was a bloody mess.

"Fifty lashes," Mark said, "Ten for the attack, forty for the rape."

Master held out his hand again and one of the officers gave him a sidearm.

The man frantically started babbling as Master stepped up to him and pressed the muzzle between his eyes.

Mark translated what one of the officers said. "As dictated by Algonquan law, swift justice and retribution is hereby carried out for the attack, rape, and breeding of the owner's pet. For unlawful breeding of another's pet during a rape, death."

Master fired.

* * * *

I didn't want to see anything else. I felt myself being transferred to Master's arms, his lips once again trying to soothe mine as he carried me through the house to his bed. He climbed in with me, softly speaking to Mark as he also climbed in, and together they held me while I cried.

I felt weak and worthless. I wanted to check out for a while, so when Mark asked if I wanted something to help me sleep, I nodded and welcomed the sting of the vet's hypo.

I awoke late that afternoon still wrapped in Master's arms. He and Mark had been softly talking, and Mark held one of my hands in his.

"Hey, baby," he whispered when he realized I was awake. He leaned in and kissed me. "Welcome back."

"Did they take it out of me?" I asked. "I don't want it in me. I want it out."

He stroked my head. "They can't, baby. There isn't a way to do that unless they operate."

"I don't care. I want it out. Now."

"Shh." Master's arms closed comfortably tight around me as he made the sound again. "Shh."

I started crying. "I want Master's egg, not that bastard's. I don't want it!"

"It's okay. It wasn't your fault. You didn't do anything wrong. He knows that. He's not blaming you."

"Dolmo, Kal."

"He feels it's his fault—"

"I get that," I snapped. "I want it out of me. Make them take it out!" I started crying again. "Please, I don't care what they have to do. Make them take it out!"

Mark took me from Master and held me, rocking me. "Baby, you don't understand what that'd do to you. If it's forcibly taken out before the drop process naturally starts, it could hurt you. You might not be able to carry any more eggs. Master took his right of revenge, and the government is compensating him for what happened. He's not mad at you."

"It's not fair!" I didn't care how hysterical I sounded. "I was supposed to carry his egg!"

Yep, totally whacked, didn't care. I wanted my Master's egg in me, a chance to redeem myself for the last time.

"It's okay. If it survives, it goes to the military to be raised. If it doesn't, no great loss. It's okay."

Master looked grief-stricken. He spoke slowly while Mark translated.

"I'm so sorry. I know I keep saying that a lot, but I am. I promise, I'll never share you ever again. If I'd known he'd do that, I never would have let him in my house, much less near the two of you. I'm so sorry."

I broke free from Mark and hugged Master. "Tell him I don't blame him."

Mark did, and Master held me tighter.

Then Mark cleared his throat. "Don't freak out."

"What?"

"Okay, first, keep in mind, you are *not* going anywhere, okay? He's not sending you away."

I sniffled and turned to look at him. "Just fucking say it!"

"The fight and rage triggered his cycle again. Part of his compensation is the government is giving him another pet, in addition to the guy's estate. He needs to breed by tomorrow night. There's another shipment arriving any minute, and he's going to go get one."

I cried, clinging to him. "I don't *want* another one!" I wailed. "I just want you and him! Why can't he go to the fucking egg farm?"

Mark tried to soothe me. "Baby, it's how their laws are. Not just an eye for an eye, but he's entitled to another one. It's okay. He told me he wants you and me to be able to choose when we want to breed, especially after this. If he's got a third one, that guy can help take over. He doesn't ever want you forced to do this again if you don't want to."

"But won't he get rid of me if I don't breed?"

"No!" He kissed me. "That's what I'm trying to tell you." He used his thumbs to brush my tears away. "He loves us. We're not just breeders. We're his pets, part of the family. He's never looked for another partner like some do who have pets. He doesn't want a partner because he had me, and now you. Once we get you through this, if you want to breed again, you can. If you decide no, that's fine, too, but he still wants you. He loves you. He just wants you to know this isn't some sort of threat to what he feels for you. It's not a punishment." He smiled. "He said we'll still be his favorites."

I sniffled but felt a laugh try to break through. "Yeah?"

He smiled. "Yeah." He hugged me. "Okay?"

I nodded.

"He wants to know if you want to go with him to help pick him out. We can if we want. They'll allow it because of the circumstances. Master gets to go in first before anyone else. They'll even let you talk to them if you want to."

I stared into Mark's blue eyes. "What do you want to do?"

"Whatever you want to do, baby. I'll go either way."

"You'll go with me if I go?"

He nodded. "Yeah. Master said he's thinking about shackling us together so we can't be separated ever again." Then he smiled.

When I laughed, Master made a relieved sounding noise.

"Okay," I said. "I'll go."

CHAPTER SEVENTEEN

So that's how I found myself in the vehicle with Master, Mark, Qhan, and the vet. An entourage. "Is this the same place where he got me?"

"Yeah. It's the regional distribution facility."

"Is it a shopping mall? That's what it looked like to me."

He laughed. "Yeah, it is."

I spent the ride in Master's lap, Mark holding my hand. Neither wanted to let go of me. "Why didn't I see any pets before, when we were there?"

"They normally don't allow pets there when the shipments arrive. They're afraid it might scare the Terrans if they see us."

"Is that why they gag them?"

He nodded.

Master said something and Mark laughed. "Guess what? We get clothes, too. So we don't spook the others."

I sniffled. I sort of preferred being naked. I never felt uncomfortable. If I ever felt too cool, I just grabbed a towel or afghan. The days were perfectly warm.

The same group of police met us there. We parked around back, where I noticed a large group of what looked like transport vehicles near a door. When we walked in, I realized it was the private room where they'd transferred me to the frame they shipped me on.

"Is that how I got to Master's?" I asked.

"Yep. Master made Qhan leash me to keep me out of the way when they brought you in." He kissed me. "They let me touch your hair before they moved you into the house. That's as close as he'd let me get to you before he knew you wouldn't hurt me." I loved Mark's smile. "I think I fell in love with you then. You looked so sweet and helpless."

"I was knocked out and strapped to the frame. I *was* helpless."

He laughed. "Yeah, I guess you were." He kissed my hand. "You pick, baby. Okay? I'll go with whatever you want to do."

Part of me worried how I'd react to a new pet. "What if I can't like them? What if I'm jealous?"

He smiled. "I'm not jealous of you with Master."

"I meant of them with you."

"Oh, baby." He slid me into his lap. "You're *mine*. Master bought you for me. You think I'm giving you up, think again. No one will ever take your place in my heart. If you tell me it's just you and me and we don't fuck around with him, that's the way it is."

"Really?"

He nodded. "Really." He grinned. "Maybe I won't want you fucking around with him. Maybe I'll be too jealous."

I laughed, sniffling again at his playful look. I had a feeling if we liked the guy, we'd both be fucking him, as horny as we got.

Maybe this would be okay. Maybe there would be benefits to this.

"Do many people have three pets?"

"Not too many. You have to be really wealthy. Some people have four or five. Master is wealthy, I told you that. Not to mention well-connected. Lots of people have one pet. Not everyone has the space for more than one, either."

Master patted me on the thigh and asked Mark something.

"You ready?"

I nodded.

The police handed Mark and myself green tunics that fell to our knees. I was surprised they didn't require us to be leashed and asked about that.

"Under the circumstances, and with the vet's testimony, they know we're tame." He smirked. "My CO from the military would never believe it. I racked up demerits like you wouldn't believe for disorderly conduct on shore leaves. I'd go to a bar fight and sometimes, if I was lucky, drinking would break out."

I laughed as he hugged me tightly and then slipped his arm around me. "You and me," he whispered. "Don't forget that."

"You and me," I agreed.

Tightly flanked by Master and Mark, we were led inside, and one of the blue-garbed techs met us. Apparently briefed by the police, he gave me a kind smile and pat on the head as he led us into the main hall where all the racks were stowed.

Had this been me? Even though it wasn't that long ago, I could barely remember experiencing the fear, the confusion, the uncertainty I read on the faces of these men. I wanted to scream at the top of my lungs that they should be grateful they were captured and about to embark on the best time of their lives!

Well, mostly that was true. I still felt that despite what I'd just gone through.

Seeing the twenty or so racks of men neatly lined up and waiting for shoppers made me remember the best of this life — the men on either side of me, both of whom I loved more than my own life.

Fuck Terrans.

Master whispered a question to Mark, who kept his voice low when translating. We'd been asked to speak in soft, calm tones.

"Do you have any questions about how to pick one?"

I nodded, and indicated I wanted the tech in close. I spoke slowly, so Mark could translate. "When Master picked me, they checked my..." I indicated my ass. "Size. How well I did. How would I know if someone had a similar score as me?"

The tech smiled as Mark translated, then the tech asked Master a question. Master nodded.

"He wants permission to scan your tag, on your collar," Mark said.

I nodded and raised my head so he could reach the one on my collar. Small and unobtrusive, it never bothered me. He scanned it into his hand-held and pulled up my records, then punched in another command. On several of the racks, I noticed little blue lights blinked.

The tech in me felt thrilled. "Those are similar?"

Mark translated, and the tech nodded.

I could tell from the look on Mark's face that he was geeking over this as much as I was. How cool was that?

"What about Mark? How did I compare to him? How about one that's equal to him, if he was better than me?"

His tag was also scanned. Some of the lights went off. "Let's start at this end," I said, pointing, now sort of excited by the prospect.

The tech led us around the racks. The men looked scared, some looked angry, some struggled against their bonds, trying to attract our attention to help to get free.

I ignored the last batch, even if their blue lights blinked, because they were invariably huge, ripped grunts with macho painted all over them.

Halfway through the hall, one of the men quietly lay there, relaxed, waiting. Younger than me from his appearance, he finally opened his eyes when he sensed us standing beside him. I stepped forward and waited until he focused on me. His brown eyes looked deep, sweet, full of hopes and dreams unrealized. His hair color was closer to Mark's than mine, but still not quite the same shade of brown as either of ours. He didn't have the hard edge of combat and the forced bravado of a grunt despite his trim body.

He looked lonely. Resigned to his fate.

"Can we, like, bookmark him? So we can see the rest first?"

Mark smiled and translated. The tech also smiled and a red light appeared on the rack's panel. We spent about an hour looking at the rest of them, and I only saw one other I might like. I wished I could take both of them home, but I wanted to talk to the first Terran I'd flagged. He was the one who really attracted my interest.

We returned to him, and Mark told Master he was a contender. Master asked the tech to go through a similar procedure with him that I went through. The captive looked at me, his eyes never leaving mine until they inflated the butt plug and his breathing quickened. His eyes closed, and I knew he climaxed.

Then his eyes opened, and he looked at me again.

I looked at Mark, one eyebrow arched.

He smiled, one side of his mouth quirked in a playful grin, and he gave me a slight nod. I caught sight of his cock trying to make itself known beneath his tunic and realized belatedly he was away from the milker and must be growing uncomfortable.

"Can we talk to him?" I whispered.

There was a brief discussion. They would pull his frame and move him to the private room so we could talk to him away from the other humans. Moving quickly and efficiently, and with us following, the techs got his frame situated in the private room and removed his gag.

No immediate screaming, no tearful pleading. No angry, empty threats. As soon as I'd entered the room, his gaze had sought mine. He stood there watching me, waiting on me.

"What's your name?" I asked.

"Cooper." That's all. No demands for information. He had a pleasant voice, too. When I reached out to touch his face, I didn't miss how he closed his eyes when I laid my palm along his cheek.

Then he leaned into my touch.

Without moving my hand I asked, "What were your duties?"

He didn't open his eyes. "Com tech. Both operations and technical maintenance."

I looked at Mark and arched my eyebrow again.

He smiled and nodded.

I returned my attention to Cooper. "What do you hate most about the military?"

His eyes popped open. "The asshole grunts. Fuckers think they're the universe's gift to humanity. Not all of us want to lay down our life for that stupid fucking war."

Mark stepped up next to me and slipped an arm around my waist. I hadn't moved my hand and Cooper made no move to try to escape my touch.

"If you could have one wish," Mark said, "right this second, what would it be?"

Without hesitation he replied, "Someone to get my ass out of the goddamned military. I fucking hate it."

My hand drifted down his neck to his collar. He didn't flinch away from me. I suspected convincing him our life was good wouldn't be too hard. There were plenty of gay guys in the service, but they tended to keep that to themselves so the grunts didn't make their life hell. His eyes stayed on mine as my hand drifted lower, down his back, to his ass.

He pushed into my hand as a delicious smirk curled his lips.

Mark leaned in and kissed me, deeply. When I opened my eyes, I realized he was watching Cooper's reaction.

I didn't miss how Cooper's lips parted, his tongue flicking his lips before he caught himself and composed his expression.

Mark looked at me and grinned. "You want?"

Surprisingly enough, I did. "I think so. You?"

"I made you a promise, baby. This is your call. All the way."

I pulled him a few feet away, wanting a private moment with him. "I like him. I think he'll do well." I didn't say the rest.

Mark stepped in and kissed me again, then whispered in my ear. "If you can't stand seeing me with someone else, I meant it. Just you and me. If you want to try him out, that's okay, too. I understand."

I studied his blue eyes. "Maybe we both could try him out?"

I felt his cock, hard and insistent, press against mine through his tunic. "Yeah," he said, smiling. "We sure can, if he's up to it."

I turned to study Cooper. I'd noticed Master, Qhan, our vet, and the techs waiting on us. Cooper waited. Patiently waited.

No doubt a man who'd had to learn patience in his life.

"You want out of the military for good?" I asked him.

He nodded. "Yeah, man." He smiled, then took what to him, I'm sure, felt like a big risk. "Wouldn't mind some of that action, either, if there's any room at the table for a third."

Mark kissed me one more time. "We always come first," he whispered. "I mean it. I love you first, baby."

I nodded. "Me too. Us first."

I pulled Mark over to Master and motioned for him to lean in close so I could whisper and Mark could interpret. "Do you like him?"

Master smiled and chuckled. "Love Kal. Love Pol." He said something else, then kissed me and Mark.

Mark smiled. "We're always his favorites, but he admits Cooper isn't objectionable. If we're happy, he's happy."

I still wavered. It'd have to be someone. Master needed someone. I walked back to Cooper, leaned in, and kissed him.

Startled at first, he immediately responded with full and eager tongue, a man who had experience with other men before, if I had to guess. No reluctance. When I let him go, I smiled.

He grinned. "Do you know how long it's been since I've been laid?" he murmured.

I liked his voice. I could imagine how it'd sound in my ear, or how he'd sound being fucked. I fought the urge to giggle. "If I can promise that will get taken care of for you, would you want to come home with us?"

"Oh, fuck yeah!"

"Do you have any family?"

He shook his head and I didn't miss the grief that flashed through his features. "No one, man. I'm alone."

One more test. "Mark?"

He stepped in and kissed him. I watched carefully, worried I'd feel that green-eyed monster roar, but honestly? It was sexy. Like watching him with Master.

Mark looked at me and seemingly read my mind. "You okay, baby?"

I smiled and nodded. "Sold."

* * * *

Despite our best efforts to convince them otherwise, they gagged Cooper again. It was their rules for transport, and while they could bend some of them, that was one they wouldn't. Mark and I quickly explained to Cooper. He obediently opened his mouth for the new gag. We managed to keep him from being drugged as long as our vet rode along for the transport, in case he panicked and needed sedation. The vet had quickly learned to trust us. He assured the techs that if we thought Cooper would be okay unsedated, they should try it.

Cooper nodded when we told him he was going home with us, and not to fight them. We practically begged him not to fight. He seemed quick on the uptake. We watched as they transferred him to the transport frame and he didn't resist in the least. The vet looked on, smiling and nodding with approval.

My logic? If he wasn't sedated, he'd get a look at his new home. Maybe see how good he had it compared to what little he'd had before.

Let the planet do our selling for us. Honestly? If I'd been awake on the drive to Master's house, I would have given a resounding "fuck yeah!" to the idea from the start.

They had to tag him, give him his other shots, and complete the transaction. They let me and Mark hold his hands and explain the tagging. He closed his eyes and even tipped his head to the side to allow them better access to his right ear, the techs pleasantly surprised by his compliance.

Master walked up to me, put his arms around me from behind, and kissed the top of my head.

"Love Kal," he whispered.

I hugged his arms around me. "Love Master."

CHAPTER EIGHTEEN

Back in the car, I felt more than happy to shed the damn tunic. After all that time going naked, clothing felt restrictive, uncomfortable against my skin despite the soft, silky fabric it was made from. Mark ripped his off and I knelt in front of him. I went down on him, knowing I was doing nothing more than taking a little edge off his need. He grabbed my head and collapsed against Master, happily moaning as I brought him over.

When he caught his breath he made me switch places with him. Master kissed me as Mark went down on me, helping me out.

Damn, I missed our milker!

I no sooner climaxed than I started laughing.

"What?" Mark asked as he rejoined us on the seat.

"Master's going to need to get another pump."

He translated. Master laughed, nodded, and replied. Mark laughed. "He said maybe he'd better buy a couple of extra ones because he has a feeling his pets are going to wear out the ones he already has."

I kept looking out the back window, watching the transporter following us in the beautiful golden late afternoon sunlight. I hoped Cooper could see Algonquan through the windows.

When we arrived home, the transport pulled up to our front door and the techs carefully unloaded Cooper. Now he looked amazed, astounded. I hurried over to him, so he could see me. "Could you look outside during the trip?"

He nodded, still wide-eyed.

Mark joined me and we walked with him through the house to our room. Mark asked for a moment to talk to him and I let him take over. He'd done a great job of calming me.

"Look, I'm Mark, this is Dale. This is going to sound freaky, but please trust us when we say you won't be harmed. Just go with it and enjoy it. Don't do anything to fight them when they move you or they'll want to knock you out and keep you tied up. Okay?"

He nodded.

"They'll take the gag off soon, too. I promise."

He nodded again.

We stepped out of the way, Master waiting with his hands protectively on our shoulders as we watched the techs and Qhan transfer Cooper to our frame, hook him to the milker, and remove the plug.

Once they checked his bonds, they had Master sign a hand-held, acknowledging receipt of his new pet. Then they took their transport frame and left.

Now Master drew close to him, and Mark talked fast. "We call him Master. Long story. He's our owner."

Cooper nodded and laid his head down on the frame, not resisting as he watched Master.

Master tentatively reached out and stroked Cooper's hair, the way I remembered him doing to me. Cooper closed his eyes and made a soft noise of enjoyment.

Then Master slowly explored his body, stroking him with his hands, relaxing the man. Mark asked Master a question, and he nodded. When Mark gently removed the gag, Cooper let out a moan.

"Please don't stop!"

Master froze, but Mark assured him that was the exact opposite of what Cooper wanted him to do, so Master smiled and started again.

Mark and I knelt by Cooper's head. "Have you ever been with a guy?" Mark asked.

"Yeah, but not nearly enough times. Please tell me someone's going to fuck me? I'm so horny I can barely see straight."

I grinned. "He's going to do a lot more than fuck you." I let Mark take over with the explanations.

Cooper looked at us when he finished. "Breeder?"

We nodded.

Master chose that moment to snake his tongue inside Cooper. His head dropped to the frame again and he moaned, bucking his hips, wanting more. "That's his cock?" he gasped.

Mark grinned. "Dude, that's just his tongue."

"Ohhh....fuuuck me!" he happily moaned. Master pulled three orgasms out of Cooper before he waved Qhan over to start the preparations. It was already time for dinner, and Mark and I were starved and horny. Efficient Qhan had already secured a third hose for the frame's milker, and Mark and me parked ourselves on a couple of pillows by Cooper's head to eat our dinner.

We explained to him what would happen. He was understandably nervous, but pragmatic about it. "I'll be honest, one of my hottest fantasies is being turned into some well-hung guy's sex slave." He laughed. "I just never figured as a breeder."

As the evening progressed, Qhan gave him the pink drink, and I held the bottle for him while he sipped. Within a few minutes, Mark and I watched as the effects hit him.

"Please," Cooper begged. "Holy gods, someone please fuck me or fist me or knock me the hell out, I need to come!"

Mark translated. Master laughed and walked around to the front of the frame and kissed Cooper. Then he stepped behind him, and Qhan brought him the stool.

Mark and I held his hands as Mark explained what would happen every step of the way. Cooper closed his eyes, happily moaning with every climax. His grip tightened on our hands when the barbs grabbed on, but he took a deep breath and before long was crying out again with another orgasm.

The process took nearly as long for him as it had for me the first time. By the time Master finished, Cooper was trembling, bathed in sweat, but wore a happy smile.

"Holy fuck," he whispered, all strength gone from his body. "That was…fucking fantastic!"

Mark translated. Master laughed and then grabbed me and kissed me, that wonderful tongue sweeping through my mouth, and he said something.

Mark grinned. "He said he won't tell his friends how good you are picking out pets because they'll want to hire you to pick theirs for them."

He ruffled Cooper's hair, patted him on the shoulder, and looked at us. "Taun."

"Master's named him Taun."

"Pol, Kal, Taun." Master kissed us. "Mine," he said. Shivers ran down my spine. I loved that, and I don't know why. I'm glad that was one of the few English words he knew.

Qhan got Cooper cleaned up, and I wasn't sure what the sleeping arrangements would be. I didn't want Cooper left alone, but now that the evening had wound to a close and I had time to think, my own demons returned in full force. I didn't want to give up Mark or Master.

Turns out I didn't have to. Master bunked with us in our room, the four of us comfortably snuggled together. Master let me pick how I wanted us situated. I decided I wanted me and Cooper in the middle, with Master by me and Mark holding Cooper.

Cooper rolled over to face me, his head snuggled against my chest. We were three happy humans when Qhan hooked up our milker pump, having already secured an extra hose for that, too. Mark laced his fingers through mine, and like that, I crashed into sleep.

* * * *

I slept restlessly. The thought of that damn egg in me when I didn't want it kept me from peaceful rest. Every time I felt horny, the memory of the attack would flash through my mind, and I couldn't enjoy the physical release.

It would be a long fucking four weeks.

Master didn't leave us the next morning. He waited with us until the vet checked Cooper and declared him bred.

I hated the pity in the vet's eyes every time he looked at me and offered me a kind smile. I didn't know how to deal with this. No, it wasn't my fault. I got that, mentally.

Physically, the fact that my body had betrayed me and eased me through the process grated on me even more. Maybe it was stupid to feel that way, but if it'd hurt like hell the entire time, been an agony to endure, it would have made it easier on my psyche.

Master had Qhan take Cooper to Master's bathroom, to the shower, telling him we'd be there in a minute.

He pulled me into his lap and gently caught my chin, making me look up at him. He spoke softly, slowly, allowing Mark time to translate for him.

"I'm so sorry you had to go through this. I'm sorry I didn't wake you up to come to bed. You looked so peaceful, I didn't want to disturb you. It's my fault I brought that animal into my home, and it's my fault you were attacked. I promise, I will never release you, never sell you, always make sure you are cared for so that no one can take you from me. I love you more than I can tell you, and even though we now have another, please never think he will ever replace you in my heart because he won't. I can like and maybe one day even love him, but you and Pol, you are my—" Mark stumbled over the next word, choking up, "—babies. I know you went through a horror, and I'm sorry. The vet told me it's natural for you to feel traumatized and have nightmares. You could not have fought him. Had he killed you, it would have broken my heart. You hold no fault."

He kissed me. I heard Mark sniffle. "Love Kal," Master said, tears welling in his eyes. "Love Kal. Mine."

"Promise me as soon as this fucking egg is out of me that you'll breed me. Please. Immediately."

Master hesitated. Mark translated his eventual response, "If it is what you want, then yes. But I meant what I said, that I will never again make you breed. Even if it means I'd have to visit an egg farm in the future. You are my pet, my love. I refuse to do anything to hurt you."

I threw my arms around him. "Thank you. I want this egg out of me, and I want your egg in me. I want to make you proud."

"You *do* make me proud." Now tears rolled down Mark's cheeks. "You and Pol are very special, don't think I don't see that. I've seen lots of other pets, and you two are unique amongst them. I suspect you have picked another who is very much like the two of you, and I will soon come to love him. But you and Pol will always be first in my heart. I swear it." He held me, soothing me.

"If there is anything I can do," Master continued, "anything you need during this time, if you need me, my attention, it is yours." He cradled my face in his hands and showered kisses over my face. "Never hesitate to ask."

I nodded and offered him a smile.

He smiled in response. Then he stood, effortlessly carrying me in his arms. "Now let's go take care of Taun and introduce him to how we do things."

* * * *

We introduced him, all right. The shower was more like a mini-orgy. When he got a look at what Master could do with his tongue as he checked Mark, his jaw dropped. He sank to his knees, eyes wide as he nudged in close. Almost without thinking, his hand went between Mark's legs and started stroking his cock as Master brought him off.

Several orgasms later, Mark was happily lying on his side on the shower floor. My cock throbbed, screaming, and Master indicated for me to assume the position.

Before I could, Mark rolled over onto his back and pulled me on top of him, kissing me while Master's tongue snaked inside me. Then I felt Cooper's hand on my cock, and I surrendered to the bliss. Master spent a long time with me, much longer than normal, and I lost track of how many times I came. When he finally finished with me, I lay there and cried with Mark's arms tightly around me. I felt weak and helpless.

Mark tried to soothe me. Cooper had no clue what was going on, but bless him, he sat down next to us and I felt him lay his arm over my back, holding me, too.

"Tell him," I said to Mark without raising my head. "Get it over with so he knows."

"Baby, it's okay."

I wouldn't open my eyes. "Just tell him."

Mark told him the basics as Master knelt there with us, his hands caressing my back. When Mark finished the story, Cooper stroked my wet hair. "What can I do to help?" he softly asked.

I finally looked up and met his gaze. I suspected those were tears, not shower spray, on his cheeks. "I'm sorry. This isn't very fair to you."

"Whoa, what?" Cooper grinned. "Dude, you guys just fulfilled my fantasy, my wish. Like I rubbed a lamp and a genie appeared. I feel bad why it happened, but I'm not complaining. I don't feel left out, trust me."

I sat up and hugged him. "Thanks for understanding." I liked the feel of his arms around me. He was about my height and size, a slightly slimmer build than Mark and me.

Mark finally gave Master a quick translation. For the first time it struck me that now he was the one left out in the cold with our conversations. I kissed him and pointed at Cooper, then flicked my tongue at him.

He laughed and patted Cooper on the ass.

Mark grinned from where he still lay beneath me. "Assume the position, dude."

Cooper did, on all fours, ass in the air. "Gladly."

Mark kissed him while I fisted his cock. A few minutes later, he was also a happy, content pet. As Master helped pull us to our feet, I didn't miss how dazed Cooper looked. He leaned against the shower wall.

"This is…wow. I owe you guys big time."

No, a grunt wouldn't have fit in with us, even if he'd been willing to accept the situation. And when after breakfast Qhan took the three of us out to the backyard, I happily lay in the warm grass, between Mark and Cooper, while Coop, as he said to call him, told us about himself.

I'd been right—Coop was a year younger than me. Like Mark and myself, his parents had died. His father died in an accident years earlier, and his mom died four years ago. He'd been drafted and despised every second of it. He'd been captured in a smaller shipment of men because he'd been on a lander going in to do recon on one of the smaller colony planets. They'd come in under the cover of darkness, thinking they'd remained unseen. Before they knew it, a huge Algonquan ship hovered directly overhead.

He stroked the grass. "I've never had anything like this before. Mom and I lived in a tiny apartment on the Neptune colony. Their idea of a park was three fake trees and a sunlamp. The only real plants were in the hydroponics labs where they produced food."

Mark rolled onto his side, propped on one arm. His other hand gently stroked my chest. "We spend a lot of time out here."

I realized that my skin had darkened to nearly the same shade as Mark's, while Coop looked painfully white and pasty. I couldn't wait for his hair to grow out like mine. Coop rolled onto his side too, looking down at me. His other hand started stroking my abs. I sensed a look pass between him and Mark and I frowned. "What?"

Mark leaned down and kissed me. "*Shh,* baby. This is your time." He kissed me while Cooper started sucking on my nipples. I happily moaned as the milker immediately pulled another orgasm out of me.

I don't know how long we lay there, them making love to me, but I felt cherished and safe and it drove negative thoughts out of my mind. Once they knew I was thoroughly and completely exhausted in a good way, Mark smiled down at me. "Good?"

I nodded, ready for a nap.

That's when we heard an unfamiliar voice.

We looked to see a blue-garbed tech talking with Master, who stood there, arms crossed over his chest and smiling. The tech looked satisfied, made some notes on his hand-held, and left. Master walked over to us and sat at my head, offering me a playful look as he said something.

Mark held my hand. "He said he's glad to see you're welcoming our new addition."

I studied Coop. I could imagine my cock fucking him, or him fucking me. Or enjoy watching him with Mark. Or sharing him with Mark.

And sharing Master with him.

I didn't have the slightest bit of jealousy over those thoughts, either.

* * * *

Master had things to attend to and wouldn't be home for a few days. We were allowed to sleep in Master's room. Mark and Coop took it upon themselves to spoil me rotten as Qhan watched over us, bemused. I fully understood their motivation and let them take care of me. Their loving attention drove the dark thoughts away, and sleeping sandwiched between them at night helped ease me through the worst of the nightmares.

I felt badly in a way that Coop wasn't the focus of our attention, the way I had been when I first arrived. Yet the fact that he so willingly jumped in to help Mark comfort me, someone he didn't really know yet, convinced me I'd made the right choice. Yes, once this fucking egg was out of me and I could think about something else again, I knew I could totally accept Coop as one of us, the three of us together.

Mark introduced Coop to the poetry of Robert Frost. We'd lie in the backyard with my head in Mark's lap and Coop rubbing my feet as he recited the poems he remembered, over and over again. I forced myself to enjoy the pleasure the egg caused in me, and soon with Mark and Coop to distract me, I could.

As the weeks wore on and Mark became more disabled by the effects of his egg, Coop took over that primary role for both of us, helping me move Mark when necessary, talking with us, telling us fantasy fairy tales and enthralling us both.

I knew I'd fallen in love with him, even though I was scared to admit it.

A bonus—Coop knew a tiny bit of Algonquan from his com duties, a few things he'd picked up here and there. Not a fraction as much as Mark, and there were some words I knew that Coop didn't just from my longer stay on the planet, but it was nice having that extra security blanket.

Yes, I'm a wuss, I admit it.

By the end of week three of Mark's time, he had reached the hardly able to walk phase. Coop helped me bathe and feed him, and Qhan would carry him out to the backyard so we could still lie out there and enjoy the sun. Both Coop and myself, at almost the same point in our cycles, felt the effects but could still function.

I'd gotten to the point where I could almost enjoy the effects of the egg without remembering the smell of that horrible man as he grabbed me.

It was fun to watch Coop beg Master for the checks. Mark teased him about being an eager slut. Coop opened one eye and stared at him as Master's tongue explored him. "Duh. Sky's blue, grass is green, I'm a slut. Congratulations, Captain Obvious."

We both started laughing, which of course triggered a series of explosive orgasms in poor Mark and left him helplessly moaning on the bed, making Master laugh even though Mark was too wiped out to explain the joke.

Three days before Mark's drop, he begged to be taken to the frame and left there. I taught Coop how to do the stretching and Qhan seemed happy to have an extra set of hands to help out. Mark was nearly unable to speak now. Master moved into our room with us, taking turns with Coop and me sitting with Mark so he wasn't alone.

Early in the morning of the estimated drop day, I was sitting with him when he let out a pained moan. He hadn't been attached to the frame, willingly lying there and not moving, unable to walk under his own power. I was getting close to that point, forcing myself to move sometimes despite not wanting to, determined I wouldn't let what happened to me prevent me from taking care of Mark. Poor Coop, however, didn't have that kind of stamina. He happily lay there and enjoyed the near-constant bliss, his fantasies made real.

I forced myself up to my knees and kissed Mark's sweaty brow. "You dropping?"

He nodded. I called for Master, who awoke immediately and crossed the room to check on him. He fetched Qhan, and we connected Mark's wrists and ankles to the frame as Coop dragged himself across the room before flopping down on the pillows by the frame in a quivering puddle. He didn't even have the strength to plug himself into the milker.

I smiled and reached over and hooked him up, earning me a happy moan of thanks.

I focused on Mark, rubbing his back, massaging his balls, helping Master and Qhan soothe him. Only a few hours later, he let out one last cry and out popped his egg.

Coop's eyes widened. "Holy fuck! That's huge!" Apparently it didn't scare him though, because his eyes rolled back in his head as another series of orgasms rendered him nearly senseless.

Mark managed an exhausted laugh as I released his hands and nuzzled his forehead. "I love you."

"Love you too, baby. Give me a few hours to catch my breath and I'll take care of you again."

My heart swelled. He did see himself as my protector, a role I was happy for him to fulfill. "And Coop."

He nodded. "And Coop." He sighed. "Although Coop doesn't seem to be in any discomfort."

I looked down at Coop, where trying to roll onto his side had triggered another series of disabling climaxes. I suspected he frequently moved just to experience the sensation. I didn't want to laugh because I knew what that'd do to me. "No, Coop seems to be a happy camper."

Coop just laid there and moaned.

CHAPTER NINETEEN

Despite his nearly debilitating orgasms, Coop still felt envious of Mark getting fucked by Master. He'd lay there in bed and happily moan as he watched Mark taking what neither of us could have yet.

"Promise me," Coop croaked, "that he'll do that to me, too!"

I managed a half-hearted laugh. "Yeah. He will."

During one visit our vet just shook his head as he teased Master about his newest pet. I liked to lay with my head in Mark's lap as he stroked my hair. Moving under my own power was now totally out of the question.

"What'd he say?" I asked.

Mark kissed me. "He said Master might find he'll have to stock up on the medicine that triggers his cycle because he suspects Coop will only be happy if he's carrying an egg."

Coop, docile and lying on his side, simply gave us a thumbs-up in reply.

Mark laughed, and so did I, which triggered another round of orgasms.

I broke down and asked to be moved to the frame. Coop couldn't do anything but lie on the bed in our room, breathe, and orgasm. He was helpless.

Happy, but helpless.

Mark did the stretching for me, talking to me, constantly touching me, making sure I knew I wasn't alone. Master would sit up at night with me while Mark spent all day at my side.

Late one morning, I felt that first cramp and almost sobbed in relief that my ordeal would soon end. With Mark holding my hands and Master and the vet there, I was shocked when only a few hours later I was told to push, and after an immense pleasure-pain of stretching, I felt relief.

I gasped. "What happened?" Scared because I didn't feel pain anymore, I worried something horrible had happened.

Mark laughed and kissed me. "It's over, babe. You're done."

"It's out?" I couldn't believe it, especially after the physical agony of the first one and the mental agony of this one.

He released my hands and rained kisses over my face. "You're done, baby. It's over. All over. All gone."

I sobbed, relieved, happy. Mark had to reassure Master I was okay. Once they finished cleaning me up, Master carried me to his bedroom and lay with me while Mark helped Qhan move a quivering Coop to the frame.

I lay in Master's arms and cried at being free while Master murmured to me. I understood a few words, but the gist was he loved me, felt proud of me, and he was sorry I had to go through that.

I pushed him back onto the bed and climbed onto him, knowing I couldn't mount him because they'd packed me with gauze, but wanting to be there. "You promised me," I reminded him, even though he couldn't understand me. "You promised." I kissed him, wishing I could ride that enormous cock. "Sedalgo," I said, having learned that was the word. "Sedalgo."

His eyebrows arched and he understood. He rolled onto his side, taking me with him. He shook his head. "Ando." He kissed me, stroking my chest. They didn't have nipples, and he loved playing with ours and seeing the reaction it brought. "Sedalgo ando."

Tomorrow. He'd breed me tomorrow.

I threw my arms around him, my body already craving the feel of him inside me. I wanted him to fuck me, I wanted his cock inside me. I wanted my memory to be of him causing that delicious pain that slammed blissful pleasure to the center of my skull.

The vet checked me later that evening and removed my gauze, declaring me healed. Mark stayed with Coop while Master gave me some more alone time. Back in his bed, I climbed on top of him, driving his cock deep inside me. I wanted to feel him fuck me, even if it wasn't for breeding. I wanted this time alone with him.

He smiled up at me, talking softly to me in Algonquan. He held my hips, helping me ride him, making me take it slow despite wanting to pound my body hard onto his cock. He didn't hook me to the milker, instead using his hand to draw several orgasms out of me. I loved it. I loved the feel of his hands on me, and I knew I could put what happened behind me for good.

His tone took on a teasing, breathy quality I knew meant he was getting close to the end of his control. His questions, despite not understanding his words, were as ancient as any race.

You ready for me? You want to feel me come?

I tried to slam my hips down against him. He finally released me and rested his hands on my thighs, letting me do what I wanted. Then I felt him swell before the delicious hot rush of his juices flooded me, filling me, triggering another climax in me.

I collapsed on top of him, happy, spent, temporarily sated as I felt the mess I'd made squishing between us.

He held me, still murmuring to me as I drifted into the first sweet, uninterrupted sleep I'd known in four weeks.

Later that night, my eyes popped open when I heard Mark's voice calling. Master helped me up, patted my ass, and pointed to the bathroom as he headed for the door.

I did need the shower.

When I made it to our room, Qhan had brought Master a damp rag to clean himself up, and he was sitting behind Coop, talking to Mark and trying to soothe Coop.

Mark smiled when he saw me, kissing me. "You look good, baby."

I leaned against him as I held Coop's other hand. "I feel good."

Together, we helped Coop through his first drop. He didn't have it as rough as I did the first time, but it lasted a while, until almost lunch the next day. After, Master lay with him on our bed as Coop dropped into sleep. Meanwhile, Mark led me outside to the backyard. I felt horny, but I didn't need the milker. I knew I wouldn't have long to wait for relief.

He pushed me onto my back and kissed me. "Let me guess, you want him to breed you again, don't you?"

I nodded.

He pushed my legs up, knees against my chest. "Then I guess I'd better get me some of this while I can." No, not as big as Master's cock, and he didn't have that wonderful swelling that pressed against my prostate and made me explode in seconds, but he knew how to satisfy me. We spent the afternoon together out there, in the sun and shade, him on top, me on top, spooning with his cock buried inside me and his hand stroking my cock—nearly every position known to man and then some. I did get to fuck him a couple of times, but he wanted to feel me, and I knew it'd be another month before he'd get the chance, so I happily let him take the top.

We lay in the shade, finally worn out, his cock growing limp in my ass and his arms wrapped around me. Sweat and cum glued my back to his chest.

"I love you, Dale," he said. "I fucking love you. I think one day I'll love Coop, too. Is that okay?"

"Yeah." I pulled his arms tighter around me. "I think I'm loving him, too. But I love you more."

"We always come first."

"Pun intended?"

He snorted with laughter. "Maybe, baby."

* * * *

Master kept his promise. Late that night, with Coop snoring on the bed in the corner, Mark stood at my head and held me while Master stepped between my legs on the frame and bred me.

I felt nothing but relief and love when he entered me. I welcomed the pain and basked in the pleasure. When we finished a few hours later, he again took me to his bed and held me as I lay there and smiled.

Contented. Yeah, the memory of the debilitating pleasure was still fresh in my mind, and while I'd miss not being able to freely get fucked when I wanted, the knowledge that I carried part of my Master within me made it more than worth it. This time, nothing would ruin my happiness.

The next day, Master called us into the dining room, where he sat at the table with a man I'd never seen before. Mark translated for us. He was the equivalent of an attorney, and now that Master had the three of us he wanted to ensure we'd always be cared for should something happen to him. He had designated the last egg Mark delivered for him his heir, should it survive to maturity, and basically set up his will.

We could never be separated, even if Master died before us. His estate, should his heir not be at maturity, would be cared for until he reached adulthood and could claim his birthright. Qhan and Mack would also be retained, and this man here would be the executor to make decisions should that happen.

Coop, desperately horny in his first post-drop days, muttered as he practically danced from foot to foot, "Okay, fine. Can I get fucked now?"

Both Master and Mark were happy to oblige him, and we all retired to Master's bed.

The days blended together that first week. When Master was at work, I was content to lay in the sun in the backyard with Mark and Coop while they fucked each other silly or made love to me. We were lying in Master's bed one evening before he returned, watching a vid news program, when Mark sat up and frowned.

"What?"

"*Shh.*"

I couldn't understand the story, obviously, but from the few stray words I could pick up, and from the video shown, it looked like the Terrans had attacked one of our unarmed colonies. We'd sustained massive civilian casualties, and some footage showed Terrans liberated from a government egg farm fighting side-by-side with their Algonquan handlers, getting killed by their "rescuers" when they refused to leave.

"Motherfuckers!" Mark screamed. "Those fucking bastards! I hate those fucking Terrans! Why can't they leave us alone?"

Coop and I tried to calm him. I didn't remind him that technically they were us, although I did consider myself Algonquan now.

Master returned home from work looking grim even though he tried to hide his mood from us. Mark tried to talk with him about the attack, and it obviously upset Master so much that he finally asked Mark to stop.

Master had known some of the people who died, including a relative.

That evening, two military officers stopped by to talk with Master. They huddled around the dining room table and discussed strategy. They were shocked when Mark walked in and sat down with them and softly started talking.

Master tried to order him away, but then one of the others stopped him and started talking to Mark.

Mark's voice grew animated, eager as he pointed to the hand-held terminal they were reviewing and discussing matters with them.

When Coop and I tried to draw near, Master called for Qhan. He gently removed us from the room, taking us to Master's bedroom where he hooked us to the milker. He stayed with us, and any attempts on our part to get out of bed were met with the warning noise and a pointing finger ordering us to stay put.

I didn't like this. I didn't like the vengeful fire in Mark's eyes and the angry tone in his voice as he talked with the military men. I didn't like the creeping suspicion trying to take hold in me.

Coop and I fell asleep snuggled together when Master and Mark finally returned to bed. Mark held me, and Master held Coop.

"What was that about?" I sleepily asked.

"Shh, baby. You don't worry about it. You just go to sleep."

* * * *

The next day, Mark still wouldn't tell me what they'd discussed. That worried me. I wanted to know. What could be so bad he couldn't tell me?

"Just giving them some advice, that's all." He smiled. "Making sure there's no way I could ever return to those Terran fuckwads even if I wanted. High treason. Spilling my guts of everything I know that could help us—Algonquans—win."

Somewhat eased, but still not convinced, I let that suffice. Unfortunately, later that night a report of another Terran attack on a different colony enraged Mark to tears, prompting Qhan to turn off the vid and take away the remote controller.

Master acted somber and moody when he returned home. It wasn't that the Terrans were even close to defeating the Algonquans, but the senseless civilian casualties grieved everyone.

I caught Mark quietly talking with Master later, and they both stopped when they noticed me watching them.

The next afternoon, the two military men who'd come by before returned and talked with Master and Mark. After they left, Mark took me and Coop out to the backyard. Coop fell asleep while Mark held me, his blue eyes looking sad.

"What's going on?"

He smiled. "Nothing, baby." He kissed me. "I love you. Deep and fierce." He held me and recited Robert Frost to me.

"'I have been one acquainted with the night.
I have walked out in rain – and back in rain.
I have outwalked the furthest city light.

I have looked down the saddest city lane.
I have passed by the watchman on his beat,
And dropped my eyes, unwilling to explain.'"

I stroked his cheek. "What does that mean? That one always makes me sad."

"It means what you want it to mean, baby." He made love to me, sweet and slow, using his hands and mouth on me to pull wonderful releases from me that, combined with the pleasure of Master's egg inside me, eased my mind.

Then he got me hard again and straddled me, impaled himself, sighing as he smiled down at me. "I love this. I love feeling you inside me. I miss this even more than Master fucking me when I'm carrying. I can't wait for my next egg, but I miss this when I'm carrying."

Sudden desperation seized me. "Ask him. Have him breed you tonight!" Unnamed terror ripped at me. I knew what I didn't want to acknowledge, and if he were carrying, no way in hell would he leave my side. No way Master would let either of us away from our safe sanctuary.

He soothed me. "*Shh*, baby. There's plenty of time for that. For now, I want you right where you are." We made love all afternoon. Coop even woke up and joined in at one point.

Still, the unsettled feeling wouldn't go away.

It returned with a vengeance later that evening when the two men returned. They handed Mark a black tunic, similar to the ones they wore.

I shook my head and grabbed his arm. "No!" This wasn't happening. I was entering the really horny phase of my carrying and Mark was supposed to be there with me for it all.

Mark said something to them and led me to the sofa, where he pulled me to him and kissed me as Coop looked on, confused.

"Baby, I told them about a guy I served with, another linguist, Louis. He was on duty with me when we were taken. They found him! He's happy with a mated couple just a few towns away, and he's learned even more dialects than I have."

"So?" I screeched. "What does that have to do with anything?"

"Baby, they need us. He hates these fucking Terrans as much as I do. They contacted him and he wants to help, too. We're going to go—"

I felt my sanity slipping. "No! You can't leave me!" I threw my arms around him as Master walked over and touched my shoulder. "No! *NO!*"

"Baby, please," Mark pleaded. "It's just for a couple of weeks. They'll keep us safe. We're going to go translate and try to help them stop these Terran fuckers from hurting our people." He captured my face and made me look him in the eye. "I'll come back to you. I'll be home before you drop."

I couldn't believe this. What was supposed to be my happiest time shattered into fragments I couldn't hold on to. "No, please, don't leave me!" I looked at Master and screamed, "Bautu dal golan pauchan!"

Mark held me tightly. "I have to do this. If I don't help, it's like spitting in the Universe's face after we were given such a good life here. I need to help them."

"Tell them you can't! Tell them you won't!"

"Sweetie, I volunteered. It was my idea." He kissed me and I felt his own tears wet against my face. "Baby, please, calm down. This isn't good for you. I'll be back."

I looked at Master and screamed again. "Bautu dal golan pauchan! Please, bautu dal golan pauchan!"

When I saw the tears in Master's eyes, I knew he wasn't fond of this plan either, but he would still let Mark go. For the greater good, if nothing else.

He sat on my other side and stroked my hair. "Dolmo, Kal. Dolmo."

Hysteria struggled to take over and frankly, I wasn't inclined to fight its grip on my system. "Bautu dal golan pauchan!"

Mark held me. "I love you. I love you more than I can tell you. You've got to be strong for me. I need to know you're going to be sitting here waiting for me so you can kick my ass when I get home, but I need you to do this for me."

"I can't lose you! What am I going to do without you?"

"I'm coming back, baby." He kissed my lips, my face, brushed my tears away with his thumbs even as I cried. "I swear, I'm coming back. You're not losing me. Qhan and Master will take good care of you and Coop while I'm gone."

"What am I going to do without you?" I sobbed. "I love you, and I can't lose you!" I was aware of Coop, now crying, moving in and trying to help comfort me.

"Baby, you'll be okay. You're surrounded by people who love you. I'll be back before you know it."

My heart felt like it was being ripped from my chest. I'd take getting raped a thousand times to this agony. "Bautu dal golan pauchan!" Why weren't they listening to me? "Bautu dal golan pauchan!"

Master eased me away from Mark as he stood and pulled on the tunic. I screamed, trying to fight, wanting to rip the garment off him.

Master pinned my arms to my side as Mark leaned in one last time. He kissed Coop, whispered something to him, and Coop nodded. Then he kissed me, long and sweet.

"I love you, baby. You're *mine*. Never forget that." Then, he whispered in my ear, "You and me first, always."

"Please don't leave me!"

"I'm coming home. I promise." He stroked my hair and I knew no matter what, that might not be a promise he'd be able to keep. "I love you."

"I love you," I sobbed. "I love you, dammit, and I cant' do this without you. You have to come back to me!"

"I will, baby. I will always come home to you." He brushed his own tears away as he kissed Master. Master whispered something to him and Mark smiled. With one last stroke of my cheek, he followed the two officers out the door.

When I tried to race after them, Master grabbed me and wouldn't let me follow.

I finally collapsed in Master's arms as Coop also moved in to try to hold me, my heart breaking.

"Bautu dal golan pauchan!" I screamed. They weren't understanding me. I couldn't be without Mark. He was my lifeline, my sanity.

My heart and soul.

I cried and sobbed and screamed and didn't even care when I heard the vet's voice trying to soothe me before I felt a pinch against my upper arm and the world dissolved into a blessed blackness where I felt no pain.

CHAPTER TWENTY

I spent the next two days in bed, not caring about anything, even the reflexive orgasms bringing me absolutely no joy.

I didn't have my Mark.

And I *needed* him.

How was I supposed to go on without him?

Coop's frantic, tearful pleadings finally brought me around. It wasn't fair to him to leave him as alone as I felt. Master bred him the next day, and while I sat there and held his hands, I didn't feel anything.

I felt dead inside.

I didn't want to play. I didn't want to talk. They all took turns, even Master, trying to coax me to eat. When I refused to go outside, Qhan used the leash on me and staked me outside in the shade with the milker attached and sat there in a chair next to me and Coop.

Coop tried, bless his heart. He held me as I cried, tried to talk to me. Tried to soothe me.

But he wasn't Mark.

I loved him, but I *needed* my Mark.

I know Master felt bad because he held me while I cried at night. I'd watch vids, not understanding the stories but praying I didn't see anything bad.

Mark said he should be back before I dropped, and by the end of my third week, I worried when he hadn't returned.

Master, unable to converse with us without Mark to translate, tried his best. He sat with me at night, holding me while I cried, murmuring to me in Algonquan. The loneliness didn't ease.

Three days before my drop, and the fact that I couldn't walk didn't bother me because I had no desire to move.

My Mark hadn't returned yet.

Coop gave up trying to get me to talk and I let him hold me. Poor Qhan was beside himself as he tried to pull me out of my funk. Master returned home that evening. As he sat down to eat at the desk in his room, while Coop watched the vid and I lay with my head in his lap, the doorbell chime sounded.

I sat up, praying that was Mark. He'd come home!

Qhan led the two military men into the bedroom. "Where's Mark?" I demanded. "Where is he?"

Master stepped out to talk with them, leaving Qhan with us.

Then I heard Coop gasp.

Before Qhan could change the channel, I saw the footage of an Algonquan ship that had crashed on what I assumed to be a disputed planet.

The somber-looking presenter said something as two pictures were displayed.

Mark, and another Terran, obviously ID pictures because they were both smiling and wearing tunics even though their collars and ear tags were visible.

I screamed. I knew in my heart, without understanding a word, what that meant.

The ship had crashed, and Mark and the other human were dead.

Qhan shut off the vid screen and tried to help Coop hold me down when Master ran into the room. I could see he'd been crying.

That was all the confirmation I needed. Funny, it didn't matter they were a different race, they notified next of kin the same way.

I screamed. "Bautu dal golan pauchan!" He'd promised never to separate us.

He'd promised to keep us together.

"Dolmo, Kal. Dolmo." He held me as I screamed and thrashed in his arms until the vet came in and gave me a shot.

* * * *

I was in hell.

I felt the cramps hit but they had me on a sedative. I think they were putting it in my water, which they made me drink. Mostly because if they let me stay too awake, I screamed and cried.

I didn't care.

I wanted to die, because my Mark was dead.

My Mark wasn't coming back, and I couldn't even hold him one more time and tell him how much I loved him.

Coop held my hands as I lay on the frame and cried as Master and the vet and Qhan helped me deliver the egg.

I didn't care.

I couldn't even tell them I wanted to die, that I wanted them to just put me to sleep for good, to put me out of my misery. I couldn't even ask for that relief.

One afternoon, Master left somewhere with Coop for a few hours. Qhan stayed with me, and I could not have cared less. If they'd only let me come out of the haze just long enough so I could walk, I'd find something to slit my wrists. Maybe then I could be at peace.

When they returned late that evening, Coop ran in to get me. "Dale, come on! You need to see what Master and I brought you!"

"Is it Mark?" I asked.

His face fell. Poor Coop. I know he tried. He didn't know how to pull me out of my grief, how to make me want to live again. It wasn't fair to him and I knew it because he also grieved for Mark.

"Come on, Dale. *Please.* I need you. I miss him too, but I need you. I'm going to drop soon and I need you."

That struck a deep chord within me. I'd needed Mark. I'd been the one who picked Coop. I brought him to us.

It wasn't fair of me to abandon him, to check out and leave him alone.

He helped me sit up and kissed me. "Please, Dale, I know you hurt, and I know you're going to hurt forever, but please don't leave me, too. I can't lose both of you. I love you."

Crying, I nodded. Would I ever be able to stop crying? Coop and Qhan helped me outside where a transport vehicle crew and our vet were unloading a human male. Part of me wanted to throw up. I didn't want anyone else.

I only wanted my Mark.

But maybe if Coop had someone, then I could figure out a way to end my pain and he wouldn't be alone once I was gone.

Coop was trying extra hard. "Master let me help pick him out. They had a tech who could speak a little English, and Master had him tell me what you did last time, so I did the same thing. I looked for someone I thought would fit in with us and asked him all the same questions you guys asked me."

I nodded and we walked over to the frame. The guy was gagged, but awake. Dark hair, blue eyes, but more grey than blue. Good, because if they'd been the same shade as Mark's I would have lost my mind.

"He was a life support tech, Dale, not a grunt. His name's Nathaniel. Nate."

I stared at him and saw the pity in his eyes. No doubt Coop told him what happened to Mark...and how I wasn't handling it.

Anger coursed through me, that Master thought simply adding another pet to our household would help me forget Mark. I resented the implication that I wasn't able to remember him, that another man would displace my grief.

Then I tried to let reason take over. Master would need to breed. He told me he wouldn't force me to breed ever again, and it wasn't fair to him to be forced to use egg farms.

And he could rescue another Terran, give them a good life when, by all rights, he didn't owe them shit. Especially now.

My Master had a good and loving heart, able to see the bigger picture and forgive the few for the sins of the many. He was a bigger man than I.

If I ever saw another Terran fighter again, a free Terran willingly fighting for the monkey men, I'd spit on him.

They killed my Mark. They were the reason my Mark left trying to help our Master's people.

They were the reason I was alone.

I nodded. "Okay." I returned to the house, crawled into Master's bed, and cried.

Coop came to me after they had Nate situated. "Come in and meet him. Please? He's in bed in there, not on the frame. He wants to meet you."

"Master's not going to give him a welcome-to-your-new-home fucking first?" I heard the bitterness in my tone and didn't apologize for it.

"Please, Dale. Please? I need you. Don't check out on me. He's going to need you, too. You've been through a lot more than we have. Please?" He started crying. "I miss Mark, too. I loved him. I know I wasn't here as long as you, but I loved him, too. He wouldn't want us to give up, and he wouldn't want you to leave me alone. Please, Dale."

It hurt. It hurt so bad, I didn't know how I'd survive the pain in my heart. I let Coop ease me out of bed. With his arm around me for support and Qhan following, he led me to the bed where I'd first met and fell in love with Mark.

Nate was tethered to the wall, Master apparently taking no chances. But I could tell from the set of his body, nervous but relaxed enough, that he wasn't going to fight.

Older than me, I suspected, but not by much.

Master helped Coop settle me on the far end of the bed. I didn't know what to say.

Nate spoke first. "Coop told me what happened. I'm sorry, man. I'm so sorry. I can understand if you hate me and don't want me here."

I closed my eyes as more tears ran down my cheeks. I didn't want to die. Coop was right, Mark wouldn't want me to quit living and I knew it. He'd want me to take over, to step in, to be a mentor to Coop and this guy the way he had to me and the other human pets I'd met that night at the party.

He'd tell me to suck it up and move forward.

To read poetry to them.

To teach them there was more than one way to enjoy life.

Master stroked my cheek as I leaned against him. "Dolmo, Kal," he said. He said that a lot over the past few days. "Love Kal, dolmo."

There was so much he couldn't say to me now without Mark to translate. A wall had suddenly appeared between us, permanent, impenetrable. I thought it temporary, to disappear when Mark returned.

Now, all the things I wished I could say to Master would forever go unsaid.

I took a deep breath, opened my eyes, and looked at Nate. "I'm sorry," I said. "I'm not at my best right now."

He nodded. "I know. It's okay. I understand. I'm so sorry."

I had to grow a set and be brave. Mark had survived alone for two years before me. I couldn't picture him all blubbery and weak and crying. He survived his breedings and drops alone.

I wasn't alone. I was surrounded by people who loved me and wanted to support me, if only I could let them.

I took another deep breath and leaned in to shake his hand. "I'm Dale," I said. "It's nice to meet you, Nate. Welcome to the family."

* * * *

Master sat with us while we talked. Nate was a nice guy, easy on the eyes, and while not gay, he'd had a few drunken encounters with men that left him open to this new lifestyle.

"If I have to choose between getting fucked for the rest of my life and getting my ass shot off, believe me, I will quickly learn to dig this."

I smiled. Coop had done well. "Why don't you let Master give you a sample of what you have to look forward to, then?"

He looked nervous but nodded. "Okay."

I mimed for Qhan to move Nate to the frame and felt frustrated by my hampered ability to communicate with him. I'd have to pull it together enough to maybe sit down with Qhan and have him try to teach me some of the basics I'd always relied on Mark for.

Coop and I sat with Nate as Master introduced him to the pleasures of the Algonquan anatomy. It wasn't a breeding, just a good, hard fucking that left Nate eager to do it again and poor Coop nearly out of his mind with pleasure as he lay on his side and watched. Coop was really horny, even though not as incapacitated as the last time.

Part of me wanted to breed again, but I couldn't bring myself to do it yet. Maybe one day my heart would be in it again, but not right now. I still needed to grieve.

When Master finished with him, I sat with Nate in the bed while Master carried Coop to his bedroom to check him and spend some time with him.

Nate was twenty-three. Nice guy, smart guy. He would fit right in with us. When I started to think about how Mark would have liked him, I had to clip that thought before I started crying again.

"Can I ask you about him?" he softly said.

"Master?"

He shook his head. "Mark."

I sadly smiled. "He was my life." I thought for a moment and then quoted Frost.

"'Something sinister in the tone
Told me my secret must be known:
Word I was in the house alone
Somehow must have gotten abroad,
Word I was in my life alone,
Word I had no one left but God.'"

He laughed and, before I could get angry, he replied.

"'I shall be telling this with a sigh
Somewhere ages and ages hence:
Two roads diverged in a wood, and I —
I took the one less traveled by,
And that has made all the difference.'"

I stared at him, my jaw gaping, my heart pounding. He eventually shrugged. "I wanted to study old Earth literature and poetry in college. Fucking government drafted me, of course."

When Master checked on us an hour or so later, he found me lying in Nate's arms, where I'd cried myself to sleep.

* * * *

I wouldn't say I had emerged from hell, but I no longer actively wanted to die. I knew I had to find some way to make myself live, for Coop, for Nate, for Master.

For Mark's memory. To honor him, if for no other reason.

To make sure every captive who entered our lives from that point forward knew Mark's name, knew his sacrifice, and honored him.

Master bred Nate the next evening. I sat there with him, softly talking to him as he writhed at the pleasurable pain. Envied him the ability to let go and feel it all without reservation, without grief, without regrets. I held Nate that night, knowing it would be a while before I could bring myself to make love to him, but already sensing I would be able to love him.

One day.

The next morning, we made Coop go outside and the three of us lay in the grass. This proved a comforting place for me, the hours spent here with Mark, the soft living carpet of green below us, the eternal sky above. I lay with my head in Nate's lap. I let him hold me, needing the strength he could give me because he hadn't suffered our loss. He had strength to spare and willingly gave it.

Coop lay with his head in my lap as I stroked his hair. His skin had started tanning, and now Nate was the odd one out, pale, with his regulation short hair. Coop's hair now resembled mine, comfortably shaggy.

Nate fit in well. He never pushed, and for that I couldn't begin to express my eternal gratitude. He offered and I took what I needed, strong arms, quiet strength, and he didn't ask more of me than I could give.

Coop got to the point he begged for the frame. I was able to be there for him, holding him, massaging his back and helping ease him through the pain as he dropped.

I could let Master fuck me without crying over memories of Mark.

Coop begged to be bred again almost as soon as he woke up the next morning, and finally, a few days after his drop, Master gave in and did it. With me the only one able to walk unassisted and form coherent sentences, it fell on me to help Qhan take care of them both. I tried to learn some Algonquan phrases, thinking how proud Mark would be of me for that.

After a few weeks, I could sit in the backyard alone while Coop and Nate napped inside and think about Mark without crying. He was here, all around me. His spirit with me. I understood the meaning of the last poem he recited to me. I, too, had been acquainted with the night. With the utter, pitch black despair I thought would swallow me whole.

But there would be another day if I chose to embrace it. I had been acquainted with the night. Now, it was time to face the dawn and join the men who loved me, who waited for me in the light of day.

I decided I wanted to live. Yeah, it still hurt like hell, and always would. One day, maybe it wouldn't hurt as much.

Master was a smart man. Yes, I resented him getting Nate at first, but I didn't resent Nate the man. I'd come to care for him, feel fondness for him, yes, love him a little, but I still had no lust. I didn't let Coop fuck me, only Master. He was the only one I could conjure true desire for because I loved him almost as much as I'd loved Mark.

I waited until a few days after Nate dropped to approach Master one afternoon. He worked at the dining room table on a portable terminal. Nate and Coop were out in the backyard playing, Coop fucking Nate's brains out, no doubt.

Master looked at me, inquiring and probably as frustrated as I that he couldn't know exactly what was on my mind and he couldn't offer more than that one word of comfort. *Dolmo.*

This time, I'd surprise him.

I crawled into his lap and kissed him. I needed to get back to living again. I wanted to. I wanted to be able to make love with Cooper, and I wanted to make love to Nate. Until I healed, I'd still be a missing man even while my body shared their bed. This was my first step toward that healing.

He smiled at me, the melancholy in his gaze no doubt reflected in my own. "Sedalgo," I said.

His eyes arched in surprise. "Sedalgo?"

I nodded and kissed him again, deeply. "Yeah. Sedalgo."

He stared at me for a long time before he smiled and nodded. "Sedalgo ando."

* * * *

I didn't want anyone else in the room with us, and finally managed to mime what I wanted and pull enough Algonquan words together to make my wishes known. Instead of the frame, I pulled Master over to the bed and I lay down on my back.

Once he realized what I wanted, he smiled and lay down with me. He made love to me, taking my mind away to that blissful place where I could enjoy him, enjoy his touch, enjoy the emotions and sensations without guilt or grief or painful memories.

He knelt over me, pulling my legs around his hips, my ass resting on his thighs. Then he pressed his cock into me, hard and thick, and when he locked inside me I remembered why I belonged here, with him. I loved him. I would live for him, even while I carried my grief within me for the rest of my life. His eyes never left mine. I enjoyed watching his face as he took me.

He lifted me up, lowering me deeply onto his shaft as I held on to his neck. He used one hand to stroke my cock as I felt the barbs pierce me, gasping with pain followed by immediate pleasure as his hand pulled an orgasm out of me. Content, I relished every bit of pain, the bliss drawing me deeper into his gaze with each round. Then he lowered me onto my back and we lay there, him holding his weight off me with his arms as his egg worked its way inside me. When I felt the burn he kissed me, swallowing my gasp of pain and sharing my cry of pleasure.

By the time we finished, he rolled onto his back, carrying me with him. I lay limp in his arms, content.

"Love Kal," he whispered, nuzzling my head as I lay cradled in his strength. "Love Kal. Mine."

I closed my eyes. "Love Master. Mine."

CHAPTER TWENTY-ONE

I had no desire to track how long I'd been there. I knew it was less than a year, but trying to calculate the time meant thinking about when Mark died and how long I'd been without him. I allowed Nate into my heart to the point I could honestly say I loved him. While he and Coop enjoyed a frisky relationship, I contented myself to simply let them hold me at night, easing the pain of my dreams, soothing me back to sleep. Nate recited Robert Frost to us, and he didn't seem to mind that I wasn't in the mood to be romantic with anyone, even with Master, other than his daily checks of me.

I had highs and lows, better days, some not so good. I knew getting over Mark wouldn't be a quick process and settled for hanging on and leaning on my family during the really dark times. At least I knew I was on the road to healing, even if some days it didn't feel like it.

Nate professed his love to me one day while Coop was asleep on the grass next to us and I lay with my head tucked against Nate's chest. His fingers lightly stroked my arm, his warm embrace a true bit of comfort working its way through my black cloak of grief. He tried. Coop was our horny, slutty clown, doing his best to make me laugh, evoke even a smile, desperate to see something other than the agony I knew still lined my face from dawn to dusk despite some days feeling better than others.

Nate was steady, quiet. Waiting.

He brushed his lips across my forehead. "I love you, Dale," he softly said. "I know you hurt, but I wanted you to know how I feel. I do love you. Thank you for not turning your back on me when you had every reason. Thank you for not shutting me out."

I looked up into his face, his blue eyes a different shade than the ones that would forever haunt my soul, and kissed him. "I love you, too. Please give me time to give you more than that. It's not you. It will happen, but I just need time to heal."

He smiled and stroked my chin. "I know. As much as you need. I'll be here whenever you're ready for me. I'm not going anywhere."

He would, too. His solid strength reminded me in many ways of…

But I didn't want to think of him right now.

I wanted to heal. At least to the point the raw pain didn't chafe my soul every time I turned a corner and expected to see Mark's quirky smile and blue eyes. I wanted to be able to give Nate me, not a ghost of myself.

I wanted to see him for who he was, and not as a replacement for the love I'd lost. I didn't want to paint him with a magical brush just to disappoint us both at some point in the future when my soul had strengthened again. One day.

I needed to just…

Be.

I didn't have those worries with Coop because he'd been there and known Mark. I'd picked Coop, and while he fit in perfectly, he was so unlike Mark that I had no trouble not putting those needs on him. Mark had been my strength. Coop was the human embodiment of a puppy if I'd ever seen one. He'd been genetically hard-wired to not only enjoy our lifestyle, but thrive in it with no "adjustment in attitude" needed. In a different time in Terran culture, he might have been seen as a male slut.

Hell, he was that now, only not needing to apologize for it.

I recognized I had to learn to be strong. I was now the "alpha pet," the one they would look to, even if I hadn't been here that much longer than them. I'd seen more, learned more.

Loved more.

I tried to let myself enjoy my carry time, helping Coop through his drop which, lucky bastard, went easy even though the egg didn't survive.

Horny Cooper wasted no time getting busy with Nate the next day, coaxing him to romp. I lay in the shade in the backyard, wistfully smiling as I watched them running around and fucking each other's brains out. Heading into my third week, I was content to curl up on my side with my old buddy the milker pump and nap. Eventually, I knew, my heart would heal enough I could enjoy that kind of playful, loving relationship with Coop again, and finally experience what he eagerly enjoyed with Nate. I wanted to.

I just couldn't yet.

Nate was a sweetheart. Not his fault he'd been brought into our house when I could least give him the best of me. I did love him. I felt thankful he was sensitive enough to understand my pain and not take it personally.

I dozed in the warm afternoon, dappled sunlight flickering through the leaves, and I dreamed. No nightmares of being back with the Terrans, either. In this sweet dream, finally able to enjoy them without feeling like my heart would break, Mark lay with me. I'd dreamed of him a lot lately as my grief ebbed and waned to a livable level while Nate worked his way deeper into my heart. In this dream, my heart fantasized that Mark came to me in our backyard sanctuary, curled his body along mine, his arm around me, whispering to me the way he had, reciting poetry to me.

"'Love at the lips was touch
As sweet as I could bear;
And once that seemed too much;
I lived on air

That crossed me from sweet things,
The flow of — was it musk
From hidden grapevine springs
Downhill at dusk?'"

I sighed, contented in my dream and hoping I wouldn't awaken from it. Mark's voice always sounded so clear, so strong in my dreams.

That's when I felt the nip on my left earlobe, and my eyes snapped open.

Qhan, Mack, and Master stood in front of me, Coop and Nate behind them. Master wore a brilliant smile, yet he'd been crying. The others all looked happily shocked.

A pair of strong arms still held me, no dream, but a reality.

A voice spoke softly in my ear. "You gonna sleep all day, baby, or you gonna welcome me home?"

I sat up, unable to believe it. A fresh pink scar crossed his forehead and disappeared up under his shaggy hair. His eyes, those sweet blue eyes stared up at me. His lips twisted in that familiar quirky smile I thought would only be seen in my dreams.

I screamed, I cried, I sobbed, and I tackled him. I think I lost my mind for a while. Mark held me and I cried, praying I didn't wake up, praying I'd died and joined him in some wonderful afterlife where we'd never be parted again.

It took them a while to convince me I wasn't sleeping, dead, or imagining it. Master took us inside and left us be alone in his bed. I sat there, at first unable to do anything but cry and run my hands over Mark's body.

"I thought you died."

"I promised you I'd come home, didn't I, baby?"

"You promised me you'd be home before I dropped." Okay, maybe it was wrong to be petulant, but dammit, I'd missed and grieved him.

He smiled and pushed me back onto the bed. "You're going to drop in about two weeks, aren't you?"

"Asshole! I thought you *died*! I saw a program about it."

"We almost did." He kissed me. "We were shot down. Louis and I both made it though. We had to hide with the survivors of our crew in the wilderness for weeks. There was a troop of Terrans after us. Our crew offered to let us leave with the Terrans, but we both refused. When the Terrans attacked us, I picked up a guy's gun and started shooting the fuckers. I took out a bunch of them. I helped lure Terrans, telling them I was a prisoner, and then killing them. We were finally rescued a couple of days ago."

I grabbed him and kissed him, deeply, desperately. I pulled him on top of me and he knew what I wanted. He impaled himself on my cock and rode me, our lips locked together as I enjoyed every last fucking climax he gave me.

When I finally exhausted myself, he rolled us over, me cradled against him. "I'm home for good, baby. Never again. I promise, never again will I leave you. Ever. But we did it. We helped them take out a shitload of Terran forces before we got shot down. We helped drive them out of our unarmed territories. They think the Terrans might ask for a truce soon."

"I don't fucking care," I mumbled. "I'm asking Master to breed you tonight and shackle us together permanently."

He laughed as he stroked my hair. "Whatever you want, baby. I told you that."

Master came to check on us. He slid into bed, and I immediately demanded it. I grabbed Mark's hand. "Sedalgo. Right the fuck now."

Master looked bemused. While he didn't understand my whole comment, he got the gist. "Sedalgo Pol ando."

I shook my head. "Now! *Right* now!"

Mark laughed and damn how I'd missed that sound! None of us had laughed much since he'd left. "Baby, he can't do it on command like that. He needs to take the medicine to trigger his cycle."

"Ando," Master repeated, then crooked his finger at Mark. Mark crawled into his arms as Master smiled and kissed him, his cock hard.

"Besides, baby," Mark gasped as Master let him come up for air, "I'd like him to fuck me the regular way before he knocks me up again. Do you know how long it's been since I've gotten laid?"

"Better be since you left here."

"Bingo. Milkers are fine to take the edge off, but nothing like feeling my ass filled. And all I had the past few weeks was my damn hand until they rescued us. Louis and I nearly fought over the damn milker on board the rescue ship until they scrounged up an extra hose for the thing."

Master and I made love to Mark, Mark lying on top of me while Master fucked him hard and deep. Our cocks rubbed together between our bellies, both of us coming several times without needing the milker, until Master finally came and we all stretched out, finally sated and spent. I snuggled against Mark, breathing in his scent.

"So tell me about the new guy?" Mark said, his tone playful. "What's with him? What's his name?"

"That's Nate." I told him the story, almost ashamed now to admit how deeply I'd sunk into the depths of my grief and ignored poor Coop and Nate.

He held me tighter. "It's okay, baby. They thought they were doing what was best for you. It's all right." He asked Master something, and it took him a while to finally reply. When he did, it was in halting sentences and with regretful looks at me.

Mark nuzzled my forehead. "They loved you so much that they were worried about you, baby. Master knew he couldn't just replace me for you. He did it hoping having a new pet would help you be distracted enough by trying to help him the way you'd helped me. And he said he didn't want to make you breed ever again, because he was worried how upset you were." Mark paused. "How's he feel, anyway?"

"Who?"

"Nate."

"I don't know. Ask Coop."

He chuckled. "You've never done him?"

"No. But he does know a little Robert Frost."

"Oh, cool." He nibbled my ear, making me pleasantly squirm against him. "He carrying?"

"No. Just me right now. Coop just dropped. I think Master's letting them have some playtime before he breeds them again."

He nibbled my ear again, knowing how much I loved that. "How about we give him an official welcome to the family of our own? You and me."

The thought excited me. "Yeah?"

He kissed me. "Yeah, baby. Him and Coop both. I think I can easily get it up a few more times. All you have to do is lie there and let them ride you."

My cock hardened. One milker for the pregnant pet, stat.

I nodded. "Okay!"

Mark spoke to Master. Master left us and sent Coop and Nate in.

Coop was eager to welcome Mark home, while Nate understandably looked nervous. "Will I have to leave now?"

Mark grinned and pulled him in close. "Nope. Master's been given permission to keep all of us because of my 'special service' to the cause."

Coop climbed into bed next to me, smiling. "You okay?"

I nodded. "Damn good." I kissed him. It wasn't long before we had Coop blissfully happy, straddling me while both Mark and I impaled him. Nate took turns kissing him and me.

"Ooohhh...fuck! That's so good!" Coop moaned.

I heard a pleased chuckle and had enough time to notice Master watching us from the bedroom door with a satisfied smile before he left us alone again.

I surrendered to the feel of me and Mark both thrusting inside of Coop, our cocks rubbing together and against his channel as the three of us rocked together. Mark's climax triggered mine, and before Coop could collapse on top of me, Mark held him up against his chest.

"Missed you, buddy."

He smiled, sated. For a few minutes, at least. "Missed you, too."

When he collapsed to the bed on the other side of me, Mark crooked his finger at Nate. He kissed him. The sight of my Mark holding him felt so damn good, beyond my ability to describe.

He was *home*. "Dale tells me you two have yet to get closely acquainted."

Nate shook his head. "It's okay, I understand, he's been—"

Mark silenced him with another deep kiss. Nate's cock throbbed, pre-cum leaking from the end. "Time to rectify that," Mark said. He turned Nate to face me and swatted his ass. "Climb aboard for the ride of your life."

Nate looked down at me, questions on his face, uncertain. I grabbed him and kissed him, glad to finally be able to give him what I couldn't before. "It's okay. Really. I want to."

He smiled and kissed me back. Mark grabbed my stiff cock and guided it into Nate. Then I heard Nate's happy groan as I felt Mark slide in, too. Together we still weren't as big as Master, but it felt sooo damn good to me, I could only imagine how good it felt to be on the receiving end.

Now I couldn't wait until my drop to experience it. I wanted it all. Every possible debauchery we hadn't tried flashed through my mind, although it was a pretty short list. Except with Nate, with whom all I'd done was kiss and cuddle.

Mark and I would have a lot of fun bringing him up to speed.

We made love all evening. After a breather, with me still on the bottom, Mark impaled himself on me again and both Coop and Nate took turns plumbing him, too. He spent the whole time kissing me, moaning with each climax that hit him, whispering "I love you, baby" under his breath.

Master finally made us stop for the night so he could come in and go to sleep. As I fell asleep in Mark's arms, I realized life was finally perfect.

CHAPTER TWENTY-TWO

Master prepared to breed Mark the next evening. We spent the time from when we got up that morning until then taking turns fucking, me always on the bottom, one man happily sandwiched between myself and whoever ended up on top while the odd man out usually tried to fuck whoever was on top.

It felt good to let go and live again.

The side effect of our efforts was Mark didn't need any preparations before Master patted the frame and he happily climbed aboard after hooking himself to the milker. "Hello, old friend," he said with a sigh as he got into position.

I sat with him. When he felt that first sharp pain, he let out a happy "Yes!" that pulled an orgasm from me. I thought when they finished he'd want to cuddle with Master, but he collapsed into my arms, content and happy.

"See?" he mumbled. "Not going anywhere now."

"Good."

Coop whined he wanted to be bred, too, but Master wasn't that good. He'd have to wait until tomorrow. Coop and Nate both had to settle for a good, hard fucking from him while Mark and I lay entwined in the bed in the corner. Mark sent them to bed with Master while the two of us lay there alone.

"I'm sorry I scared you, baby," he said. "I'm so sorry you had to go through that."

"I don't want to talk about it. I've got you back." I didn't want to talk about it, either. I wanted to forget it and enjoy having him home and finally being able to open my heart again to the other two men who'd patiently waited for me to return to them, just as Mark had returned to me.

When I dropped, it was Mark's arms I went to and spent the night in. And when Mark dropped a few weeks later, it was me he wanted, not Master, to hold him. Not that we ignored Master, and not that he ignored us. He held us both, recognizing we needed the time together and not begrudging his two favorite pets their clingy behavior.

* * * *

Time blurred. Mark and I loved Coop and Nate, and depending who was where in their cycle, we all enjoyed making love to each other, sometimes in a group, sometimes in pairs. Mark and I got to go places with Master, while Nate and Coop usually stayed home with Qhan. It was a natural pairing, the two of them and me and Mark. We all loved each other, but as Mark had said, it was me and him first. Coop had picked out Nate, and their bond grew strong, as it should.

Life became a pleasant routine that left us all content and happy. I lost track of time and didn't care how long we'd been there, although we knew from meeting one newer pet at a party at Bob's owner's house it'd been at least three years since I'd been there. Coop truly felt happiest when carrying, and he rarely went longer than a week between his drop and next breeding. Usually, he bugged Master until he gave in and did it. Not even the largest vibrating butt plug, now teasingly dubbed "Coop's pacifier," would satisfy him for more than a few hours.

Ironically, I realized had Coop ended up at one of the egg farms, or even on a ship servicing troops, he still would have been happy.

Coop and Nate were both at various stages of carrying, and Mark and I weren't, when we had visitors one day. The man wore a silver tunic and had a young Algonquan with him. Coop and Nate napped out in the backyard. Master called Mark and me into the living room to meet our guests. He never separated us. If he wanted one of us, he called both automatically. It was a given we were each an extension of the other. Usually he simply called out "PolKal," as if one word.

Master looked pleased, smiling as he introduced us to the boy. Boy wasn't the right word, both because they didn't have genders and because Algonquans reached maturity so damned rapidly. He could have been nearly full-grown, for all I know. By Mark's estimates, Master was over sixty Terran years old, even though he looked much younger.

Mark's face dropped with shock as Master talked.

I felt panic threaten. "What?" I squeaked. "What's wrong?"

Mark shook his head and regained his composure, taking a moment to absorb whatever information it was Master had just imparted.

Mark spoke with the young Algonquan for a few minutes, then the boy and the man in the silver tunic turned to leave. I knew Mark would tell me when he recovered from his shock. Master ruffled Mark's hair, kissed him, and then smiled and ruffled my hair before he went to show the guests out.

Mark turned and slowly walked to our room. I followed, now worrying. Master never took me away from Mark, not even just to go on an outing. Not after what I suffered when we thought he died. I worried about something else maybe being in the works and was near tears when Mark lay on our bed in the corner, staring at the ceiling.

I crawled in with him. He put his head in my lap and held my hand. I stroked his hair, unable to read his expression.

Finally, he looked at me. "Remember after we got Coop? Remember how the lawyer came and Master drew up his will?"

"Oh, gods, he's not dying, is he?"

Mark smirked. "Stop. No one's going anywhere." He kissed my hand and his voice grew quiet. "Before...we left the

Terrans. Before we were drafted, did you ever dream of having kids?"

This was an odd tangent. "Well, yeah, I guess I did. But I knew it would never happen for me. Not with the breeder laws and marriage bans. No way I'd ever be able to get permission. For all I know, some of my sperm from the mandatory deposits and the breeders they paired me with might have taken. But I'll never know if they did or not."

He squeezed my hand. "Think back, babe. Think back to when the lawyer was here. What did Master say?"

I had to think about it. "He said he'd designated an heir or something."

Mark nodded. "At the time, the last egg I carried." He closed his eyes. "That kid was that egg."

We lay there in silence. Mark would talk when he was ready. I knew better than trying to push him. Mark had proven to be the strong one, and I was more than happy to let him own that role. Sometimes, he just needed silence to think.

He rolled to his side, his face pressed against me as I held him. "You asked me when you first got here what happened to the eggs, and I didn't really know. While I was gone, I learned a lot about all of that. You know why it's so peaceful here usually? No crime?"

"No."

"Remember…*that* guy?" That's how we referred to the fucker who raped me. To my dying day, I'd never forget the protective rage on Master's face when he threw the guy to the floor for me to identify.

"Yeah?"

"Their laws are draconian in some ways, to a Terran, but think about it. They have lots of freedoms despite their rigid laws. Lots of rights. We didn't have a fraction of the rights and freedoms and choices as Terrans. Hell, we've got more freedoms and protections now as owned pets than we did as 'free' Terran men."

He sighed. "Eggs are raised by the government. They have a very controlled system, to try to minimize the egg mortality rate. It also ensures they're all raised the same way, equally, with no bullshit politics or the kind of garbage you and me grew up with. Normally, before this fucking war, partners only reproduced when they wanted to create an heir. The egg would go to the regional center to be raised. If it survived, obviously, it became the heir to their sire. If not, they tried again.

"With the war, the government took over raising the extra eggs to create troops. Once the war is finally declared over, they'll colonize some of the planets in their territory and let them absorb into other colonies, if they want. The government trains them regardless, educates them, teaches them the laws, drills respect for the law and for their fellow Algonquans into them from literally the day they're hatched. There are no prisons because judgment is swift, as we saw. They can prove if someone committed a crime or not by using the truth serum. If they're innocent, they're released. If guilty, they're punished, and the harmed party is allowed to carry it out if they want, or the police do it."

"Like Master did?"

"Right." He stroked my hand. "Because extra eggs usually go to raise troops, someone has to designate a specific egg as an heir. Which Master did, because he wanted to ensure we'd always be cared for." He looked at me. "It was just sort of a shock."

I stroked his forehead. "Master seemed happy about it."

"He is." He kissed my hand. "He said how proud of me he was, and that one day I might belong to his heir." He laughed. "Kind of weird but makes sense when you know how their culture works. I mean, he's not my son, but he's here because of me."

We cuddled like that for a while. A lot of our relationship was like that now, contemplative, quiet. Sure, we still made love every day, but without the frantic energy Coop and Nate shared. We were content to hold each other, knowing how precious that simple contact truly was above all else. We could come whenever we wanted, but a milker couldn't caress you.

A milker couldn't whisper thoughts of love and longing.

Mark had brought back a hand-held with him of files they'd hacked from a Terran ship they took over. In it, Earth books, including poetry, that he and Nate desperately enjoyed sharing with Coop and myself. Some nights, the four of us would sit cuddled together with Master, while Mark and Nate took turns reading to us.

Nate and Coop loved each other, but they hadn't endured what we'd survived.

Mark and I knew what was truly important.

CHAPTER TWENTY-THREE

Master's heir moved in with us not too long after that initial introduction. Because they were unisex, they didn't have words for "son" or "daughter," "mother" or "father." Just "sire" and "heir."

Normally a juvenile Algonquan wouldn't move home that young, but Master's status and the success his pet had created for the Algonquan empire earned him special privileges. Marzan, which was as close as we could come to pronouncing his name, was only a few years from maturity. We could see him growing taller with every week that passed, already taller than us. Special tutors came in to educate him in everything he needed to know while Mark worked with him to teach him Terran Standard English. Marzan would read poetry to us as part of his lessons, especially our beloved Robert Frost, as we gathered around him like enraptured puppies and listened to his rich voice speak a language we could understand.

I suspected Master wanted him to know English not just for political and military purposes, but so he could better care for his beloved pets.

We loved Marzan. Not as a child, because he wasn't a child. We loved him because he was our Master's heir, to be our Master by birthright one day. We loved him knowing, as the spitting image of his sire, he would love and care for us the way his sire cared for us.

Master pampered us. Mark and I both chose to breed, usually on the same cycle within a day or two of each other, so we could enjoy everything together. Master installed a swimming pool, and soon he was holding parties for his friends and their pets.

Mark and I frequently sat off in the shade during these parties, alone, smiling and watching Nate and Coop enjoy themselves with the other pets. We didn't want to be with the other men, but we didn't mind Nate and Coop doing it. It made us happy to see them having fun, and usually inspired us to drift off together and make love.

Master never shared any of us with his guests, although he welcomed guests who wanted to share their pets with others to do so.

None of us pets kept track of time beyond how long until our drop date. We didn't want or need to. One morning, Mark and I were lounging next to the pool while Nate had Coop bent over the edge and was fucking his brains out.

Some things never changed.

I played with the shaggy hair along Mark's temples and he noted my smile. "What, baby?"

"You've got a couple of grey hairs."

"I'm sure you've got a few in there somewhere, too." But he didn't look any older in my eyes. I searched for lines, stress, and found none.

We had no stress.

Well, except poor Coop begging to be bred or fucked. Our sweet little slut.

When Marzan had to go away to attend some classes and take tests as a requirement of his schooling, we missed his presence. He played with us pets in his spare time, romping with us, wrestling, although that's all that happened.

Upon his return several months later, it struck us all how much like Master he looked, a younger version, certainly, but the same strength and steady nature, now as tall as his sire.

He looked at us with the same love and passion his sire had for us.

I didn't have to look to know Mark's body reacted the same way to him mine did, an instant longing.

Coop and Nate were both in their third weeks and had gone to bed, to sleep, after dinner. Master called Mark and me into the living room and pulled us into his lap on the sofa. Then he started talking to Mark, Marzan listening and obviously the subject of this conversation.

I knew if I needed the information, Mark would translate. Otherwise, I'd wait until we were done to interrupt. I knew it wasn't a bad conversation because I sensed no tension in any of them.

A smile creased Mark's face as he tucked himself against Master's chest and replied. We were sent to our room to wait. Coop and Nate had already curled up in Master's bed to sleep, so we had the bed to ourselves.

"What's going on?" I asked.

"Algonquans reach the age of their majority and are considered adults. But designated heirs aren't eligible to claim their birthright for a year after that, or their first natural cycle, whichever comes first." He smiled. "Marzan is, as of last week, the age of majority."

"So?"

"The first natural cycle can't happen until after..." He laughed and pulled me to him. "He's gotta lose his virginity."

I snorted. "Master's going to take him to a brothel or an egg farm?"

Mark looked shocked. "Fuck that!" Then he laughed. "Um, that's not what I meant."

But comprehension dawned as I understood what he meant.

"You okay, baby?" Mark looked worried.

I nodded. "I'm okay. Are you?"

"He's not my kid." He kissed me, deeply. "Master loves us. He's proud of us. He wants his heir to appreciate what he has." I sometimes forgot that as much as Mark and I loved each other, the strength I received from him, he received that same love and strength from Master. If we lost Master, it would be worse for Mark, who'd bonded even more closely with him than I had. "I want to do this. He asked if I was okay with it." He looked into my eyes. "Are you okay with it?"

I smiled. "Why wouldn't I be?"

"It's not sharing us. He's Master's heir. And it's not creepy like if it was those fucking Terrans and how they do things. It's different."

Those fucking Terrans. That's how we thought of "them." We were Algonquans now, all four of us, in our minds. "I know."

Master and Marzan soon appeared with Qhan, who stepped away to the corner, waiting. Master spent a long time talking with Marzan, quietly, solemnly, before clapping him on the shoulder.

Then he called for Mark.

Mark kissed me. "Stay here. Please?"

"I wouldn't miss it for the world."

Master walked over to me, caught my hand, and pulled me down to the bed with him. I thought he might make love to me, but he sat with me in his lap, his arms around me as we watched.

Mark went to Marzan and, despite the difference in age, I couldn't help but see my Master standing there. He could have been the man I first saw in the distribution center that day, when he rescued me and brought me home.

And that's how I thought of it—a rescue from a life sentence as a Terran. Only by becoming a pet had I finally gained my freedom and the accompanying happiness.

Mark softly talked with Marzan, drawing his arms around him, kissing him. They worked their way over to the frame and Marzan finally caught on. We were simply voyeurs as Mark softly spoke with Marzan before hooking himself to the milker and climbing onto the frame. I wished it was Marzan's large hands running over my body, caressing my back. When I started stroking my own throbbing cock, Master chuckled in my ear, gently grabbed my hand, and held me immobile in his lap.

I softly whined, wanting release. He chuckled again as he nipped my right ear, by the tag.

I prayed this meant he had plans for me, because held like that, it only amped up my need to a fever pitch.

Marzan's instincts took over. I heard Mark's happy moan and the Algonquan's satisfied grunt as his cock plunged home inside my love. I tried to squirm in Master's lap, to maybe impale myself on his cock, but he nipped me again on the ear and held me still.

There would be no quick, loveless fuck between them. Whatever talk Marzan's sire had given him, he took to heart. I saw his love in every gentle touch, every slow move, heard it in every breathless sigh and passionate moan. I don't know how long it took, because by the time they finished I felt nearly as frantic as Coop a day after dropping and would have given anything to feel something up my ass.

When they finished, Qhan stepped in to clean Mark up. Then Marzan pulled him up, into his arms, cradled against his chest as he whispered into his hair.

I'd rarely seen Mark look happier than at that moment. It surprised me that I didn't feel jealous, either of Marzan for earning that loyalty, or of Mark for being the recipient of his joy.

After a few minutes, Marzan carried him over to where we sat on the bed and gently laid him down beside me. Master let me go, and I kissed him.

He wore a sleepy, satisfied smile. Neither of us had bred for several weeks, and our urges were usually easily sated. "Love you, baby," he whispered to me.

My heart felt full to bursting. "Love you, too."

Master touched my hair and said something that sounded like a question. When I looked and caught sight of his playful smile, my pulse surged as my cock throbbed.

Marzan held his hand out to me. "Would you?" he asked. His English, though heavily accented, was always understandable to me, his voice still a nearly identical reproduction of Master's.

Would I? Oh, *hell* yes!

He laughed as I jumped up and threw my arms around

him. He led me to the frame, kissing me, whispering to me in English how much he loved me, would cherish and care for me the way his sire had. It struck me that all these years, the whispered endearments Master had spoken to me in that same voice, but in a language I couldn't understand, were likely most of these same words.

He didn't rush, taking his time before letting me plug in and climb onto the frame. The touch of his sweet hands, before his cock ever entered me, brought me several climaxes. When he finally pressed home, claiming and filling me, I couldn't imagine a more perfect existence than this.

Fuck Terrans, indeed.

Later, he carried me over to the bed and laid me next to Mark, then stretched out on my other side. We were two happy pets. Mark pulled me into his arms. "Okay?"

I nodded, too sleepy and content to answer. Master softly spoke to us. It was Marzan who translated.

"You two are my loves, my favorites. I love Taun and Dal, you know I do, but after all we've been through together, you two are most precious in my heart and soul. I feel secure knowing that should I not be here for you, you shall be loved and cared for by someone who will cherish you as much as I."

Master stroked Mark's cheek, then mine. "I have never felt the need to take another partner after mine was killed. At first, before Pol, I didn't know if I could ever love a Terran. But I am so glad I opened my heart and saw not one of them, but the spirit I can truly call my partner. And then to be doubly blessed by you, Kal, is a gift. Marzan has sworn that if he ever takes a partner, he will be sure they meet with your approval before he commits. He would rather spend his life without one than to take someone who would not be able to appreciate and love you all as much as we both do."

Mark and I were both crying by the time he finished. Master gathered us both into his arms and hugged us.

"Love Pol," he said, kissing Mark.

Then he turned to me. "Love Kal." He kissed me.

I cupped his cheek. "Love Master."

CHAPTER TWENTY-FOUR

Nate and Coop had to wait until after their drops to enjoy Marzan. Because Marzan's first cycle had to trigger naturally to enable his birthright, unless the year was up first, Master finally stilled Coop's begging to be bred by doing it himself the next morning. After, Coop lay with a happy smile on his face. Master made a joke, which started Mark immediately laughing, but Marzan interpreted.

"We should look into finding him a better pacifier. Maybe one shaped like a hard egg he can wear all the time."

Nate and I joined in the laughter. Coop simply smiled and gave us a thumbs-up.

When Master had to be away overnight on business, it was Marzan we all snuggled up with now. While he deferred to his sire, and when Master was home we slept with him, Marzan still received our attention and affection.

We were six months from the deadline, and Marzan had not naturally cycled yet. I'd learned if an Algonquan's first time was with a partner they loved and mated with, usually that would trigger their cycle. Since we were Terrans, it didn't create the same effect.

I sought Marzan out one morning in the living room, where he sat on the couch reading, the vid screen on but unwatched. Coop had talked Mark into playing with him, but I didn't feel like doing that. Nate was taking a nap. I lay next to Marzan and watched, my head in his lap while his hand absently stroked my hair. I knew a little more Algonquan than I did when I arrived, but mostly household commands and, of course, sexual terms. So when I saw an Algonquan in a black uniform shaking hands with a Terran, who appeared to wear a military uniform, I tugged on Marzan's sleeve. He looked up, his eyes widening in shock as he turned up the volume and watched.

I didn't like seeing scenes of anything having to do with the Terran military. We pets worried Marzan would have to go into the military, meaning we'd risk losing him. Master's job didn't take him away into battle, or even off-planet. But Marzan was young and from a prominent line, meaning he could be tapped for command duties in the field.

After a few minutes of him watching and not translating for me as he usually would, I sat up. "What happened? What are they saying?"

When the story ended, he looked at me, stunned. "It's over," he softly said. "The war. The Terrans have surrendered and agreed to completely withdraw their troops from our territories."

That was good. So why did he look like it wasn't?

"But what's *wrong*?" I felt the old hysteria threatening to take over. The fear I would be taken away from them.

"Nothing. Our government says any Terrans who wish to stay, who are already homed with private owners, may remain if they wish. Others without private owners are free to leave or stay. But the egg farms are no longer needed and will mostly be disbanded or converted into adoption centers for Terrans who wish to stay but who don't already have owners."

"We don't have to leave?"

He kissed me. "No, Kal. You are free to leave if you wish, but you do not have to."

I threw my arms around him. "Please don't make me leave."

He held me, reassuring me. "I will never make you leave. I love you."

When Mark and Coop wandered in a little while later, they found me sobbing in Marzan's arms as he tried to comfort me.

Panicked, Mark raced over to take me from him. "What happened? What's wrong?"

Marzan looked amused as he rapidly explained in Algonquan.

Finally, Mark laughed and kissed me. "You are a big baby, you know that?"

I sniffled. "I won't go back."

"Neither will I."

Apparently, Coop told Nate. I thought Nate would be as happy as we were about this development, but he retreated to the backyard with a confused Coop trailing him.

Master returned home a short time later to break the news but found we already knew. Only minutes after his arrival, the door chime sounded.

I don't care how nice they were to me, or how well they treated me, the sight of the blue-garbed techs always sent a skitter of fear through my bowels. Mark looked grim as Master sent Qhan to bring Cooper and Nate in from the backyard. When I tried to ask what was going on, Mark shushed me.

The four of us pets were led out the front door, Master and Marzan taking the lead. Outside, with the tech, stood a Terran colonel. No tag or collar on him, he wore a battle-ragged uniform of the people I despised. Inside the Earth transport vehicle he'd apparently arrived in, I spotted three Terrans, former pets, if I had to guess. However, they wore green tunics, lacked collars, had holes in their right ears where their tags had been, and wore no manacles on their wrists or ankles.

Who in their right mind would *want* to leave if given the chance to stay? Then again, maybe they were from an egg farm. Maybe they hadn't been lucky enough to have loving owners who pampered and cherished them.

Marzan translated the tech's words for us. "The Terran wishes to speak to your pets, to offer them a chance to leave and be repatriated. By law, you have to allow them to speak with him, if they wish it."

Master nodded and indicated the colonel could speak to us. Then Marzan continued softly translating the colonel's English for Master.

The Terran stepped forward, eyeing us, pity and more than a bit of disgust in his gaze. "Look, the government is offering you all back pay and bonuses if you return. You can even get a civilian job if you want, and an apartment."

Mark's hand remained tightly gripped around mine. I felt anger coursing through him. "A job? An apartment?" Mark pointed at our home. "What kind of fucking apartment can compare to *this*? Are you *shitting* me? What can the fucking Terrans give me that I don't have here?"

Apparently, we weren't the first Terrans to react like this. "Look, the government is also guaranteeing you marriage slots. The breeder laws are being lifted. The marriage bans will be lifted in a few years, but all you guys, you'll get first chance to marry."

Mark snorted in disgust. "Fuck you." He released my hand, walked over to Master, and sat at his feet. "I'm not getting in that transport. You murdered our people, you lied to us about the Algonquans, and you have nothing to offer me. Get the hell out of here."

I felt the same way but didn't bother reminding Mark he'd mixed his references. We were Algonquans by choice, but Terran by birth.

The Terran stared at him, loathing filling his gaze. Perhaps sensing he'd have no better luck with me, he turned to Nate. Since hearing the news our Nate had worn a look I couldn't interpret and didn't want to.

"What about you? Want to go home?" He glanced at Coop. "Guy like you can have nearly any woman you want."

"I won't go back in the military," Nate said.

My heart ached. I didn't want to lose Nate or Coop. I loved them. If Nate left, I had no doubts Coop would go with him.

The Terran grinned. "See? A reasonable man. No, you'll get an automatic honorable discharge, if you return and want out of the military. The Terran government isn't going to say what happened to you guys while in captivity. They'd rather keep that quiet, and they know you guys probably don't want the whole universe knowing what these perverts did to you, either. Everyone has to sign privacy agreements not to talk about it. I mean, if you're...you know, got one of those things in you, our docs know how to take them out and reverse the effects of what they did to your bodies."

Coop looked frightened and stared at me and Mark, then back to Nate. Nate gently shook Coop off when he tried to talk to him before stepping away from us for a moment. The Terran commander followed, whispering to him.

Suddenly, I wondered if the Terran made bonuses based on how many of "their guys" they could convince to come back. It wouldn't have shocked me if they did.

I walked over to Coop. "I can't force you to decide either way. I won't guilt-trip you to stay, either. But Mark and I, no way in hell we're going back. I love you and Nate both, and it'd hurt like hell to see you go, but I won't stop you, either."

Agony washed over Coop's face as it looked like the Terran commander made in-roads with Nate. I knew Coop would be lost to us, too.

I stepped over to Mark and sat in front of him, my back resting against his chest, my arms holding his around me. Anger still radiated off him and he nipped my left ear.

"Baby, did I tell you yet today how much I love you?" he asked.

I leaned my head back. "You did now."

He nuzzled his face in my hair and I felt his breath along my scalp. Somehow, I suspect he was drawing as much strength from me in this moment as I was from him.

After a few anxious minutes, the Terran commander looked triumphant. He walked over to the transporter, as if waiting for Nate to follow.

Nate eventually turned back to us, staring at Mark and me, then Coop.

Coop's lip trembled. He was carrying. Hell, he was almost always carrying. He loved it, lived for it.

More than once, Coop had said how grateful he was to be with us. That it was an amazing life he never wanted to give up. He truly enjoyed everything to do with our life, including breeding.

Nate studied the ground for a few long moments, not revealing anything. In that way, he was sometimes different from the rest of us. In our new life, we learned we could be open, free with our emotions, but sometimes Nate still held back.

"Well? You coming with us, or not?" the Terran asked.

Nate released a deep breath he'd been holding and walked to Coop, where he took Coop's hands in his and held held them. "If I leave, will you come with me?"

He choked back an anguished sob but tearfully nodded.

Nate smiled and stroked his hair. "You're happy here, aren't you?"

Well, that was a fucking no-brainer.

Coop nodded again.

Nate pulled Coop to him, holding him, whispering to him. Coop sobbed one more, nodding, clutching at him, and my heart sank.

Then Nate held Coop's hand and, together, they took a step toward the Terran. "Get the fuck out of here," Nate said. "And if you ever set your filthy Terran boots on my Master's property again, I'll *personally* kick your damned ass."

Mark and I both gasped, and it was only then we realized Coop wore a happy smile, his tears ones of joy, not good-bye.

The Terran frowned and stared at us. "You're sick fucks. All of you. They've brainwashed you, don't you know that? What man in his right mind wouldn't want a woman? Who wouldn't want to go back?"

Marzan and Master stepped forward. Marzan spoke. "They have told you what they want. They are happy and loved here. Leave. Now."

Finally, he did. I didn't miss how the former pets inside the transport looked at us with envy, their faces pressed to the back window as the transporter left. I wondered again if they'd been at an egg farm. I'd since talked to several other pets who'd been former egg farm inhabitants, and while none of them missed that life, they all preferred it to their Terran lives.

Mark and I jumped to our feet and threw ourselves at Nate. "You asshole!" Mark said as he hugged him. "You scared the crap out of me! I thought you were leaving!"

Nate snorted. "*Fuck*, no. I just wanted to see what kind of bullshit they were trying to spread." He stroked Coop's cheek. "Like hell I'm leaving any of you, and like hell would I make Coop leave. My boy's a happy camper."

Nate met my eyes and held my gaze. "The Terrans have nothing to offer me. I've always been welcomed and loved here, from day one. I just needed to have those questions answered so I'd never have a 'what if' thought." He kissed Mark, then me, his eyes still fixed on mine. "*This* is where I belong. This is my home, and I belong with all of you, because you're my family."

* * * *

If the Terrans thought they had an uphill battle convincing the "prisoners" to leave with them, they soon found it was even more difficult than that. Master returned home from work the next afternoon with the latest reports. Terrans slated for repatriating were low in number to start with. Of those, most escaped their Terran "liberators" within a few hours and demanded to be returned to wherever they'd been, even the egg farms.

It left the Terrans frustrated, to say the least.

Master laughed as he related one case where a transporter full of Terran repatriates actually convinced one of the Terran liberators to escape with them, and the man was now requesting political asylum from the Algonquans at one of the former egg farms.

After two weeks of dismal efforts, the Terrans gave up and left after losing dozens more of their men to the "Algonquan perverts," as they called them.

I didn't care.

We had a beautiful autumn afternoon with lazy clouds drifting across the sky as the four of us lay on our backs in the grass and listened to Marzan read poetry to us. Coop was, of course, hooked to the milker because he was in the third week of his cycle. Mark occasionally corrected Marzan's pronunciation for him. Master, Qhan, and Mack joined us.

One thing the brief interruption of our lives gave us was a timeline. The Terrans turned over all records to the Algonquans regarding the missing men, so we now had the official dates of our "capture."

It turned out I'd been there over eight years, Mark ten. We still had a few months until a planned celebration of Marzan's birthright, unless he came into his cycle first. With the war over, Marzan would begin going to work with Master in preparation to take over Master's duties, leaving Master free to retire. I couldn't wait. The prospect of having Master home all day, every day, thrilled me. The fact that Marzan wouldn't be placed in jeopardy pleased all of us.

While there were many days almost as good as that one, if I could have picked one to define my life, my most complete happiness, it would have been that day.

I would think back on that perfect afternoon in years to come, wishing I could have frozen it in time.

CHAPTER TWENTY-FIVE

Three months and counting until Marzan's celebration. That day, Master came home not feeling well, and Mark and I curled up with him in bed. It wasn't very long until he asked Mark to call for Qhan and Marzan.

The stricken look on Mark's face didn't bode well, and Mark wouldn't answer my questions.

By late in the evening, a doctor had been called and a prognosis issued, stunning all of us.

Master's face grew pale as the night deepened. He spent a little time talking with Qhan, Mack, and Marzan. Calling all four of us pets to him, he kissed Nate, Coop, myself, and then Mark. "Love all." His eyes lit on each of us in turn. The doctor wanted to make us leave, but both Qhan and Marzan nixed that.

Master pulled Mark and me close on either side. "Love Pol. Love Kal," he whispered so softly only Mark and I could hear.

This couldn't be happening. This couldn't be real. It wasn't until he finally took his last breath, Mark and I both sobbing, that I realized I was once again acquainted with a night that had no dawn. This time, there would be no magical return.

The four of us consoled each other as best we could. Apparently, Master knew about his condition, an Algonquin word I couldn't pronounce similar to our Terran cancer. The doctor told us Master kept it from us because he hadn't wanted us to know about it. Master had also known there was no cure, and that it would take his life eventually, but he'd thought it wouldn't happen until after Marzan had claimed his birthright. The doctor assured us nothing would have changed the course of Master's death or extended his life.

According to their customs, we buried him the next morning as the dawn broke, beneath a tree in the backyard. He loved it out there, spending time with us all, laughing and smiling as he watched his beloved pets play with each other or even with him.

Marzan tried to stand tall, but the tears streamed down his face as much as any of us. Later, in numb shock, we all gathered at Marzan's feet in the living room as he sat on the couch and the attorney outlined what had to happen next. Marzan could not legally claim his birthright yet, but because Master had outlined everything in detail, Marzan could still continue working in Master's former position and the estate would be preserved.

Unfortunately, we were now stranded in a type of legal limbo until Marzan could actually claim his birthright in three months, and therefore draw an income. The estate still needed to be funded. While we pets could not legally be separated as part of the estate, we were technically still property of the estate, not of Marzan. There were laws that had to be followed concerning our care, complex regulations clearly stating how pets could be cared for and by whom.

Mark tuned out, numb with grief. He held me more for his own comfort than mine as I rested my head against his chest while I held hands with Coop and Nate.

Marzan paced, thinking. The bulk of the estate's vast funds were untouchable to him until he inherited his birthright. The money was there, but could not yet be used. He could release Mack and Qhan and have money to keep us, but no one to care for us. Which, by law, he had to have. He couldn't do it himself when he had to work. He didn't want to fire them, though, because they were family.

Getting rid of us was, of course, out of the question, as far as he was concerned.

I had no idea of the legal complexities the Algonquans set up regarding us pets.

After hours of discussions between Marzan, the attorney, and Qhan, most of which weren't translated for us because Mark wasn't able to function, Marzan sat on the floor with us.

"He says there is an option that would allow a solution. I am not fond of it, but it would only be for a short time. He said there is also a chance the ruling body may allow a dispensation due to my father's high status, but the case must be heard and it could take several weeks, at the earliest.

By this time, Mark lay cradled in my arms as I stroked his hair. I nodded for Marzan to continue.

"If I am not able to care for you all, or provide someone to care for you all, they would remove you from me. The attorney said he knows a mated pair who would be willing to..." He struggled to come up with a word in English. "Lease you from the estate until I can officially claim my birthright. The legal requirements of caretaking would be satisfied because Qhan would go with you. It is a temporary option until either he can get the ruling body to hear a plea for dispensation to allow me to trigger my cycle and therefore claim my birthright, or the time is up by law and I can claim it if my cycle doesn't naturally occur first."

"What does it mean?" I asked.

"They would not be allowed to breed any of you, but you would temporarily be their pets until I could legally reclaim you." This next part pained him, I could see from his expression. "There are two heirs in their home who have reached the age of majority. Their sires would prefer them to cross over and begin their claiming period with a pet rather than a partner. Apparently there are..." He struggled again for the right words. "Political implications. They prefer no partners, so no one else can have a claim on the estate when they reach their year or start their cycle."

Cross over.

In other words, have sex with us.

"What about me?" Coop said, obviously stricken. "I'm carrying..." He sobbed. Nate pulled him close and tried to soothe him.

Marzan smiled. "Qhan would be with you to help you through it, and of course if the egg survives, it would be cared for."

Nate and Coop stared at me, waiting on me to make the decision. Normally, we would all look to Mark for guidance, but he lay in my lap, a glassy stare on his face. He hadn't spoken since Master died.

I knew all too well how he felt and gently raked my fingers through his hair.

"What are our other options?" I asked.

"The only other option I would have is to surrender you to the government until my birthright claiming, and they do not have to abide by my sire's will. They might separate you. There is no guarantee they would return you all to me upon claiming my birthright. They might see fit to re-home you, and I could not claim you." He looked near tears again and I prayed he didn't cry yet. If he did, I wouldn't be able to keep it together.

"And if we do this?"

He nodded. "You would remain mine. I do not wish to do this. I know my sire did not anticipate this. He thought he would live until I had already claimed, or he would have set aside more funds outside of the protected birthright estate, I'm sure. Our laws, unfortunately, are very strict. If I can get the dispensation, they will let me trigger my cycle sooner so I can breed and claim my birthright. But meanwhile, Qhan would ensure you're cared for, and, as soon as possible, you would all return here, to me. At the very latest, three months."

"And they can't separate us from each other?"

"No. There would be a clear contract. No breeding, no separation, and Qhan present to care for you."

Mark's eyes had dropped closed. "How soon would we have to go?" I asked.

Marzan asked the attorney. "He said he will have to confirm with them and negotiate the contract. Three days at the most."

"And then we're with you for good once we're back?"

He nodded.

"What if you'd died before him and there was no heir?" I felt a little angry. "What would have happened to us then?"

"He designated Qhan as your caretaker, the estate to go completely for your care for the rest of your lives. Qhan has already reached full status, so he could have taken over with no delay. But I am the heir, with a birthright claim in process. It is a different and complicated matter. He cannot step in because my claim is in process." Marzan looked as horrible as I felt. "I'm so sorry, Kal. I do not want to do this, but I do not wish to lose any of you. He will file the dispensation request tomorrow. If they do hear it, it could take weeks."

I didn't want to make this decision. I looked at Nate. "What do you think?"

Weary grief filled his face. "We've gotta stay together. I can't lose any of you. It's only a couple of months. What the hell, we can do that if we have each other, right?"

"They can't mistreat or abuse us?" I asked Marzan.

"No. Contractually, they will be obligated to abide by Qhan's care. There are many families, apparently, in a similar situation. Before, they could use the egg farms. Without them, many sires and their mates are trying to avoid their estates becoming entangled with the partners of heirs." He sighed. "This conflict with the Terrans created many issues we never had before, a larger population the government is still trying to equitably distribute throughout the colonies."

Fucking Terrans.

"No forced breeding?" I confirmed.

He nodded. "No breeding at all. Not even if one of them reach their cycle. He says they used to have a pet, but he died a couple of years ago of an illness. He says they are kind. They knew my sire, so they would prefer to strike a deal with someone they know rather than strangers."

I brushed my fingers through the small patches of grey at Mark's temple. I couldn't bear to try to rouse him from his grief to make this call. He needed my strength.

"Okay," I softly said. "As long as we've got Qhan and for sure we're coming back here to you."

Marzan nodded again. "Absolutely."

* * * *

If we weren't cuddled in Master's bed with Marzan, we were out in the backyard. Nate took over reciting Robert Frost and other poetry for us, his smooth voice settling over us like a comforting blanket as he held Coop and I held Mark. The two of us sat up, leaning on each other, the men we desperately loved in our arms. Mark still wouldn't, or couldn't, speak.

I could sympathize.

Our last night there, I found I couldn't sleep, so I walked outside to stare up at the night sky. Over the years the constellations had become familiar to me even if I couldn't pronounce their Algonquan names in most cases. I walked over to Master's grave and sat at the foot of it, staring at the small stone marker engraved in a language I mostly couldn't decipher. Any Terrans passing by, they might think it was a pet's grave, or simply a garden marker.

I wanted to cry, but my body felt desiccated, empty. I recognized this grief, at least, and while it hurt, I knew I would eventually process and survive it. Master would never return to us, but we had Marzan and Qhan and Mack, and each other, of course.

This, too, shall pass.

If only I could find a way into Mark's shell of pain, to love him, to help him know he would survive. I had thought him dead and while yes, I wanted to die and would gladly have done so if I could, I was glad everyone who loved me kept me going until I survived the pain and eventually wanted to live again.

I heard a noise and looked up to see Nate making his way from the house. He didn't speak as he walked over to me and sat behind me, pulling me into his arms and resting his chin on my shoulder. Poor Coop was almost as inconsolable as Mark. He was our sweet, emotional boy, our normally playful, horny, slut-puppy. He wouldn't have survived a return to Terran society. He was born to breed, and not as a stud, either.

I pulled Nate's arms tighter around me. "Thank you," I said.

He kissed me. "For what?"

"For staying when you had a chance to leave."

He softly laughed. "I never had a chance to leave. Not from the moment I met you and Coop. And then Mark, of course," he added. "I love you guys. I loved him" — he nodded toward Master's grave — "and this is the life I want. I just needed that closure. That's all."

"Promise me I'll get through this?" It was something I'd asked him countless times after his arrival, in my darkest days when I didn't think I'd find the strength to breathe, much less make it through another minute in as much pain as I felt.

He held me tighter. "I promise. We'll all get through this. Just hold on tight to me." It had been his answer, every time.

"I'll never let go."

Love Nate? Absolutely. Make love to him? Over the years, countless times.

Each of us had a different relationship with each other, beyond the sex. The first and most obvious level was Mark as our leader, if we could be said to have one. The true Alpha pet in the hierarchy. Then there was Mark and me, and Nate and Coop, as couples. And so on.

One of the special things between Nate and myself was that residual lifeline he held for me, my back-up. When I needed a steady shoulder, I had Mark, or if he was unavailable for whatever reason, I had Nate. I didn't begrudge Nate sought a similar kind of dynamic with Mark, needing strength to lean on. I could take Coop off his hands for a few hours and he would spend time with Mark, and everyone was happy.

Or Mark would distract Coop—not hard if you had a penis—and Nate and I would spend time alone. That flexibility made us all stronger, in some ways. It certainly strengthened our bond, with never any jealousy between us.

"How do I bring him back?" I asked. "How did you bring me back?"

"I didn't. I just held on and knew one day you would be ready to love me as much as I loved you. You'd already started coming back to us when he returned." He kissed me. "He'll come back to us. Remember, he was with Master longer than us. You bonded first with Mark, but he bonded first with Master."

I looked into his blue eyes. "Who'd you bond with first?"

He stroked my cheek. "You. I love Coop, you know that. I love all of you. Coop made it fun. You made me see I could live here."

I snorted. "How? I was a wreck when you got here. I could barely talk to you."

"I saw how much you and Coop loved Mark. But especially you. I knew if you could come to love him so strongly in such a short time, and I saw how anguished Master was over losing Mark and worried about you, then this was the only place I ever wanted to be. I'd never had love like that before in my life."

He let out a harsh laugh. "What, I'm supposed to pick some Terran woman out of a catalog and hope she likes me? Fuck that shit." He kissed me again. "There's a reason why the Terrans had to give up trying to repatriate us, and I don't just mean because most of us didn't want to go. Their guys wanted what we had. Not the sex, but yeah, sure, that's cool. They wanted the love. I didn't give a shit about anything before I got here. Nothing. I got here and I learned how to care. Wanted to care." He nuzzled my forehead. "Cared about all of you."

I took a deep breath and let it out. "Please keep telling me I'm gonna make it."

"Every day, in every way."

I smiled. Another familiar mantra.

"What did you think when Mark returned?" I asked. "Honestly?"

He didn't need me to clarify. After a minute to consider his response, he said, "Well, you remember I asked if I'd have to leave."

"Yeah? But what else?"

"I worried he might hate me for loving you."

I turned in his arms. "Really?"

"Don't worry, we talked about this, me and Mark." He kissed me again. "He thanked me for keeping you going. That's what I mean. He loved me for loving you. Because you loved me. He could have easily been pissed or jealous about it and he wasn't. Can you imagine that happening back on Earth?"

No, frankly, I couldn't. I'd seen guys get into bar fights over taking someone else's chair.

A lover? That would have been a to-the-death fight.

"Do you think what they did to us changed us?" I asked.

He smiled. "Yeah, I do. But it changed us because we decided to change, not because of what they did to us. We adapted. We'll adapt to this, too. It'll hurt, but once we're back with Marzan, life will settle, Mark will heal—"

"Coop will beg for an egg," I snarked.

We both burst out laughing. "Our poor guy's such a little slut. Jesus, I love him for that."

Truth be told, so did I.

CHAPTER TWENTY-SIX

Poor Mark. Marzan sat with him that morning in the garden by Master's grave and quietly talked with him, just the two of them, while I watched from the patio. Mark finally nodded and Marzan kissed him before helping him to his feet.

I wouldn't say Mark looked better, but at least he'd finally broken his silence.

Nate, Coop, and I embraced Mark in a group hug. Mark ended up with his arms around my waist, his head on my shoulder.

"I love you, baby," he whispered against my neck.

I kissed his forehead. "I love you, too."

Marzan said good-bye to us and kissed each of us. He had to go to work and couldn't accompany us. Poor Coop openly wept, whether from emotions or the effect of the egg on his system, I wasn't sure. Maybe both. We learned Marzan had been welcomed to visit us anytime he could, so that took a fraction of sting out of this situation. Our temporary family was simply grateful their estates wouldn't be put in jeopardy.

The attorney, our vet, Qhan, and a blue-robed tech rode with us as Mack drove. The house was, comfortingly enough, not far from ours. I paid attention during the ride in case I ever needed to find our way back home.

On our drive, we passed a few human pets with their handlers. Most off-leash, a few on. I suspected the leashed ones were in a particularly horny part of their cycle and their handlers wanted to prevent straying. Gods knew Coop would bend over and beg to be fucked by anyone the first day or two after a drop.

I watched Mark's face, worried for him. He closed his eyes and rested his head against my shoulder during the ride. He'd never spent a night away from home without Master, except for his time on the mission. None of us had, for that matter.

I felt further reassured when we pulled up to their house. While their front yard wasn't as big as ours, the house was just as beautiful, large and well maintained. Two older Algonquans met us out front and warmly greeted everyone who escorted us. Then they turned to us.

I wasn't so out of it I missed the kindness in their faces. Their sympathy. I couldn't pronounce either of their names, but the first one, slightly taller and slimmer than the second, stepped forward.

"Welcome," he said in thickly accented Terran Standard.

That caught my interest. Mark immediately spoke to him in Algonquan, then translated. "He knows a little. Very little."

How much he knew didn't matter so much as we appreciated his effort.

Our room lay situated in the back of the house with a door leading to a shaded patio that overlooked their backyard. No pool, and not as large a space, but still nice.

Then my eyes lit on a small white marker under the shade of a tree. I realized that was most likely where they had buried their beloved pet, as we had buried Master.

Well, that made sense. That they had given their pet a marker worthy of an Algonquan further comforted me.

Qhan left us in our new room while he went to discuss things with our foster family. The room wasn't quite as large as the one we had at home, but it was clean and light, airy, with an attached washroom of our own instead of just a sink. The large corner bed felt soft and comfortable and struck me as new, for some reason. Big enough for the four of us to cuddle together in our familiar, comfortable way.

Their frame looked similar enough to ours, and they had a portable milker.

It finally struck me that I hadn't used a milker for several days, since before Master's death. Neither had Nate or Mark, to the best of my knowledge.

Poor Coop. He spotted the portable milker by the bed and collapsed with a groan, hooked himself to it, and flopped onto his side. Nate smiled and sat down with him, pulling his head into his lap and stroking his hair as Coop succumbed to the device.

I noticed the flicker of a smile crossed Mark's expression.

Qhan eventually returned with our lunch and began discussions with Mark. We would be given a couple of days to settle in. The heirs were away at school, and once their sires felt we'd grown more comfortable in our surroundings, they would recall them to meet us and do what we'd been rented to do. Coop, of course, would be exempt from anything while carrying.

We had the run of the backyard and common areas of the house. Qhan's room lay directly across the hall from ours.

Mark talked with Qhan while I sat next to Nate. "They seem nice," I whispered to Nate. "Not too bad, then."

Nate shook his head and caressed Coop's hair. "No. Not too bad." He looked at me. "What the hell, it's not like it's going to hurt. I mean, yeah, this sucks, but..." He shrugged, not saying it, but glancing down at Coop in his lap.

He didn't have to say it because I'd already thought it.

But it's not like we have to breed and drop for them.

Poor Coop. This would be murder on him. Part of me could see the ironic humor in the situation. I would laugh, except that it would make an already emotional Coop even more distraught. He liked predictable routines and rhythms in his life. Disruptions messed with his head.

Fuck, breed, carry, drop. Repeat.

Until we returned home, he didn't have that comforting schedule.

* * * *

Mark didn't retreat as deeply into his grief as he had before, although his quiet resignation frightened me more than if he'd openly grieved. What if he didn't fight to stay with me? What if he died of a broken heart?

That night, as if reading my mind, he rolled onto his side and stared into my eyes. "I promised you, baby," he whispered, "I won't leave you. I mean it. I...just don't know how to deal with this. I never thought he'd die before us."

I kissed him, relieved. "Let me help you. Kind of have experience in this area."

He sadly smiled. "I'm so sorry, baby. I knew you were hurting, and I felt guilty about putting you through that, but...*fuck*."

He snuggled in my arms, but this time he remained there with me, mind and body, not just a physical shell holding a bereft, wandering soul looking for comfort. "I'm so sorry," he eventually whispered. "I'm so sorry you suffered like that."

"You came back. That's all I needed. That's all I ever need. If I have you, I can get through anything."

The next morning, Nate and I left Mark napping in bed with Coop and went exploring. The well-maintained backyard felt welcoming. We both wandered down to the stone marker and wished we could read the markings. Mark knew a little of their complex written language but not nearly as much as he could speak it.

One of the Algonquans, we'd settled on calling him Harn since that was the closest any of us could come to saying his name, emerged from the house and walked down to us. He was the one who could speak a little English. He sadly smiled as he stood in front of the marker and then leaned in to pull up a tall piece of grass that had missed being trimmed. His hand fondly caressed the marker before he straightened, still looking at it. From the lush grass in front of it, I guessed it had been a few years since the burial, not recently.

"That was Gal," he said then turned to us. I didn't miss the tears in his eyes. "Our pet."

Nate and I shared a glance. I knew for a fact the same exact thought ran through our minds. We both stepped forward and hugged him. He tentatively put his arms around us, and when he realized we weren't afraid of him, he hugged us tighter.

I think I knew at that point I could easily endure this stay. Any man still in that much emotional pain over a Terran pet's death couldn't be a bad man.

He finally stepped back and smiled at us as he wiped his eyes. "Thank you."

The second man walked down from the house and the two of them conversed for a moment. We called him Jord. Again, the whole difficult language issue.

Harn turned to us. "Room comfortable?"

I smiled and nodded. "Yes, thank you."

They both smiled. Then they patted us on the heads and returned to the house. Over the years, I'd come to enjoy that expression of affection, whether from Master or Qhan or any of Master's friends. Hell, most Algonquans stood nearly two feet taller than me, if not more. I felt like a kid compared to them.

Nate looked at me. "You thinking what I'm thinking?"

"Probably."

He watched as they disappeared into the house. "Look," he said, "I don't know about you, but I'm willing to shoulder the burden of our duties, so to speak. That way Mark doesn't have to do anything."

"Me too."

Nate sighed. "Coop's gonna need a bigger pacifier."

We burst out laughing. "I don't think there's one big enough for our boy," I joked.

* * * *

Mark spent a lot of time sleeping. I knew that was due to his grief and depression. Nate and I left him and Coop cuddled together on the bed.

When Marzan came to visit us that night, after he spent time with Mark and Coop, Nate and I got him alone outside to speak with him.

"We want to tell them that Nate and I, we want them to use us, not Mark and Coop," I said.

He stroked my face and I fought back a wave of sadness. I missed him, wanted to be home with him, not here and beholden to the kindness of strangers.

"Are you sure?"

Nate and I nodded. "We can do it," Nate said. "We'd prefer they leave Mark and Coop alone. They need time to heal."

Marzan hugged us. "I'll speak with them before I leave."

We went with him to the living room, and I listened as he spoke to Jord and Harn. The two men nodded in agreement. I went back to check on Mark and Coop and found them asleep already. Softly closing the door behind me, I returned to the living room where Marzan prepared to leave. Qhan had already retired for the night. When Marzan left, I fought the urge to cry.

We needed to be strong.

Jord and Harn settled in to watch vids. They indicated we were welcomed to stay if we wanted. We did, curling up on comfortable pillows on the floor next to their sofa.

I dozed off at one point. I awoke with a start when they turned the vid screen off and stood to go to bed. We sat there, watching, waiting. Harn turned at the doorway. It didn't matter what the species, uncertainty is a universal expression.

"You are welcomed to join us, if it is your wish. Both."

Well, we had to start sometime. I preferred a quiet, low-key introduction to intimacy with them, if possible. It'd sure make it easier on me and felt a lot less clinical. I'd be lying if I denied I could pretend one of them, at least, was my Master. I felt adrift in the Alpha pet role, but I wouldn't force Mark to step back up unless or until he was ready.

I checked on Mark and Coop again. Still asleep. They'd be okay, for a while, at least.

Nate and I crawled into their bed with them. It was as large as Master's bed, and as comfortable. I ended up with Harn, while Nate settled into Jord's arms. Nervous didn't begin to describe what I felt.

If nothing else, I knew they wouldn't hurt us. I suspected my body would predictably react as I'd been trained, even if my heart and mind couldn't get into it. I ignored whatever happened on the other side of the bed and instead decided to focus on Harn's eyes. Large and brown, like the others of his species. He started by lightly caressing my face, tracing the line of my jaw, brushing his fingers through my hair.

When I spotted his tears, I realized we weren't the only ones adjusting to this new arrangement. We weren't their beloved pet any more than they were our beloved Master.

Tonight, maybe all of us could escape into comforting fantasies of the loved ones we mourned.

His hesitance colored every action despite his obvious wish to go further. Finally, I reached up, caressed his face, and when his lips parted, I pressed one finger between them.

Rewarded with a tentative smile and a cock-hardening swipe with that delicious tongue, he finally realized I felt okay with this.

We both closed our eyes and let go of our collective pain, easing the other's grief. I lost myself in the feel of his warm arms holding me, his tongue exploring me, pulling the first orgasm out of me that I'd had in a while. Beside us, I heard Nate having a similar good time, and at one point his hand blindly sought mine. Our fingers laced together as we allowed the men to use us, sating their needs as well as slaking ours. They took us on our backs, face up. When Harn entered me after giving me two climaxes that still left me hard and wanting, he slowly thrust, giving me that sweet fullness I'd longed for.

Nate and I let go and enjoyed it, our hands squeezing the other as we came, until finally we all lay still and quiet in the room. I felt Nate's tension ease as he fell asleep and his fingers went limp.

I couldn't sleep, despite the comfortable post-sex contentment struggling to drag me down into rest. Once I felt Harn also fall asleep, I carefully climbed out of bed without waking any of them and returned to our room. Mark had curled his body around Coop's, both asleep but neither looking restful. I lay behind Mark, my arm draped over both of them. I couldn't suppress my smile when, in his sleep, he wiggled tightly against me and I felt tension ease from his body. Coop too, as one of his hands found mine and held on tight.

I pressed a kiss to the back of Mark's neck. "Don't worry, baby. This time, I'm gonna take care of you," I whispered.

CHAPTER TWENTY-SEVEN

Nate returned to our bed the next morning before Coop or Mark awoke, but I'd already heard noises as the household stirred. He smiled sadly at me as he lay on Coop's other side. Without waking, Coop immediately rolled toward him, like a piece of iron drawn to a magnet. With him there to watch Mark and Coop, I went to take a shower, needing one. A few minutes later, Mark appeared. Without a word he stepped under the spray with me and kissed me, fiercely, possessively.

We made love, hard. He bent me over and drove his cock inside me, making me cry out with the closest thing to joy I'd felt since our ordeal started. Before he came he reached around me and grabbed my cock, stroking it as he thrust. "You're mine, baby. All mine. Never forget that, no matter what."

Desperation tinged his tone. I met every thrust with my hips, needing him. "Yes!" We both came nearly the same time, and he backed against the wall, pulling me up and tight against his chest, his arms around me.

He bit my left ear lobe, harder than normal, immediately hardening my cock again. "Us first, always. Right?"

I turned in his arms and kissed him, our tongues fighting and stroking and fucking, until I dragged him down to the floor and pulled him on top of me so he was impaled on my cock. "Always," I gasped.

He rode me as I stroked his cock this time. Once we were spent he finally collapsed on top of me as we lay there under the warm spray, both of us exhausted.

I held him as he cried. What could I say to him? I myself had learned first-hand there were no words to make this better, to fix it. I had nothing but my love and my body to offer him for comfort.

"I'm sorry," he whispered, barely audible over the sound of the water. "I'm so sorry, baby."

"For what?"

"That I'm not stronger for you when you need me."

I made him look at me. "You're here for me. That's all I need. If I have you, I can handle anything."

His sweet blue eyes studied mine. "Did they hurt you?" he finally asked.

I shook my head. "No. They were nothing but gentle with us. Nate and I made an executive decision that you and Coop are going to take it easy and let us deal with things. Okay?"

He sniffled and laid his head back down on my chest. The tile wasn't exactly comfortable, but I wouldn't make him move. "Okay," he softly said. "Thank you."

* * * *

A new routine of sorts took over. I'd be lying if I denied I enjoyed sleeping with the men. Before my incident, Master would share Mark with a select few because he was proud of his pet. I could rationalize this in my mind as something similar. With my fears assuaged, I could let go for a while in their embrace, enjoy their cocks possessing me, their tongues exploring my deepest recesses in that delicious way that's beyond any description.

I never fell asleep with them, always returning to Mark and Coop in our room. My heart lay there, with them, and that's where I wanted to be.

Nate would return every morning before Coop awoke. Coop had to understand what was going on, but if he ever awoke in the night to find Nate missing, he never questioned it. He would drop soon, then we'd be faced with that situation.

Every morning, Mark would join me in the shower and reclaim me the only way he could, sometimes even marking me with love bites as I reassured him I was and always would be his first. I loved it. I let myself go with him, enjoying his brief return to the dominant role in our dynamic.

It wasn't until a few days later Nate shed light on this.

"He's afraid you'll want to stay here with them." Mark lay inside with Coop while Nate and I sat in the backyard, in the shade, eating lunch.

"He said that?"

Nate shook his head. "He didn't have to." He turned his blue eyes on me. "He's afraid you'll want to stay here because he knows he's not strong right now. He's struggling with his grief and doesn't have the strength to deal with this too, and he knows it. He's worried you'll want them instead of him since he's not helping us out."

I stared at him, stunned. "How could you possibly know this?"

He shrugged. "Coop kind of felt that way after I first arrived. He told me later, after Mark came back. He was afraid you'd want me instead of him because I was more like Mark than he was."

Guilt washed over me. I'd been so self-absorbed during that time I honestly didn't feel much of anything for anyone. "That's not true. I loved him."

"I know that, and you know that. Grief can short-circuit rational thought." He met my gaze again. "No, I'm not one hundred percent sure that's all that's going on with Mark, but I think he's looking for a sign not just that you're his, but that he's still yours."

I chewed on that during the afternoon. I left Nate with Coop and coaxed Mark out into the backyard where, once lying in the grass, I rolled on top of him.

I kissed him and felt the tension flow from his body. "You're mine," I told him, my lips working down to his left earlobe where I nipped him the way he liked to nip me. His fingers dug into my back as his hips rocked against mine.

"Yes!"

I worked my way lower, sucking his nipples, driving him half crazy with need until I pushed his legs up and plunged home inside him, fucking him hard and fast, the way I knew he loved.

"If you think I'm ever going to give you up," I told him, "think again."

He held on to my arms, his gaze never leaving mine. "I love you, baby."

I smiled. "I love you, too. Once we're back home, trust me, I'm going to spend every day and night showing you how much, all the time."

He pulled my face down to his and kissed me, the taste of desperation thick and fierce. Nate had been right.

I fucked him harder. "And until we get home, this ass belongs only to me, doesn't it?"

"Yes!" He closed his eyes and tried to roll his back to take me even deeper.

I grabbed his arms and pinned them over his head, staring down into his eyes. "All I need you to do for me over the next few weeks, or however long it is, is take care of Coop for me and Nate. That's all. Let me and Nate handle the rest. Got it?"

He nodded.

I kissed him again, crushing his lips with mine, pounding my cock into him to leave him no doubt how I felt. I didn't need to grab his cock and help him, I hit his sweet spot every time and after a few more thrusts he exploded.

"That's what I wanted to see." I finished, enjoying the feel of filling him with my cum even more than my own climax.

When I released his arms he grabbed me and we rolled onto our sides. I held him close, stroking his back as the sun warmed us. "No more worries or guilt, right?"

He nodded.

* * * *

The two heirs, Ang and Neri, were recalled home by their sires. Nate and I enjoyed meeting them. They both knew a little Terran Standard, not as much as Marzan, but more than Harn. We could have waited and dragged out the inevitable, but with Coop's drop time growing closer every day, I wanted to make sure we were both available for that. The first evening they were home, I suggested Nate and I go to bed with the heirs that night instead of the sires.

I almost laughed, which wouldn't have helped the situation. While adult Algonquans and towering over us, they both looked nervous, nearly terrified. I felt sorry for them, in a way. Before the war, Algonquans usually waited until they found a partner, even if they didn't permanently mate with them. Because of their complex laws, however, that could lead to family entanglements, which before didn't matter as much due to the fact that they didn't need to rush things and could carefully select a partner. During the conflict, with the population explosion, the dynamics changed.

The two sires had a talk with their heirs, and after a little while, Nate and I retired with them. I'd ended up with Ang. While sex was an open topic of discussion among Algonquans, and he'd no doubt witnessed the sires with their pet before his death, the poor guy seemed at a loss.

Thank the gods he knew Terran Standard. I coaxed him out of his clothes and to his bed. Before long, nature finally took over. Fortunately for me, he had a naturally gentle nature and was willing to please.

After we wore each other out, he rolled onto his side and looked at me. "Good?"

I snorted with laughter. "Very good." I wanted to stay there until he fell asleep, but as worn out as I felt, I was afraid I might fall asleep.

I wanted to sleep with Mark.

He reached out and touched my arm, a hopeful look on his face. "Stay?" He'd met Mark and Coop and been made aware of the situation with them. Both he and Neri agreed they would honor our wishes.

Part of me wanted to. Part of me craved curling up against one of those large, hard Algonquan bodies and sliding into a dreamless sleep. "They need me."

He nodded and wistfully smiled. "Okay." I started to get out but he leaned in and caught my hand, kissing me. Damn, those fucking Algonquan tongues could melt me! "Maybe tomorrow," he said before lying back on his bed.

I made my way down the dark hall, pausing outside Neri's door and smiling at the sound of Nate enjoying himself before I returned to our room. Far enough away, I couldn't hear what was going on at the other end of the house.

For that I felt extremely grateful. It certainly made it easier on my conscience.

It didn't help that Ang's parting kiss hardened my cock again. Sliding into bed tonight wasn't as easy as I thought it would be. Mark, either awake and waiting for me, or barely asleep and disturbed by my return, wiggled his ass at me as I tried to find a comfortable position.

Fuck it.

I pressed home, my heart enjoying his satisfied grunt as I bottomed out inside him. I didn't want to wake Coop, though. Mark carefully untangled himself from our boy and we ended up on the other side of the bed, him face down with me on top. I slid my hands down his arms and laced my fingers through his. He squeezed, not about to let go.

I fucked him, hard and fast and deep, enjoying the way he tried to work his hips in time with my thrusts despite being covered by my body. Before I exploded I slowed the pace, found his left earlobe, and bit down.

His whole body went rigid beneath me. He muffled his scream against the mattress, and his ass muscles clenched around me as he climaxed, the friction of his body against the sheets bringing him off.

That was all I needed. I pounded into him, briefly forgetting we were trying to be quiet. When I came it felt better than a simple release. We lay there for a moment, sweaty, panting. I felt his body tremble, and at first I thought he was crying, until I realized he was laughing.

Rolling off him, I pulled him to me and he muffled the sound against my shoulder.

"What's so funny?" I whispered, trying not to wake Coop who, somehow, had managed to sleep through it.

He grinned. "You just laid that kid, and he left you horny?"

A switch flipped in my brain, illuminating a key truth I hadn't fully understood before and bringing it fully into focus for me. I nuzzled Mark's nose. "You're the only one who can satisfy me, mister."

He rolled me on my back, and before I knew it, he was fucking me. "I am, huh?"

"Yeah."

Aha.

He grinned, then leaned in and nipped my ear. "I've gotta keep my baby satisfied."

"You do keep me satisfied." I felt a frantic energy in his fucking, but he still brought me over. Damn, I missed carrying and the perpetual orgasms, but it was nice having the ability to think and move freely and be filled by Mark's cock. When he came he collapsed on top of me, this time sated, emotionally as well as physically.

As we laid there and I stroked his back, he pressed his face against my chest. "I love you," I softly said.

He rubbed his cheek against my skin. "Love you, too, baby."

"I love both of you," Coop groused. "Can you *please* go back to sleep now since I can't get fucked? This is torture!"

Dissolving in a fit of laughter, the two of us snuggled our grouchy boy between us. Before we both fell asleep, Mark winked at me.

I grinned and winked back.

We'd all be okay, we just needed to get through this.

CHAPTER TWENTY-EIGHT

Marzan brought good news on his next visit. The government agreed to hear his request for dispensation, but it would still take a couple of weeks to wind through their system. With our purpose fulfilled, Nate and I could relax and enjoy the intimacy we shared with our temporary owners and their heirs.

Coop was due to drop any day now, and his nerves got the better of him. Not being in his familiar home, he whined, complained, and we did our best to soothe him. Even the minor differences in their frame nearly drove him to tears.

Harn and Jord had a gathering of what Ang told me were family. Three of them spent the night, two partners and their heir. We pets spent the evening together in our room after being briefly introduced to everyone. The heir, Scal, seemed fascinated by all of us, but especially Mark's ability to speak their language. Ang told me their cousin had never had a human pet before and spent very little time around humans. To him, we were a delightful oddity.

Tonight we wouldn't be going to other beds. That meant I could comfortably fall asleep in Mark's arms, which was what I did until Coop awoke me with a pained groan from where he laid on the frame. I nudged Mark and Nate awake, and Mark went to fetch Qhan.

Poor Coop. Most of his drops went like clockwork, but every so often he had a difficult one. It wasn't until an hour into the process I realized Mark hadn't followed Qhan back to our room. Ang and Neri, and Harn and Jord had all gathered in our room to support Coop. I turned to Ang. "Have you seen Mark?"

He frowned, also now realizing we had a missing man. It wasn't like Mark to disappear, especially during a drop.

Leaving Qhan and Nate to care for our boy, the rest of us started looking for Mark. It didn't take long to establish that not only had Mark gone missing, but so had Scal.

The sires, when notified their heir had apparently taken off with Mark, acted horrified.

I grabbed Ang's arm. "You've got to find him!" I didn't know why I felt so afraid, why my balls felt like they wanted to crawl inside me.

Within an hour, our vet arrived to help with Coop. Marzan, his attorney, and Mack had been summoned, and I was ordered by both Marzan and our hosts to stay with Coop while the police joined in the search. It didn't help my mood when one of the blue-garbed techs showed up with the police. While I'd learned not to fear them over the years, some reactions aren't that easy to suppress.

I sat at Coop's head with Nate and tried to soothe him even while my heart raced. Our sweet boy was in a lot of pain, and I felt utterly helpless to do anything while he begged and cried for relief throughout the night.

Around dawn, the vet said my given name. "Kal."

He waved me around to Coop's ass and pushed me down onto the seat he'd occupied. Then he started miming something. I felt like screaming at him until Qhan, in his frustration, said, "Pol." He mimed the same thing and then pointed at me. "Kal."

"I don't understand!" I yelled at him, near tears.

"They're showing you what to do." Harn's voice from the doorway startled me. He looked exhausted.

"Did you find Mark?" He shook his head and walked in.

"No. Still looking. No Scal, either."

"I don't understand what they want me to do!"

Coop let out another scream of pain, followed by a moan of pleasure.

Harn talked with them. I sensed his frustration as he tried to think of how to translate their instructions. He finally grabbed my hand and placed it on Coop's ass. "Egg...stuck. Small hands. Said Pol did it for you."

I nearly sobbed with relief as I realized what they wanted me to do. "Okay, Coop, buddy, you've gotta push for me."

He did, and I got one hand in there. Fortunately for both of us, that was all I needed. I could feel the connective tissue on the top of the egg and managed to work it free with my fingernails. "One more push, buddy."

With Nate holding his hands, Coop managed another push and the egg popped free. Both the vet and Qhan slapped me on the back and gave me happy smiles as Coop cried with relief.

I cleaned up and helped Nate move Coop to the bed while the vet and Qhan did whatever they had to with the egg. I turned to Harn. "Thank you."

He nodded. "They say it is viable. Sometimes...sticks."

Coop would be happy that it would survive. It was the last egg Master ever produced.

Now back to my other concern. "What's going on? Why would Scal take Mark?"

Harn shook his head again. "Don't know." He looked distraught. "I'm sor—"

"If you tell me dolmo, I'll fucking kill you!" I screeched. I didn't need this. I didn't need this surreal complication in my life. I needed my Mark *here*, with me. I couldn't do this. This was his job, taking care of us.

"Kal." Qhan shook his head at me and guided me to the bed where Nate held Coop. His implication was clear: sit down, shut up, and take care of them.

Nate's eyes met mine. I sank to the mattress beside him and took Coop from him. Then Nate wrapped his arms around me.

I wanted to be out there, helping search for Mark. No matter what, Mark wouldn't willingly leave this house and us. Never. He didn't run away. Maybe my thinking jumped the gun, but I'd already tried and convicted Scal in my mind as my own incident returned to haunt me.

Mark promised he'd never leave me. Ever.

That meant someone *took* him.

It was late in the day when they finally found Mark, battered and bloody but alive, under the trees in our very own backyard, beside Master's grave. Unconscious.

Bred.

Marzan took me to the clinic, holding my hand as I trembled, terrified.

No sign of Scal had been found, but from evidence the police discovered, it appeared Mark had dragged himself home from a small park very close to our house.

Marzan wouldn't release my hand as we walked inside, holding me back as I tried to pull ahead to find Mark. I needed him. They had put him in a single room, like I'd seen before, restrained to a bed.

The restraints weren't necessary because he was still unconscious. I reached over and unstrapped him. I couldn't stand seeing him like that.

Crying, I sank to my knees beside his bed and held his hand, begging him to wake up. Marzan spoke to our vet as I rested my head on the mattress and waited. Both his eyes were blackened and swollen. I doubted the right one would even open, as bad as it looked. His upper lip was swollen and split. Bruises and cuts were scattered all over his face and body.

He had to come back to me. I couldn't lose him like this, not so senselessly. Why would anyone attack him? If they wanted to rape him, he would have let them have him, wouldn't have fought them. They didn't have to brutalize him like this. This spoke more of hatred than simply wanting a piece of ass.

After consulting with the vet, Marzan returned to me. "He is under sedation." I cried again, relieved. He wasn't in a coma. He wouldn't slip away from me without hearing me tell him I loved him. "He awoke after they brought him here, and he panicked. They worried he'd hurt himself, so they sedated him while they treated him." He kissed my forehead. "We can take him home to heal, with our vet's blessing, after he awakens."

Barring Mark's return to me the first time, I'd never heard words so beautiful. Marzan and I sat there with him and I recited as much Frost as my tortured brain could recall. The police came to talk with Marzan. "They need to talk to me. You stay here with him. It is routine. I will be back."

I nodded. I had my Mark back. That meant I could deal with anything.

When his eyes fluttered open a few minutes later, I forced a smile. "Hi, handsome." I gently brushed his shaggy hair away from his forehead. The scar he'd returned with had faded over the years, little more than a pale line in his flesh, and barely noticeable now with all his fresh injuries.

He closed his eyes again and breathed a sigh of relief. He tried to speak, licked his lips, and tried again. "How's Coop?"

It took me a moment to absorb what he said. "You get abducted, attacked, and look like hell, and you're worried about Coop?"

"Baby, please."

"He's okay. Who the fuck did this to you? Was it Scal?"

He didn't exactly shake his head, but he moved it enough. "He didn't attack me. He wanted to show me to his friends. They had come over and were outside and heard the commotion when I got Qhan. He wasn't supposed to be talking to them, and his sires didn't know they were out there. They decided they wanted to play with the human. Scal didn't want to go along with them, but there were three of them. He didn't know they were going to hurt me. One of them — apparently his sire was killed by Terrans in the war — he hated Terrans."

Fuck. Me. My poor Mark.

"What happened?"

"I don't know. Scal tried to fight them when he realized what was happening, and when he ran to get help, two of the others went after him. The fucker who raped me knocked me out, and when I woke up, they were all gone. I recognized the park and managed to drag myself home."

Marzan returned with one of the policemen. He looked grim.

"What?"

"They found Scal's body."

* * * *

Mark told his story. Because of the circumstances, we were all immediately returned to our home. Harn and Jord felt horrible about what happened and offered to continue paying for our care. None of us held them responsible but it didn't change the facts.

When we got home I couldn't help but think there was something wrong beyond the obvious. Marzan seemed out of it, like something else was wrong.

Unable to take it, I pulled him into our room and closed the door. Coop and Nate were in Master's bed — now Marzan's bed — with Mark. "What's going on? Are they going to take us from you?"

He sat on the bed in the corner. "No," he softly said, tears in his eyes.

I didn't like this. "What's wrong? Please tell me."

"I...I think I'm in my cycle. The rage I felt when I saw what they did to Pol. I think it triggered it."

Stunned, I stared at him. Then I started laughing as I threw myself at him. "That's good, right?"

"I'd always wanted it to be with Pol," he said. "To continue on the tradition of my sire. What would he say to me that I couldn't protect Pol? He would be so ashamed of me."

"No! This isn't your fault." Oh, Jesus, I *so* didn't need this. I crawled into his lap and kissed him. "Use me. Please."

Desperate? Me? Yeah. All I could see of this was a one-way ticket to getting our security back.

"I promised my sire I would never force you to breed."

"Does it look like you're forcing me?" I kissed him, hard, refusing to let go. "Do you need to do anything, like get a witness or something?"

"No."

I ripped his tunic off him and pushed him back onto the bed. "Do you have any questions before we get started?"

That earned me a sad smile. "You are a pushy pet. I thought Taun was our breeder."

"Shut the fuck up." I kissed him again and nearly moaned when that delicious tongue entered my mouth. I encouraged him to roll over, on top of me, and before he could change his mind I grabbed his cock. Oh yeah, it felt like a piece of living steel in my hand. No mistaking that.

I guided it to my ass. "Do it!" I wrapped my legs around him.

He did. I bit my tongue to stifle my happy cry as that cock buried itself deep inside me. He wasn't sure what to do from that point, but I knew. I put his hands on my hips and made him pull me tight against him, forcing his cock as far in me as it could get.

I nearly sobbed with relief when I felt that first bite of delicious pain when his barbs grabbed hold, immediately followed by a rush of pleasure.

He pulled me up into his arms as I writhed on his cock, and he kissed me and whispered to me. In his passion he switched back to Algonquan and my reality slipped. I wasn't in Marzan's lap, but Master's. His voice, his face, even his scent the same as his sire's.

When the egg started moving he laid me down on my back, covering me, kissing me. Time blurred for me. As the burn of the egg attaching to me turned into mind-shattering pleasure, I threw my head back and sobbed with joy.

His body trembled over mine as he completed the process. As his sire had so many years earlier, he rolled onto his back, taking me with him, his softening cock still embedded inside me. Warm, strong hands stroked my back.

"Thank you, Kal," he whispered.

I smiled against his flesh. "Thank you, Master."

* * * *

Nate found us there late that night, worried when neither of us had returned. We'd both dozed off. When he found out what happened he clapped a hand over his mouth to stifle his cry of joy and threw himself onto the bed with us, kissing us both.

Marzan smiled. "I'm glad to see your feelings aren't hurt, Dal."

He grinned. "No, but get yourself a supply of those pills because Coop will bug the crap out of you to breed him next."

Mark awoke when we returned to bed. He looked at me, then Marzan, and Nate's silly grin.

"What?"

I nuzzled his forehead, not wanting to hurt his already bruised lips. "Everything's going to be fine now," I whispered. Coop had slept through our return and I wanted to avoid waking him yet.

His blue eyes studied mine in the dim light. Slowly, a smile creased his face. "Yeah?"

I couldn't help but smile back. "Yeah." I leaned in and nipped his left ear before I whispered, "We can be horny together."

He knew. He turned to look at Marzan and grinned. "That's my boy."

* * * *

Three days later, and the culprits hadn't been apprehended yet. The police told us Scal had been strangled to death. Qhan wouldn't take his eyes off us pets. He hovered like a vigilant mother hen, never letting us out of his sight.

Master, as we all now called him, finalized his birthright claim after the vet verified I'd been bred. The next day, he triggered his cycle again and bred a very happy Coop. Coop enjoyed being plugged back into his familiar frame and milker. Nate stayed with him during the process while I stayed in bed with Mark. It'd be a few days before Mark would comfortably be up and around, but despite the hell he'd endured, emotionally he dealt with it better than I had, considering we were now securely at home with our Master.

I suspected in his mind he talked himself into pretending Marzan was the sire, our old Master. If that fantasy brought him comfort, none of us would deny him that.

Harn and Jord came to check on us. Qhan didn't want to allow them near us at first, until I interceded on their behalf with Master.

The men sat outside with us. Nate and I didn't miss the sadness in their expressions, more than just a failure to protect Mark. They'd been able to relive a little bit of their lost past with us in their bed, just as Nate and I had been able to close our eyes and relive a little of ours.

Just as Mark could now comfort himself by calling Marzan Master.

They were preparing to leave when Mack raced out the back door, his rapid-fire Algonquan startling all of us.

Harn and Jord jumped to their feet and ran inside. Nate and I helped Mark to his feet. Coop reluctantly unplugged himself from the portable milker to follow, not wanting to be left behind.

"What's going on?" I asked.

Mark shook his head. "Something about the police. That's all I understood."

Master met up with us as we reached the living room. He took Mark from us, carrying him the way his sire had carried me so many years earlier, out the front door.

Three Algonquans, stripped from the waist up, were tied to the back of a police vehicle. My knees nearly buckled but Qhan and Nate caught me, holding me up.

I knew what would happen. I didn't want to see it, but I wouldn't abandon Mark to witness this alone, either.

Scal's sires arrived and Master handed Mark over to Qhan. Despite Mark insisting he could stand, Qhan wouldn't let him down. There was a huddle with raised, angry voices as Master, Harn and Jord, Scal's sires, and the police conferred over the situation.

"What's going on?" I asked Mark.

"I think they're arguing over who has the right to demand retribution. Scal's sires want to do it because of the murder. Harn and Jord want to do it because we were in their care. Master obviously wants to do it."

The arguing continued until Master's attorney arrived. Then the huddle broke. Master returned to us, looking grim.

"What?" I asked.

He stroked Mark's face. "Death to all three. Fifty lashes to the one who bred Pol. Twenty lashes each to the other two. They've agreed I can punish the one who bred Pol."

Scal's sires drew out the twenty lashes they inflicted, taking turns with tearful, angry taunts as they took their pound of flesh. I thought they would execute him, but they didn't.

"They want them to suffer," Mark said. "They'll execute them all after the whippings."

Harn and Jord also divided the punishment between them. As much as I hated what happened, and hated even more watching this, the protective anger on their faces as they whipped the prisoner only sealed in my mind that they were good men. I made a note to ask Master if, when he wrote his will, he'd make sure us pets and Qhan could be left to them if there wasn't an heir.

Master went last. Time blurred. I was no longer standing there next to Qhan and holding Mark's hand. I was in Qhan's arms and watching Master whip the man who raped me.

Except Marzan drew each stroke out, his fiery anger radiating from him as he pulled scream after scream from the prisoner. When he finished he returned the lash to the police and received the sidearm.

This time, I didn't look away.

CHAPTER TWENTY-NINE

It didn't surprise me that Master's rage triggered his cycle again. This time, three of us pets gathered around the frame that night as Nate writhed in pleasure under Master's hands. With all four pets barely a week apart in their cycle, Qhan had his hands full as we all closed in on our drop dates.

I personally had a lot of fun teaching Master how to check our progress. Okay, so I encouraged him to take his time and play with me when he did it. So sue me. If you ever had an Algonquan tongue up your ass tickling your prostate, trust me, you wouldn't blame me.

Harn and Jord welcomed the opportunity to help play midwives to us as Master went to work, fully taking over his sire's duties. One afternoon the four of us lay in the backyard, all hooked to our beloved milker. Coop, then Nate, dozed off as Harn sat on the patio and read. Unless we were inside the house, an Algonquan always stood watch over us. I hoped once Mark dropped he could talk to Master to ease up on that, but for now it made us feel secure and loved.

Mark carefully rolled over to me, into my arms. "You okay, baby?"

I kissed his forehead. The injuries to his body had long since healed. "I'm okay. You okay?"

"I will be."

I knew the feeling all too well. "No running off to war on me now, once you've dropped."

A lazy smile creased his face. "I'm thinking of trying things Coop's way for a while."

"I hope you wait long enough for me to get to fuck you." We could still walk under our own power, barely, but neither of us could muster the strength needed to play together. That required movement, which incapacitated us.

He snuggled closer. "This ass belongs to you, baby. You know that."

"Damn right it does."

Over the past few days, I'd noticed my Mark coming back to us. Hints of his former personality returning, as I'd suspected they would with our stability restored. We slept every night in Master's bed with him. None of us begrudged him holding Mark every night.

Harn and Jord started spending the nights at our house as Mark approached his due date. They had become close friends with our Master, bonded by their common love for us. When Mark's drop began, the room grew crowded as I lay at his head and held his hand while the Algonquans encouraged him.

Within a week, things had returned to normal around our house. Nate, Mark, and I had dropped. Coop had dropped and was already bred again.

Yep. All was well.

Master never shared us with anyone, but Harn and Jord became extended family. When an owner died without an heir the next year, and their pet needed new owners, Master was the first to testify to the techs that the human wouldn't have a better home, except perhaps our own, than with Harn and Jord.

It was at the party Master threw for them at our house, his friends and their pets in attendance, that we received sad news.

Bob was happily splashing around in the pool with Coop when I realized Carl wasn't there.

"Have you seen Carl lately?"

Bob shook his head. "Olco's here, but I haven't seen Carl in a while."

Mark slipped away from the festivities. When he returned a few minutes later, he looked sad.

I knew.

I waited to ask him until we could be alone. "When?"

"Last year." He held me. "He died in his sleep."

We stood in the shade of the trees. Over the years they had grown larger, fuller, providing a cool hideaway from the rest of the yard. Master's grave, the grass now full and lush over it, lay nearby. Many times I'd watched Mark walk out here alone and spend a few minutes sitting by it.

"Well, that's not so bad," I softly said. "He didn't suffer, right?"

"Nope. He lived long and died well." He pressed his lips to my forehead. "That we can be so lucky."

"You're not getting away from me that easy."

"No, baby. I have no intention of leaving you."

* * * *

Coop plopped down next to me in the grass. Two days post drop and he was crawling out of his skin horny. We really did need to get that boy a better pacifier, but he spent so much time carrying anyway, we suffered through his brief empty periods.

"Hey, Dale."

"Go ask Nate or Mark," I mumbled. "I can't move." I lay on the grass, three weeks into my own cycle. Life had settled down in our house, back to our comfortable routine. I'd waited nearly a year to be bred again since I'd dropped Master's first egg, which he designated his heir. I guess because it'd been so long, the effects this time around were nearly as debilitating to me as the first time. Mark and Nate, or Qhan, had to move me.

I didn't begrudge Mark and Nate spending a lot of time together, neither of them carrying. It meant I could lie there with my buddy and sleep without being molested.

"No, not that. Besides, they're asleep. Who's the guy?"

I forced an eye open. "What guy?"

"Master's got a guy in the house. Never seen him before."

I groaned. I didn't want to get up. "Is he a tech?"

"No. He's a civvie."

Fuck. "You're not really going to make me get up, are you? Why don't you go ask Master who he is?"

Coop looked nervous. Coop never looked nervous.

That made me nervous. "What's wrong?"

"I don't want to interrupt them."

"This coming from the man who tried to hump Master when his boss came for dinner?"

"Okay, look, I told you I couldn't help it. I was horny."

"You're always horny." I desperately fought the urge to laugh. If I laughed, it would trigger a spasm of orgasms that would nearly render me unconscious.

"They're…busy."

"Busy how?"

"They're on the couch making out."

That got my attention. "What?"

Master never dated. He never had another Algonquan in his bed.

"Yeah. They're sitting there talking, but they're all cuddling and shit like you and Mark do when you get all mooney over each other."

I didn't want to be a jealous pet, but dammit, he was our Master. We'd gone through too much to lose his affections to someone else.

I started summoning the strength to sit up and investigate the situation when Master and his friend walked outside. I hated him on sight. He reminded me of the man with the hungry eyes who'd raped me.

Master looked nervous as he sat next to me. He pet me and Coop on the head. "Kal, this is Galden. He's a friend of mine."

Galden didn't sit. His eyes narrowed as he looked down at Coop and me. I nodded. "Hiya." Coop remained silent, letting me take the lead.

The man said something in Algonquan, which Master replied to.

"He doesn't speak Terran Standard?" I asked.

"No."

Galden studied Coop and asked something. The hair on the back of my head stood up.

"Did he just ask to fuck Coop?"

Master frowned. "Why?"

"Did he?"

"Yes, but I told him no. Why?"

I forced myself up into a sitting position despite the sensations rolling through my body. Hanging on by the skin of my teeth as each shift in position rubbed the egg against my prostate, I leaned in toward Master and kissed him.

Out of the corner of my eye, I watched Galden glare at me.

"Be careful," I whispered in his ear. "Please."

Master nodded. I knew he'd want to talk to me later, alone, to find out why I felt like this.

Turns out I didn't need to object to Galden. Before dinner that night, Master joined us by the pool, where we were eating our dinner. Mark and Nate had missed out meeting our guest, but I told them flat-out why I didn't like him.

Master leaned in and kissed me. "My sire told me you were gifted at picking out pets."

Okay, weird tangent, but whatever. "Yeah?"

"Perhaps I should let you pick my partner, too."

"Why?" My heart raced. I prayed Master didn't have more than a passing interest in the guy.

Laughing, he stroked my cheek. "I sent him away. When he asked how often he'd be allowed to breed my pets, it put me on my guard. When I told him you all sleep with me, he felt that was improper and said he didn't allow pets to sleep in bed with him."

Mark sat beside me, his arm draped around me. "Improper?"

"Yes." Master kissed him, too. "If someone thinks my pets are improper, they have no business being my partner. I swore to my sire I wouldn't take a partner unless he could love you as much as I do. And that's a promise I will always keep."

It was another year before Master brought someone else home to meet us. Coop was happily immobile early in his fourth week, while the rest of us weren't carrying.

This time, it was Mark who sounded the alarm when the asshole muttered how human animals weren't good for anything other than fucking or breeding.

Master hadn't yet told him Mark could speak the language.

When Mark asked the guy, in Algonquan, why he felt that way, his face turned red.

Master took great pleasure throwing the guy out on his ass.

Love Master, love his pets.

A few months later, one of Master's co-workers came home with him and spent a few days as our houseguest. Just to work, not for any kind of romantic getaway together.

We loved him. Corin, and that was as close as we could come to saying his name, was soft-spoken, kind, and had been carried by his sire's beloved human pet.

Master had never seen Corin in a romantic way before, but we didn't miss the looks Corin snuck at our Master as they sat at the dining room table and worked on their project together.

We appreciated that while Corin's Terran Standard sucked, he made the attempt to speak to us using it.

Leave it to Coop to force the situation to a head. I blamed it on the fact that he was three days post-drop and his testicles overrode his brain. Master hadn't had time to breed him with our guest there. It was the second day of Corin's visit, and Qhan had the day off. After Corin and Master took a lunch break and sat at the table talking, Coop climbed into the guy's lap and threw his arms around his neck.

"Master, when are you going to let me play with your guest?"

I didn't know Algonquans could blush, but both men did.

Mark, Nate, and I rushed in to peel Coop off the guy. Mark quickly offered mortified apologies to our guest in Algonquan as we tried to get Coop to let go of the man short of bodily dragging our horny little slut out of the guy's lap.

"No, wait." We all froze at the sound of Master's voice and turned to him. He stared at us, including Coop, who had a death grip around the guy's neck.

Poor Corin didn't know how to react. He looked scared to death, holding his arms away from Coop as if afraid to touch him and piss off Master.

Master looked to me. "Kal? Your thoughts."

I hated being put on the spot. "We like him," I mumbled, my own face red. "He's nice."

"Pol?"

Mark replied in Algonquan.

Master smiled. "Dal?"

Nate grinned. "How does he feel about pets in your bed?"

Master laughed and asked Corin in Algonquan.

Despite his red face, Corin smiled and nodded. "I like. Pets are family."

After we convinced Coop to release Corin, we forcibly dragged him back to our room, hooked him to the frame with the milker and a gag, and Mark stuck the largest vibrating plug we had into him and turned it on high.

Mark slapped him on the ass. "That'll hold you. Jesus, Coop, you can't do that kind of stuff when Master's working. It makes him look bad."

Coop lay there and happily moaned.

We turned at the sound of a throat clearing, startled to find Master standing in the doorway. From the smirk on his face, I knew he wasn't upset.

He walked over to us and in a low voice said, "If I was to ask Corin to do more than just stay over as a houseguest, would that be objectionable to any of you?"

We shook our heads.

He leaned around us. "Taun?"

Coop gave him a thumbs-up.

Master didn't rush things over the next few weeks, but we were always happy when Corin came over to visit. It actually took him longer to win over mistrustful Qhan, who worried about any strange Algonquan getting to close to "his" beloved pets.

We were thrilled when Corin asked Mark's help to learn Terran Standard, and he started trying to read Robert Frost to us. He never asked to fuck us, even though Master left the door open for that. It was Mark who finally broke the ice there.

One night in bed, when Corin slept over, Mark crawled on top of the man and kissed him, officially welcoming him to our family. The rest of us followed suit, and, with the exception of egg-carrying Coop, we had fun taking turns getting fucked by both him and Master that night.

We'd definitely need a bigger bed. Mark and I snuck away later after everyone wore themselves out from the mini-orgy and curled up together in our room.

He kissed me. "You okay, baby?"

I grinned. "As okay as you are."

He grabbed my ass. "This still belongs to me."

I slapped his. "Yeah, well, ditto."

His blue eyes stared into mine. He now had a few creases at the outsides of his eyes, lines that hadn't been there when I first arrived. I knew I did, too. A little more grey in my hair, too, but so did we all. I didn't want to look away from Mark's eyes. I could spend hours locked in his gaze. A few times we'd done just that when too debilitated from carrying to move. We'd lie there, holding hands and staring into each other's eyes. "I like him," he said.

"Me too."

"I think our family just got bigger."

Master bought a larger bed the next week. He threw a party a couple of months later for his friends and their pets, officially welcoming Corin to our family. Bob's owner arrived, but Bob was nowhere to be seen.

I wished I hadn't mentioned it to Mark. Over the years, we could almost read each other's minds just from the look in our eyes. When he asked Bob's owner where our friend was, I knew.

We didn't tell Nate and Coop, who were both too happy splashing in the pool with the other pets.

Mark and I walked over to the shade and sat holding each other.

* * * *

Mark carried the first egg Corin had after joining us. When Master's heir, Malkan, came of age, it was Mark who helped him cross over into his claiming period, and again a year later Mark was the one who took his first egg. The dark times had faded into memories we didn't want to revisit. We'd been acquainted with the night, but we preferred to enjoy the days we'd been blessed with.

Corin did love us. It wasn't fair to compare his love for us to that of Master's, not when Master had known us all his life and been through so much with us. We pets felt secure in Corin's presence, sought him out if Master was busy, and enjoyed making love with him as much as we did with Master.

Master's heir moved in with us. My Algonquan wasn't nearly as good as their Terran Standard, but thanks to Mark's patient tutelage, I didn't feel totally adrift.

I never bothered to calculate how long we'd been there. I didn't need to know. It didn't matter. I would die here, with the people I loved who loved me. If the universe were kind, it would take me first.

Unfortunately, the universe is rarely kind.

CHAPTER THIRTY

It happens to all of us, regardless of how you've lived over the years, or what you've done with your time in this universe.

You wake up one morning to realize life has, literally, passed you by. Even though the living felt long and filled with happiness beyond measure, the reliving as you look back upon it all brings to mind how fleeting time is compared to the stars in the sky above us.

These thoughts drifted into my mind one afternoon as Mark and I enjoyed a beautiful afternoon out in the backyard. We were alone out there, because Coop and Nate were napping inside. Mark rolled over in the sunlight and laid his head on my chest.

"What are you thinking about, baby?" he asked, looking up at me with those beautiful eyes of his.

A soft, puffy cloud lazily drifted overhead. "I don't miss it. At all. Or any of *them*."

He knew what I meant.

Terrans.

"Neither do I, baby."

"I feel sorry for the ones who never had this chance. All the people who died fighting that stupid war, or who are stuck grinding away in jobs they despise just to stay alive."

He chuckled. "Feeling philosophical today, are we?"

I slowly shook my head. "It's all so...pointless. Why can't they see it? Who wouldn't want to come live like we do?"

He rolled over, smiling. "Do I need to distract you to get you out of your head?"

I smiled back. "Maaaaybe."

And that's what we did.

Neither of us had bred in years. Even Coop had slowed down to a couple of times a year. Malkan and his partner Brul lived with us, but never sought us out sexually, only as beloved family pets. Only Master and Corin used us in that way, and I turned a blind eye to how infrequently those times had become over the past several years.

We still slept with them every night, the four of us draped over each other and our beloved owners, but there were many nights we were content to lie there in bed and doze while our energetic Algonquan owners, still in the prime of their lives, fucked each other's brains out before falling asleep.

For pets of our advanced age, we were relatively healthy. I sometimes had problems working the stiffness out of my joints in the mornings. And even on the largest font setting, Mark could no longer make out the text on the hand-held containing our beloved poetry. Master, Corin, or Qhan would read to us.

Nate sometimes slipped into unsettling periods of ominous quite, or, worse, repeating himself several times when he said something. Other times, our other sweet blue-eyed boy acted his normal, loving self.

Coop's hearing had faded somewhat. Despite his hair being almost completely grey now, and the deeper lines in his face, I could still clearly see that patiently waiting man I'd picked out from all the other humans, the sweet eyes, the silent plea to me. The man who wanted to help me heal from unimaginable loss.

The man who'd done everything possible to keep me alive when all I wanted to do was die.

The man who'd made us laugh countless times throughout the years, and who brought us joy beyond measure along with his unconditional love.

We didn't speak about the other pets we'd known in the past, some who we never saw again at gatherings of owners at our home.

We didn't want to know their fates. It was too easy to imagine that as our future. Humans aged and died much sooner than our Algonquan owners, many of whom looked barely older than when Mark and I had first seen them at that party so many decades earlier.

Besides, the four of us were happy to never leave the safety of our beloved home. I think if they'd forced me to go somewhere now, it would have terrified me. The vet came to our home to check us out periodically, and the techs made regular mandatory visits to ensure we were still well cared for and happy.

Outside, the world had moved on and changed. While human pets were still strictly protected and had become more of a rarity since the war ended, we were now an oddity. I didn't want people staring at me like we were fascinating freaks of nature.

We were beloved pets, and that's all I wanted to be.

If a story appeared on the vid about Terrans, I changed the channel, or, if I wasn't by myself and others were watching, I left the room. My years in the military were now a lifetime away and those memories deserved no place in my thoughts.

We tended to sleep later than our owners, who had to go to work. One morning, after they kissed us good-bye for the day, I rolled over to Nate, who I'd ended up closest to, and draped my arm around him.

His skin felt warmer than normal. He also didn't snuggle against me like he normally would.

I gently shook him. "Nate, you feeling okay?"

His grumpy reply didn't sound normal either. "Leave me alone. Don't feel good."

Mark sat up from where he'd slept on Coop's other side, now instantly. "What's wrong?"

I sat up and pressed the back of my hand against Nate's forehead. He felt feverish. "I think Nate's sick."

"Not sick," he groused. "Just leave me alone."

For the first time in my life, I wished Mark hadn't looked at me. I saw it in his eyes. We were all somewhere in our mid to late sixties, and while the vet knew a lot about Terran physiology, he wasn't a miracle worker. Fortunately, Terrans rarely fell ill.

Unfortunately, sometimes they did, usually succumbing not to human ailments, but Algonquan pathogens our aging bodies couldn't fight off any longer.

"Go get Qhan," Mark quietly told me.

With fear in my heart, I did.

* * * *

Sitting out in the backyard, Mark and I forced ourselves to hold it together for Coop. Numb with grief, he lay in our arms and held Nate's collar in his hands as Master and Corin dug a grave for our sweet Nate.

Nate had left us earlier that morning, while we held him and after we all had a chance to tell him we loved him.

"I won't let you go," I'd whispered to him. "I picked you, and you belong here, with us. You can't give up. I love you."

He'd smiled at me, resignation in his eyes. "Love you, too. Hold on tight."

After giving us time to cry and hold him, his body had been reverently wrapped in a funeral shroud, just as Master's had. It now lay beside us, waiting.

Qhan and Mack, and Malkan and Brul sat flanking us, trying to comfort us through their own grief.

When the grave was ready, Master and Corin both gently placed our Nate's body in it and then sat beside the grave, reciting what sounded like the identical rites spoken over Master's sire. Eventually, the grave was filled by them, and they placed a stone marker, both of them kissing it before turning to us.

I tried to convince myself that Coop's body didn't feel warmer than normal, that it was just stress and grief and the afternoon sun.

Mark looked at me, then back down at our sweet Coop. His grief was ours.

But I didn't want to acknowledge what I saw in Mark's eyes.

* * * *

Could I survive this?

I had my Mark. My one constant mantra throughout the years.

As long as I had my Mark, I could survive anything.

Two days later, Qhan and Malkan held us as we clung together, stunned silent in our shared grief as Master and Corin dug another grave. I now held Nate's collar, and Mark held Coop's.

The vet said it was the same fever that took Nate from us, but you'd never convince me a broken heart didn't kill Coop. Or, at the very least, it contributed to his rapid decline and death.

Mark and I didn't want to move when they finished filling the grave. We wanted to lie there beside their final resting places and talk to them, recite poetry to them.

Finally, late that night, Master and Corin gently picked us up and carried us inside the house and into their bed, where the two of us clung together between Master and Corin, who held us.

"I love you, baby," Mark whispered. "Us first. Always."

"I love you, too. Always."

The next morning, I noticed Master and Corin didn't leave for work. They stayed in bed with us, quietly talking to each other as Mark and I lay there in each other's arms.

By late afternoon, I knew.

Mark stared up at me, his blue eyes forever embedded in my soul, part of me. "You promised you'd never leave me," I whispered. "You promised."

"I know. I'm not leaving you, baby." He touched my chest, over my heart. "I'm staying right here with you. Always. I'll never be far away."

Again, as so many years earlier, I knew that wasn't a promise he might be able to keep.

Before dawn the next morning, Mark smiled at me. "It's not so bad, baby." His skin felt hot against mine, the fever raging through him. He didn't have long. "There's no pain."

"I don't care," I sobbed. "I can't lose you. I can't live without you."

"*Shh*, baby. It's okay. I'll be waiting for you close by. I can feel them waiting for me. Master and Nate and Coop. It's okay. I'll be waiting for you, too. We all will."

I stroked his face. "You promised me you wouldn't leave me. Never again. You promised."

"I know. I love you, baby."

I kissed him. "I love you, too."

They let me hold Mark, crying over him long after I knew he'd taken his last breath. I couldn't think. I couldn't breathe. I could speak but one thing.

"Bautu dal golan pauchan."

I repeated it over and over again as I watched Master remove my Mark's collar and put it into my hands, where my fingers were already tightly wrapped around Nate and Coop's.

Master was crying almost as hard as I was.

He had to hold me to keep me from throwing myself into the grave with Mark. I couldn't bear this. I couldn't live without my Mark.

I didn't eat. I prayed for the fever to take me, but it didn't.

As I said, the universe is rarely kind.

I laid outside in the backyard and whispered to them, my body stretched across their graves.

"Bautu dal golan pauchan."

Three days later, Master and Corin carried me outside to the backyard. Normally, I would have thought it was a beautiful day, the perfect kind that had brought me so much joy throughout the years, but all I could think about were the three fresh graves and those four words.

"Bautu dal golan pauchan."

Master held me cradled in his arms as I clutched the three collars to my chest. Corin stroked my forehead and whispered things to me I didn't listen to.

My heart and soul lay buried in the dirt beside us.

Everyone was there with me, even our vet.

Master kissed me. "Love Kal."

I looked up at him and finally managed to take in a breath. "Love Master," I said.

Corin, his tears gently falling upon my face, leaned in and kissed me, too. "Love Kal," he said.

"Love Corin." He sadly smiled and brushed his tears and mine from my cheeks.

The vet bent in and I felt a slight sting against my arm.

Master smiled, and I no longer lay in his arms. I was in the arms of his sire, so many decades before. The next words he spoke to me were my Master's voice, but in Terran Standard and not Algonquan.

> *"'Love at the lips was touch*
> *As sweet as I could bear;*
> *And once that seemed too much;*
> *I lived on air…'"*

My body felt light, like I was floating, and my hands relaxed around the collars. As Master's sweet voice recited "To Earthward," one of my absolute favorite poems, I turned my head and looked at the graves.

They hadn't left! I saw Master, Nate, Coop…and my Mark. Smiling at me. Waiting for me.

Just as he'd promised.

Master's voice in my ear grew softer, as if coming from a distance.

Mark held out his hand to me and playfully smirked, those delicious blue eyes twinkling at me.

"Come on, baby. You gonna lay out here all day, or are you gonna let me welcome you home? We've been waiting for you. We can't wait to show you what comes next."

I took a deep, final breath, feeling the smile on my face as I stood and joined them.

EPILOGUE

I'd always dreaded this day. I never imagined in my worst nightmare I would lose my precious pets so close together in time, but I knew maybe one future day I would see that as a blessing. That they didn't suffer, in the end.

Thank the spirits for Corzin's strength to hold me. He and Malkan took over digging the grave while I sat there and sobbed with my beloved pets' collars in my hands, clutched against my chest. I couldn't stop staring at Second's still-warm body, now shrouded and waiting to join the others in the earth.

I know those who'd never owned a pet couldn't understand our love for them, or why we buried them in our custom, as if they were us. They weren't merely mindless animals, despite the things some of their kind are admittedly capable of.

They were intelligent, loving, beautiful beings who chose to stay with us when offered a chance to be free.

And losing them broke my heart into a million pieces that I suspected would never fully heal.

I didn't want to make the decision. Unfortunately, Second wouldn't eat and had lost the will to live. The vet said it appeared he was immune to the fever, but I knew in my heart he was dying inside of a broken heart.

What kind of life would it be to force him to cling to an existence he was so obviously ready to leave?

His pitiful, mournful cries over the past several days gutted me.

Please don't take me from him.

It became a heartbreaking dirge, whether whispered or

sobbed, one of the few of our phrases Second knew by heart. Qhan told us Second had sobbed that same phrase over and over again when First had left on his brave mission to help defeat the Terrans for good.

Please don't take me from him.

What kind of owner would I have been to force him to survive when his grief was already killing him in a far crueler and more painful way?

Qhan sat next to me and draped his arm around me. "It is what your sire would have done," he said, his voice also hoarse from crying. "He loved them all so much, he would not have wanted Second to suffer. If First hadn't died, he and Second would have had each other. It would have been cruel to make Second live alone after all these years. He would not eat, would not drink. He had lost the will to live in a way I did not even see in him when First left that time. He was already dying. You simply released him from his agony, and that was the greatest kindness of all."

I nodded as I fingered their collars. All I had left of our precious pets, beside my memories and a few images and vids we'd taken over the years.

When they finished digging and we spoke the Old Rites, they gently buried the last of our beloveds. Corzin held me as I cried in his arms. I needed him, his strength, to get me through this. I did not fail to remember if it hadn't been for Third's intervention, perhaps I never would have seen the love and heart inside Corzin's carefully guarded ways.

I desperately loved this man and knew we would go on, sadder certainly, but we could heal.

One day.

"He's out of pain, love," he whispered to me. "They all are."

Malkan sat beside me and wiped at his own tears. "I wish we could get another one someday."

I shook my head. "It wouldn't be the same. No one could ever replace them. They were truly special."

I didn't bother telling him what he already knew, that the

few Terrans who occasionally escaped their government's clutches and made their way here looking to be adopted already had hundreds of people waiting to give them homes. Even my high status wouldn't get me bumped to the top of that impressive waiting list.

Our doctor knelt in front of me. "You did the right thing."

"He didn't feel any pain?"

He sadly smiled. "No. He simply went to sleep. Did you not see his smile at the end? He was thanking you for releasing him from his misery."

I looked at the five markers, for my sire, for First, Second, Third, and Fourth. It brought a smile to my sire's face when I'd once asked him why those names.

"They care not what we call them, as long as it's done with love. I wasn't any good at picking out names, and he was the first pet I'd ever owned, so I named him First. When I got Second, I decided to continue with that theme. They called themselves by their Terran names, but you know I can't speak their language the way you can."

I stayed out there all day with Corzin. I needed time to grieve. I wasn't a spiritual man, but for the first time in my life, I prayed the old myths were true. I wanted to believe that, unlike others who claimed Terrans had no souls, they were together once more. That somewhere in the stars, my sire and our four beloved pets were reading poetry to each other, loving each other, and maybe waiting for me to one day join them.

That was the comforting thought I tightly clung to, easing me through the dark nights ahead, until my grief lifted enough that I could smile again when I thought of them.

THE END

Please keep reading for a note about how this book came to be.

AUTHOR'S NOTE

(This is my original Author's Note from the 2010 edition.)

Normally I know, Gentle Reader, this is a note at the front of the book. But I wanted to put it back here. I wanted it read after.

Sometimes as a writer the "voices" in my head drown out everything else, not willing to shut up until I write what they tell me to. (Fortunately, I've found I'm not alone in that. I would have worried if I was.)

This is one of those stories.

As a writer, I don't do this just as a hobby or just as a profession. I am a writer. It's a definition of my soul and my heart, not just a designation on a Facebook profile, or on a line on an IRS form.

Some people drink or use drugs to escape or self-medicate.

I write.

As with *The Reluctant Dom*, there are hard books to write. Sometimes they have to be written, whether to preserve one's sanity or to peel open an emotional wound so it can heal. This is one of those books, although as with any book, that didn't make itself known to me until midway through the writing process.

As strange as this sounds (and for me to admit that, you know it's frakking strange), I feel this book was my way of working out some grief. We lost our beloved black Lab, Holly, on April 1, 2010, while she was in surgery for cancer after having survived several other surgeries.

A couple of weeks later I was standing in my shower and the "what if" door opened.

What if a man was turned into an alien's pet?

Not a new theme, granted, but the starter's pistol fired and my brain took off running before I could hold it back.

Six weeks after we lost Holly, we had to put our sixteen year-old golden retriever, Tessa, to sleep. And I was dealing with health issues of my own.

So no, this isn't your typical story. I'm sure there will be some who say damn, why didn't you just end this story a few chapters earlier and let me imagine it? Why didn't you give them their "happily ever after?"

Because I couldn't.

But in a way, truly, they did get their happily ever after, did they not? A long life, loving owners, and in the end, they were together again. At least in the telling of this fairy tale.

When you finish this book, Gentle Reader, I hope if you have furbabies you give them a hug. If you don't, give your two-foots a hug instead. Because any of us who've loved and lost before, we're all "acquainted with the night," in our own ways.

Lesli Richardson

ABOUT THE AUTHOR

Author Lesli Richardson, who is better-known by her more prolific wild-child Tymber Dalton pen name, lives in the Tampa Bay region of Florida with her husband (aka "The World's Best Husband™") and too many pets. She writes a wide variety of heat levels and genres, from mainstream sci-fi all the way to scorching ménage.

The USA Today Bestselling Author (as Tymber), two-time EPIC award winner, and part-time Viking shield-maiden in training loves to shoot skeet and play D&D with her friends. She's also the bestselling author of over two hundred books and counting, including *The Reluctant Dom*, *The Great Turning*, *Cross Country Chaos*, the Bleacke Shifters series, The Great Turning series, the Suncoast Society series, the Love Slave for Two series, the Triple Trouble series, the Coffeeshop Coven series, the Good Will Ghost Hunting series, the Drunk Monkeys series, and many others.

She lives in her own little world, but it's okay—they all know her there.

She loves to hear from readers! Please feel free to drop by her website and sign up for her newsletter to keep abreast of the latest news, snarkage, and releases.

Honest reviews are always welcomed. They help with a book's visibility and can boost its placement on book retailer sites. Even a few lines about what you felt reading the book will help. Thank you so much, it's greatly appreciated!

Visit my website to sign up for my newsletter, find out what's coming soon, and more!

http://www.tymberdalton.com

Printed in Great Britain
by Amazon

58912956R00149